bombshell

ROWAN MANESS

Simon Pulse

NEW YORK LONDON TORONTO SYDNEY NEW DELHI

SIMON PULSE

An imprint of Simon & Schuster Children's Publishing Division

1230 Avenue of the Americas, New York, New York 10020

First Simon Pulse paperback edition July 2018

Text copyright © 2017 by Rowan Maness

Cover photographs copyright © 2017 by Thinkstock

Also available in a Simon Pulse hardcover edition.

All rights reserved, including the right of reproduction in whole or in part in any form.

SIMON PULSE and colophon are registered trademarks of Simon & Schuster, Inc.

For information about special discounts for bulk purchases, please contact Simon & Schuster Special Sales at 1-866-506-1949 or business@simonandschuster.com.

The Simon & Schuster Speakers Bureau can bring authors to your live event. For more information or to book an event contact the Simon & Schuster Speakers Bureau at 1-866-248-3049 or visit our website at www.simonspeakers.com.

Cover designed by Regina Flath

Interior designed by Greg Stadnyk

The text of this book was set in Neutraface.

Manufactured in the United States of America

2 4 6 8 10 9 7 5 3 1

The Library of Congress has cataloged the hardcover edition as follows:

Names: Maness, Rowan, author.

Title: Bombshell / by Rowan Maness.

Description: First Simon Pulse hardcover edition. | New York : Simon Pulse, 2017. | Summary: High school sophomore Joss Wyatt maintains several alternate, online lives—usually with a corresponding long-distance romantic relationship—until she receives anonymous messages threatening to expose all her secrets, she alienates close friends, and she has problems distinguishing reality from fantasy.

Identifiers: LCCN 2016052869 | ISBN 9781481441643 (hc)

Subjects: | CYAC: Online identities—Fiction. | Impersonation—Fiction. | Friendship—Fiction. | Dating (Social customs) —Fiction. | Stalking—Fiction. | Bullying—Fiction. | BISAC: JUVENILE FICTION / Social Issues / Dating & Sex. | JUVENILE FICTION / Social Issues / Bullying.

Classification: LCC PZ7.1.M36465 Bo 2017 | DDC [Fic]—dc23

LC record available at https://lccn.loc.gov/2016052869

ISBN 9781481441650 (pbk)

ISBN 9781481441667 (eBook)

to my queens, Ottilie and Cosima

to Brian, who makes everything real

and to Mom and Dad, for your endless love and support

CHAPTER 1

All right, I'm Anna. What am I up to?

There's a full moon tonight, and in Paris it's hanging bright and low behind the Eiffel Tower. My face is covered with ultra-futuristic Ziggy Stardust-style makeup, and the golden café lights are shining all reflected in the Seine like fallen stars. I'm exhausted after a long day of back-to-back runway shows, but this is only my second time in Paris, and it's the first quiet moment I've had since the plane landed three days ago. Despite the setting—or maybe because of it—I'm lonely. (Anna is always a little bit lonely.) *So I take out my phone and text Max, who's been waiting.*

Me: **Damn, this is beautiful.**

The streets have a cartoon van Gogh quality and from a restaurant open late "La Vie en Rose" filters out into the street just like in Sabrina. Max writes back **Show me?** *and I'm already* searching "full moon paris night" on Flickr. It takes only a second to find the right photograph, and just a few more to crop and filter, turning it into Anna's Full Moon Paris Night. I send it off to Max.

Max will wonder at the pretty picture, and though he won't think of it consciously, the girl who sent it to him will become a bit less abstract. She is across an ocean, but he's seeing what she's seeing right now. The face he fell in love with is placed in time and space, and in his mind, through his longing for her, she is made more real.

I never slip up, but if I do—if Anna takes a misstep beyond the realm of possibility—these solidifying moments will help Max instantly forget. When he doubts, he will soothe himself, repeating: *But I've seen so many pictures. She has so many Instagram followers. If I ask for something, she supplies it. It is not impossible that I could be loved this way by a woman like her.*

Max's capacity for denial is a bottomless well inside him, like it is for everyone.

A text from someone else interrupts. I leave Anna standing on the moonlit bridge while I look at the clock—not the clock on my phone, but the clock on the classroom wall. It reads 3:40 p.m. That's 6:40 p.m. in New York, forty minutes after midnight in Paris, and five minutes until the bell rings.

New message from GEORGE

George: **Skype?**

Another woman, Emma, stirs restlessly in the bedroom of a mansion in Savannah. Asleep next to her, the duvet-covered

ROWAN MANESS

mound of her abusive husband, Ron, snores and farts, a detail she has been waiting to share with George.

But the phone's red light is blinking, beckoning, telling me that Max has seen Anna's picture and has something new to say. *Sorry, George, not now.*

Max: **Wow, that's pretty.**

Anna, paused, takes a deep breath back to life.

Me: **They offered to have a driver take me back to the hotel, but I felt like waiting. It should be romantic, strolling along the Seine way past midnight, but I'm lonely without you. And I've been thinking about our fantasy all day. . . .**

Max: **Naughty girl. Get back to your hotel and take another picture for me. I'm stuck in the lab, and I need a distraction.**

Me: **Hmm, I don't know. I'm feeling pretty uninspired.**

The red light's blinking.

Now Mary-Kate's saying **ANSWERRRR CAREY NOW AGHGHHG**

Oh shit, I thought, and tried to diffuse the haze that's been comfortably separating me from sixth-period precalc for the past forty-five minutes. My phone, hastily shoved back inside the desk I'd been slumped over, made a sad little scraping sound. I missed it as soon as it left my hands.

I looked up, but the equations covering the SMART Board at the front of the classroom blurred and spun and refused to come into focus. My eyes landed on the phrase "real zero," and it became an anchor. I hauled myself up from the abyss.

It was clear I should say something, so I said "Yes?" but I was thinking, *Wait, what's an unreal zero?*

There was no precalc in Paris. There was no Anna in Ms. Carey's class.

"Joss, is there something more interesting you'd like to share with the class?"

Pretty much everything is more interesting than a sophomore math class, but how could I explain that I had just been five thousand miles away, inhabiting the body of a woman who doesn't exist? Or that she does exist, just not with the name and history I gave her? *Hey, Ms. Carey, I took a candid Polaroid of an Estonian girl from a modeling agency's website and turned her into a whole new person?*

I looked at the clock again—3:44 p.m. (That's 6:44 in New York, 12:44 in Paris, where the early-summer night is warm enough for a riverside stroll.) I drew a triangle between the three of us—me in Arizona, Max in New York, and the ghost of a made-up girl in France.

"No. I'm sorry, Ms. Carey. I was just reading ahead." I touched the open textbook in front of me. "Real zeroes, right? They're really—"

Across the room, Mary-Kate stifled a laugh. At the beginning of the school year we'd been forced to move our desks apart because we couldn't stop talking to each other, like hyperactive third graders.

"—exciting." I finished the sentence, dragging it out as far as

I could toward the last remaining tick of the clock.

Three forty-five came as slowly as ever, two seconds forward, one second back. But the bell rang, setting me free. Everyone stood up, and I slid the phone out of my desk and into the sleeve of my sweatshirt. Before I could make it out the door, though, Ms. Carey called to me.

"Joss? A minute, please."

Suddenly, the room was empty.

I took the tiniest step possible toward her desk.

"Hmm?" I mumbled.

"Hand it over," she said. *Coldhearted troll!*

"Excuse me?"

"Your phone. Hand it over."

"But it's in my locker."

Here's where she knows I'm lying but can't do anything about it because she's a high school teacher and she's tired and can't exert any real power over me.

"Honestly. It's in my locker."

You're walking the Seine right now. It's the dead of night in Paris. There's no precalc, no speckled linoleum tile and water-stained ceilings. The city's asleep, but everything's humming, and you're a beautiful girl in a beautiful place, in love and beholden to no one.

The bags under Ms. Carey's eyes were showing. I wondered how many episodes of *Grey's Anatomy* she binge-watched on Netflix last night instead of grading our pop quizzes.

"Oh, by the way, do you have the quizzes from Monday ready yet? You said we'd have them back by Wednesday, but—" I said, trying to avoid looking at a faded, ruler-shaped poster with MATH RULES! printed across it in lime-green Comic Sans.

The look on her face said she suspected I knew about the Netflix. The look on mine said I'd put a firm bet on the probability of a software engineer boyfriend who plays video games all night while she looks at pictures of baby nurseries and oatmeal in mason jars on Pinterest.

"I can't do my job if I'm competing for attention with cell phones. Show some *respect*."

I hate it when people talk about respect like that, like we should all just automatically respect someone because they happen to be our teacher, or older than us, or a priest or a cop or a politician. That reduces the whole concept into nothing. I don't know whether or not Ms. Carey's a good person. I don't know if she is wise and righteous. I don't even know what a respectable person would look like. Probably some little kid playing in the mud somewhere is respectable.

Ms. Carey yawned at me. *How much better would her life be if she were a fake doctor in a fake hospital with heartfelt traumas and romantic intrigue? No insolent teenagers, Pinterest crafts in her spare time—*

"Look, I like precalc," I said. "I do my homework. I got an A on my last progress report. Okay, maybe I have problems paying attention sometimes, and you know I hate talking in class—"

Resigned, she waved me away, and I caught the beginning of a sigh of defeat as I bolted out the door.

In the bustling hallway, I moved through a sea of identically dressed girls, slipping the phone out of my sleeve—six new messages from Max.

Max: **I could help you.**

Max: **Here's something to add to our fantasy** 😜

Attached, a photo. Despite everything I'd learned about men in the three years I'd spent lying to them on the Internet, I got excited. That private thrill. A photo, just for Anna/me.

It could be a photo of anything—Max's face, his hands, the view outside his window, the cover of the book he's reading. Something immediate, something that would make him more vulnerable, something to give me the upper hand.

Slowly, I scrolled down.

And . . . my hopes for something deep and meaningful evaporated. Same old, same old. Full frontal, totally lacking in creativity, a demented still-life painting. *Penis and fruit bowl.*

But after he'd made his bold move, his valiant foray, Anna hadn't responded quickly enough. Max felt wobbly. He sent three messages in a row.

Max: **You like?**

Max: 😊

Max: **. . . ?**

Classic ellipses-only text. Always a sign of a great mind. And do not get me started on his use of emojis.

"Hey," Mary-Kate said—she was waiting at my locker, smiling her permanent faint smile. She wore it as protection, like a talisman, but it never looked forced.

"Can you tell me something, my genius, levelheaded, dearest best friend? My angel?" I stroked her cheek, tucking a strand of her dirty-blond bob behind her ear.

"Of course." The smile widened a bit, and she rolled her eyes.

"Why, oh why, do guys always send these—"

I flashed her the photo of Max's member, artlessly cropped and badly lit, sitting there all proud and pathetic.

"—without any invitation whatsoever?"

"Oh God, Joss! Warning, please."

"I'm sorry. It's hideous, I know," I said, shaking my head.

"So hideous," echoed Mary-Kate—but she grabbed my phone to get a closer look.

"Which guy is this?" she asked, swiping her fingers across the screen, zooming in until the picture was nothing but orangey, flesh-tone pixels.

"What the hell is Ms. Carey's problem?" I asked, ignoring the question.

"All she wanted was to whine at me. I'm on the honor roll every damn day, man," I went on, emptying my backpack, stuffing books and binders into my locker. "How did I offend her? I think she's jealous of me, in a really sad, creepy way."

Mary-Kate laughed. "I'm on her side. You didn't even know she asked you a question."

"You're stone-cold, Mahoney."

"You should have gotten into trouble for staring at your Internet boyfriend's boner, Wyatt."

"I wonder what Ms. Carey would do if she saw all the dick pics stored on my SIM card."

Mary-Kate made a face.

"But yeah," I said. "I get what you're saying. I should do like you do. Fly under the radar. Get good marks, no confrontations, keep my rep clean. Just like in prison."

"Why are you so obsessed with prison?"

"Why are you not?" I said. "It's an apt metaphor. You think it's insensitive? Off-color?"

"No, *this* is off-color," Mary-Kate said, waving my phone—and Max's penis—through the air.

"It's dancing!" I laughed, speaking with a bad, overwrought, old-British-lady accent. "Oh, it's so happy, it's dancing! It's dancing and it's laughing!"

Mary-Kate was a good five inches taller than me, and she held the phone out of my reach.

"I don't know. If this were my penis, I'd at least try to make it prettier," she said, squinting at the screen.

"Penis? Where's penis? Show me now," said a familiar voice.

There's this thing that happens when you're about to close your locker for the last time on Friday. You hook up to a universal teenage feeling—the third person in your sixteen-year-old-girl trifecta has just walked up, and there's an open weekend on the horizon with a couple interesting prospects. You're thrilled to near euphoria by the thought of the next two days stretching out in front of you. A tinge of sadness to it all, a romantic sheen. The weekend is never going to be as long as it seems it will be on a Friday afternoon.

Mary-Kate handed the phone to Rhiannon, who looked at it, frowning. "Another guy who can kiss his political career good-bye."

"Slight moral transgressions are a net positive in politics," I said. "Sexting scandals hardly even register anymore. It's just assumed everyone has one. I chatted with this state senator for a few months, and—"

Rhiannon interrupted, as usual, so I didn't get to finish my sentence—*and it would have been so easy to blackmail him.*

"I see what you mean about making it prettier, though. He's not looking his best here. A nice Instagram filter and he'd be good to go. That's basic politeness," Rhiannon said, sighing as she untucked her white uniform polo from her plaid skirt, which was already hiked up so impossibly high that the untucked shirt nearly covered it.

She swiped her finger across the phone's screen.

"No response for ten minutes? You're making him suffer," she said disapprovingly.

"The moment's ruined," I said. "I can't get inspired by another hairy penis. He has to be punished a little."

"Aww," Mary-Kate said. "But what are you going to say when you write back?"

"I'm not going to say anything," I said. "Anna the model, however—"

"So what will Anna the model say?" Mary-Kate said, a hint of annoyance behind the enigmatic smile.

I'm telling a story, I want to explain. But they know. They know all the stupid things I do. They've heard all my stories.

"Nothing!" I shouted instead, slamming my locker door shut.

"You're such a professional," Rhiannon said, finally handing me the phone.

We began to make our way through the hallway, and after a moment Mary-Kate asked, "Wait. Why nothing?"

"Because he bored me," I answered, pushing through a heavy metal door.

"That doesn't make sense," Mary-Kate replied skeptically. "If he likes you—I mean, if he likes Anna—then won't he be upset that she's ignoring him?"

"You're so cute, MK," I said.

Mary-Kate furrowed her brow. "But what if he gets mad? Like Crazy Guy?"

My whole body started to blush, like it does every time something reminds me of Peter.

"That was"—I hesitated before deciding—"a mistake. It wasn't even my fault. He was sick. I was, like, thirteen. I'm a lot more careful now."

Remember him, staring at you? And not staring at you. Staring through you. Wanting a ghost. Needing her.

"Are you talking about the guy who called your dad?" Rhiannon asked, reliably pouncing on anything resembling a lurid detail. Mary-Kate and I met Rhiannon the middle of freshman year, when she transferred to Xavier after being home-schooled her entire life, so she wasn't around when everything happened. I tried to remember which details I'd shared with Mary-Kate and which I'd shared with Rhiannon.

They don't know his name. Just Crazy Guy. I've even never said "Peter" in front of them.

"Yeah," Mary-Kate said. "And she got her phone and computer taken away for months, and her parents sent her to that weird therapist she used to see. Before she switched."

"Oh yeah! That's how I knew we were going to be friends. You were messing with those smiley-face How Are You Feeling? cards and it was so fucking funny," Rhiannon said, smiling at the memory.

I was feeling nothing.

Rhiannon gasped, adding, "Do you still have those? I want to use them for something."

I didn't respond.

"Uh-oh," said Mary-Kate. "We've displeased our mistress."

"Do you want to talk about it, Joss?" Rhiannon asked, throwing her arm around me, pulling Mary-Kate in on her other side. "Do you need your angry-face card?"

"Guys," I said, stopping in the middle of the hallway. "Can we please not?"

Rhiannon shrugged. "I'm just sorry I missed it all."

"It was not that dramatic."

"It kind of was," Mary-Kate whispered to Rhiannon.

"Whatever, Anna-Joss," Rhiannon said. I wriggled out of her side hug and kept walking.

"But still, I don't see what you're trying to accomplish by waiting so long to respond to Max," Mary-Kate said, with an awful lot of conviction for someone who, for as long as I could remember, had never even had a crush on a boy.

"It's the best move," I said. "Trust me. I'll text him tomorrow and say Anna met up with the male model from her shoot as she crossed the Pont des Arts. It'll drive him nuts."

Outside, we were met with a blast of ninety-two-degree heat, like stepping into a furnace, so hostile your mind goes straight to cremation.

"Oh, fuck this place!" Rhiannon muttered.

"Fuck this place," I repeated in solidarity, taking off the sweatshirt that I wore so I could hide my phone in its sleeves during class.

We had to cross through the main courtyard of our school, Xavier Prep, to get to the parking lot, where Rhiannon's car waited, heated up like the inside of an Easy-Bake Oven. It could be a treacherous walk for lesser girls, full of invisible fault lines carved into the ground by ancient, made-up social separations.

The fault lines didn't bother us—we'd banded together. We

were protected by the shared, unshakeable sense that We Did Not Belong Here. We were three very different people, who felt out of place for very different reasons, but it turns out that's a pretty solid basis for friendship.

Halfway across the courtyard, someone called my name.

As I turned toward the sound, I thought I saw something dart across the courtyard—a kind of undulating flash. Paws in the dead grass. Gone before I took a breath, sun-blasted.

Jackrabbit, I thought, hoping that was all.

Mary-Kate and Rhiannon walked on without me. I grabbed for my sunglasses.

"Hey, Joss!" the voice said again, closer. This time I could place its sickeningly sweet enthusiasm, which, to my ear, never failed to sound absolutely hollow. It was Leah Leary, a girl I'd had three sleepovers with in elementary school because our mothers were on the same committee.

I watched her walk toward me, wheeling a gigantic rolling backpack. It hit the back of her ankles with a *thunk* when she stopped moving.

"What do you want?" I asked. She never seemed to get offended, which was why I couldn't help but try my hardest to offend her.

She fiddled with the backpack's plastic handle, which was decorated with ribbons in Xavier Prep's signature blue-and-yellow plaid. I pictured her braiding them together, at home, alone.

"Shane said you might be interested—"

"He's wrong," I interrupted.

"We're going to this movie tonight—"

"I'm not interested."

"Sorry," she said, her voice rising ever so slightly, to the frequency of a boiling teapot. "I was just trying to be nice. Shane wanted me to ask you."

"Tell Shane I'm busy," I said, leaving before she could say anything more.

Just because she's dating Shane doesn't mean I'm available for re-friending. She should know better, anyway. She should be protecting herself.

Rhiannon's hand-me-down Volkswagen pulled up to the curb at the front of the school. Across the parking lot, streams of gross little steroid monkeys from the boys' school, Brophy, descended on their huge pickup trucks and ugly-era Mustangs.

Rhiannon was blasting a Blondie song when I climbed into the backseat, and her off-key voice competed with Debbie Harry's perfect one as they both screeched against the roar of the air-conditioning.

"Mr. Lauren, behind us," Mary-Kate shouted from the passenger seat as we started driving.

Mr. Lauren, my AP bio teacher. Friend of the youth, on the side of the angels. British, weirdly attractive. Drives an intensely cool little car—small, red, foreign, old, but not too precious or showy—a dented Volvo coupe, teacher's salary paint job. He lets me play music during class and doesn't mind if I look at my phone while we're running experiments. I smiled at him through the back window. He looked surprised and smiled back.

"Mmm," Rhiannon said, watching him in the rearview mirror. "He makes me feel all *Dateline: To Catch a Predator.*"

I laughed. "That show was an insult to teenage girls everywhere."

"Here it comes," Mary-Kate said.

"I mean it. They have these people whose job it is to pretend to be teenage girls, and they all do the same thing—dumb themselves down by ninety-five percent and type stuff like 'I'm so horny 4 U' in some dark lair of a Yahoo chat room. There's no style, no nuance, no character development. And they're scraping the bottom of the barrel. Picking up creeps like that is the easiest thing ever."

"Joss is defending the child molesters again," Mary-Kate scolded.

"I am not. I'm defending us. What does it say about society if the mark of authenticity—for both perverts and pervert catchers—is that teenage girls must talk and write like complete idiots?"

They didn't respond. Rhiannon rolled the windows down and turned the music up as we slowly coasted across campus.

My phone buzzed.

New message from JAMES

James: **Are you there?**

I checked the clock, cursing daylight saving time for

throwing off my calculations. I couldn't remember if it was an hour behind or ahead in Los Angeles.

"Let's get coffee!" Rhiannon sang.

Am I here? Am I here?

"Drop me off first?" I asked.

"What?" she and Mary-Kate both complained.

I searched my phone for the right time zone.

"I have a—a thing," I said.

They groaned.

"Fine," said Rhiannon, making a hard U-turn that sent me flying across the backseat.

"Rhiannon!" I shouted.

"Fine," she repeated. "But you're coming out tonight. No way you're staying home to chat with Random Weirdo number 2,863."

"Yeah, yeah, yeah," I said, fastening my seat belt.

Rosie is sitting in the café at her exclusive art school, look-ing out at a tree-covered hill. A tiny brown rabbit appears, just at the edge of the tree line. The rabbit twitches his nose. Rosie watches—there's something strange about this animal. He is small, but he looks heavy. Not fat. Held down by a force. Rosie looks away. It takes effort. She looks at her phone.

I texted James.

Me: **I'm here.**

CHAPTER 2

***Church, mall, school, prison. Church, mall, school, prison.* In** the desert they're indistinguishable—a never-ending row of big stucco boxes pumped full of freezing, artificial air. Windowless monoliths. I watched them zip by, judging the churches by the size of their crosses, the malls by the size of their parking lots.

The only break in the chain of stucco boxes is the occasional lush, rolling golf course, landscapes so out of place they are like a gash in the desert floor, spilling neon green. Lakes with cement beds.

Rhiannon merged onto the freeway, headed north. Beneath the overpasses there are mosaic depictions of Kokopelli, the ancient Native American trickster god, paused mid-dance, playing his flute. A god reduced and cheapened, banished to rush-hour traffic for eternity.

As we drive past, I swear I see the turquoise tiles shift

as the Kokopelli lifts his head out of the concrete.

Trickster.

Arizona can be beautiful, though, if you take away the boxes and asphalt. The valley is surrounded by patchwork mountain ranges—some red and round, some scrubby and low, and the biggest, distant and snowcapped. Every night there are brilliant sunsets, and in the late summer, monsoons like color-shifting mood rings full of pink and purple light come barreling across the desert at a hundred miles an hour. A high wall of dust envelops everything, bringing with it the smell of rain on hot concrete and an aura of wild electricity, and it's like you're on another planet.

On days like that, on days when it's not too hot or too hazy, it almost makes sense that humans should live here. But most of the time, it doesn't. Why anyone would settle here instead of plodding on just three hundred miles west and living in paradise, I will never understand.

Off the highway now, moving out of Phoenix up through the vast burbs, way out, all the way to my neighborhood, nestled against red-dirt foothills. Rhiannon and Mary-Kate are talking, but the music's so loud I can't hear them, and I'm thinking of James, anyway—James and the Kokopelli, James in the middle of a monsoon.

James is my favorite. James is my favorite? James is my favorite, right now. He's twenty-eight and heads an art collective—I've thoroughly stalked each member on their fantastically non-ironic social media feeds. He is shy about his own art and forthcoming about his insecurities in a way that isn't tiresome or narcissistic. He lives in New York—not upstate, where Max lurks in a grad school laboratory, but in Brooklyn.

He messaged my avatar Rosie on Facebook a year ago. Rosie is nineteen and goes to art school in LA. She's kind of a mess, but well-read, a flirt with a dry sense of humor. Not light-years away from the truth, at least compared to Anna the model, Emma the married former beauty queen, Rebecca the anthropologist studying remote Alaskan villages, Jessica the pro surfer, Lucy the dissatisfied housewife who lives in a trailer home in Nevada, or anyone else I've ever made up. I even used my real pictures for Rosie's profile.

From the first notes James and Rosie exchanged, they were able to talk about real stuff without worrying the other person might not understand. I am acutely aware of how unusual that is.

Me: **We can do it, though. We could walk in a dream forest together.**

In his last nightly e-mail, James said he didn't believe that we could meet on the astral plane—that our bodies could follow the trail of our words and manifest in front of each other in a new dimension. He didn't say "Rosie, that's crazy," but he was definitely thinking it.

But I know it's possible. I've done it before.

He is quick to respond, and I can feel the hunger there.

James: **You're teasing me with this whole idea. You know how much I want to meet you.**

Me: **Why don't you think it's possible?**

James: **Let me think about it.**

I know to wait before responding. He is going to change the subject.

James: **Hey, have you read that Alan Watts book yet?**

Me: **I checked it out from the library, but I haven't started it.**

That's true.

James: **You have to. It's so good.**

Me: **Cross my heart. I've just got to get my dumb show finished and ready before I can think of anything else.**

I was on the edge of a sweet James daydream, ready to jump into it and escape, to distance myself from six classes of boredom and clock-watching, from the stubborn heat and my frustration with Max. I wanted to walk in nature as Rosie, who would notice the subtle beauty of pale green moss on a dark tree trunk, who would record it with an artist's eye, in that special way she had of describing. She would tell James, and he would see, too—

My phone buzzed. The text with James was obscured by a new notification.

New message from BLOCKED NUMBER

I love the moment after you get a new text, before you open it. Sometimes when I'm feeling self-indulgent I let them sit awhile, so I can just exist with the knowledge that there's an unread text waiting for me. It's like mini Christmases all day. Despite the heat, I got goose bumps.

But the text wasn't right. It was wrong.

XXX: LIAR

The wrongness was somewhere between the screen and the four black letters. Serrated pixels sent on bad vibes, reaching out from a remote, unseen place.

I remembered other texts. The first had come about three weeks ago, and since then, there'd been one every few days. **New message from BLOCKED NUMBER.** Blank when I opened them. Maddening, an empty text. I thought it was a glitch.

But now it was talking.

It could be any of them, Joss.

Joss. Whose voice was that? My own, but removed, as if the thought had jumped ahead without me. My thumb hovered over the reply box, and I realized my hand was shaking.

"Joss!" Rhiannon shouted.

"What?" I snapped, startled, deleting the text from Blocked Number. I could not think about the unseen place and who might be reaching out from there.

"We're here, you horny little liar."

"Here?" I asked, then realized the car had stopped and was idling in front of my house. "Oh. Here."

"Yes. Where you live. In the real world. Get out. Go do whatever it is you do," Rhiannon said.

"I like to refer to it as 'decompressing,'" I said, reopening the conversation with James.

Me: **Can we switch to Chat? My phone's about to die. No idea where the charger is.**

Get the phone away. Put it out of your mind.

"So go. Decompress. I will collect you later. To go to a party. With real people, who have faces and feelings."

I climbed out of the car and slammed the door, giving Rhiannon a big fake smile as they drove off. From the passenger seat, Mary-Kate shot me a worried look.

I hurried to the gate and punched in the access code: 1113, my birthday. People like gates here. Gates and access codes and security guards patrolling in tricked-out golf carts. The gate clanged shut behind me, and I ran through the tiny front yard and punched the same code into another keypad to get into the actual house. Saltillo tile, stainless-steel appliances. A tract home with all the upgrades.

Just like every day, I passed by my dad's studio and pressed my hand to the door. It's always shut now—what a cliché. Someone dies and you shut up the room like a coffin. That big home office with oak built-ins. He'd stacked the shelves with canvases and ripped the carpet out. "I need a glass room. I need more light," he said once, when my mom caught him about to take a mallet to the back wall. "For God's sake, Jay, we'll hire a contractor." But here we are. There hasn't been any light in there for months.

Enough. Up the stairs to my room, past another closed door—my older brother Dylan's bedroom. It's empty too, but not because of death. Shoes off. Uniform off. Mind racing with a thousand thoughts to tell James, all the things I'd been thinking about while staring at a splotch on the wall in French class, or the back of someone's head in US history.

I pulled on a pair of pajama bottoms and a tattered Kinks T-shirt, grabbed my laptop, and sprawled across the bed, throwing the computer open, impatient as it labored to wake up. The screen flickered and the dashboard appeared with a shudder of mechanical protest.

I skimmed through my long list of screen names, chose **RosieRose**, and signed in. James was already on—he messaged me first.

sharkliver: **Someone left it in the stairwell of my building.**

RosieRose: **Left what?**

sharkliver: **The Alan Watts book. That's how I found it.**

RosieRose: **It was me. I left it there for you.**

sharkliver: **(Some small part of me thought so.)**

RosieRose: **The part that sees me, sometimes, walking ahead of you on the street, or across a crowded restaurant? Even though you know I'm here in LA?**

sharkliver: **That part, yes.**

RosieRose: **The squishy part.**

sharkliver: **The part that belongs to you.**

sharkliver: **We are god in disguise, pretending not to be himself.**

What was James saying? Did he know? Was it him, controlling things? *James and the Kokopelli.* A flash of blue as the car drives by, a mosaic made of turquoise planets, each

ROWAN MANESS

spinning, each a world. James in one, figuring me out.

sharkliver: ^ That was a quote. From the book.

Mary-Kate and Dr. Judson would say, have said, that lying so much and so easily makes me paranoid.

RosieRose: Woah. Deep.

RosieRose: But it should be "herself." God is a girl.

sharkliver: You've met Her?

RosieRose: She is cruel, but fair when supplicated.

sharkliver: I want to read this book to you.

RosieRose: You can, on the astral plane.

sharkliver: DON'T SAY "ON THE ASTRAL PLANE"

The last two messages, sent at the same time. Down to the last fraction of a second on the timestamp.

sharkliver: In our bed.

Sometimes, with James, in the pauses between our messages, it feels like he's in the same room. Distance becomes fluid, and I can bring him closer just by looking at the words on the screen.

RosieRose: If we were in Our Bed, we wouldn't be reading.

sharkliver: Our brains already fit together. Imagine what it would be like if our bodies could catch up.

I clicked over to Rosie's Facebook account and found the page for James Constant. In his profile photo, he was standing on a balcony looking out—at what, I didn't know. I always picture the ocean. Short brown hair, a shadow of stubble, eyes turned up at the corners by an easy smile. Artistic, smart, evolved. That a guy like him existed made every forced interaction with a Brophy boy all the more depressing.

Thank you, Goddess Internet, for showing me the way.

sharkliver: **Tell me about your show. Did you decide what you're going to do?**

I looked around my room for inspiration. Everything neat, orderly. Rhiannon would say "anally organized." A corner full of houseplants I was trying to keep alive. My bearded dragon, Bueller, in her tank, hiding beneath a faux dinosaur egg. Posters—Dalí's *Galatea of the Spheres, Christina's World.* Four squares of color on the wall from the time I almost decided to paint the walls blue. Hanging near them, a small collage.

What was that from? Seventh grade? Personal mandalas.

RosieRose: **I'm trying to find a way to fabricate these sculptural personal mandalas I designed. Since my last crit I've felt so shitty about it all. People were mean. I want the work to protect me from that.**

RosieRose: **I'll show you when I have something made. I can't really focus right now though. There's all this other crap going on.**

sharkliver: **What crap?**

RosieRose: **I think I have a stalker.**

RosieRose: **I keep getting texts from a blocked number. They just say LIAR, that's all. Nothing else. For a few weeks now, like five times a day.**

sharkliver: **Why LIAR?**

Was that too much? I should have changed the word.

RosieRose: **No idea.**

sharkliver: **It's probably a friend fucking with you.**

RosieRose: **Yeah. But it makes me edgy. And I did have an incident, when I was thirteen. This guy was obsessed with me. But it couldn't be him. At least, I think.**

Maybe James can help.

sharkliver: **Shit. I gotta go.**

sharkliver: **I'm sorry.**

I didn't expect that.

sharkliver: **Rosie?**

I watched the blinking text box.

sharkliver: **You know you're the only one for me, right?**

I slammed the laptop shut. He'd won that round. I was thinking of him. I wanted him.

I thought of how his hands might rest on my shoulders, what it would be like to look into his eyes as they met mine for the first time. The idea of having a real boyfriend paralyzes me—it seems so much more satisfying to imagine something perfect instead.

The doorbell rang, and I ignored it. Probably a delivery—files for one of my mom's cases or the monthly shipment of contraband wrinkle cream she orders from China. I started searching for a top to wear to the party later, but it seemed so tedious a task that I gave up immediately and went downstairs in search of food.

The doorbell rang again. I stomped into the kitchen and

threw open the refrigerator doors, grabbing a carton of leftover Chinese and a bottled iced coffee. I set them on the counter and pushed the talk button on the intercom mounted on the wall.

"Yes?" I said.

"Hey, let me in."

Shane.

"I'm busy," I said, grabbing two pairs of wooden throwaway chopsticks from a drawer stuffed full of wooden throwaway chopsticks.

"No you're not," Shane answered.

I buzzed him in. I heard the door open down the distant, tiled hallway, then his footsteps squeaking—he'd been wearing the same pair of hideous Hush Puppies for the past two years. Predictably, the soft jingle of Ferris's bell followed. Ferris was my dad's cat. She hates women. And men too, actually, but she really likes Shane—maybe because he is neither.

He was holding her when he came into the kitchen. He grabbed a soda from the refrigerator and sat on the stool next to mine, at the kitchen island.

"Chinese, huh?"

"Want some?" I offered. The cat settled down in his lap.

He took the carton and I handed him the second pair of chopsticks.

"Is there any of that stuff?" he mumbled. "The purple stuff?"

"Fridge," I answered. He put Ferris on the floor, and she

followed him as he retrieved a tiny plastic cup of plum sauce.

"I don't get that cat," I said when he sat back down and Ferris jumped into his lap again.

"She's a complex creature."

"Stupidly complex." I reached out to pet her, and she swatted at me. Shane cleared his throat.

"So, this is you 'busy'?"

"I'm preparing my body for tonight's adventures. Caffeine and MSG are integral parts of my ablution process."

"Oh," he said, and stopped talking.

"What, Shane?" I snapped, annoyed he was making me ask.

"I'm kind of surprised you weren't Skyping with a serial killer, like usual."

"James is not a serial killer," I said without thinking. I didn't mean to use his name.

Shane raised an eyebrow.

We ate in silence for a while. The cat purred. Shane dripped plum sauce all over his shirt.

"Heard from Dylan?" he asked finally.

I laughed.

"Last time he called he said he was someplace in Chile waiting to get on a ferry to an island with 'a shit-ton of happy cows.' My mom was not amused. Probably because she knows cows is code for shrooms."

"Ah." Shane sighed. "God I miss him."

I missed my cue to say *I miss him too.*

"Speaking of cow mushrooms," Shane went on. "You have something to do tonight?"

"Oh yes," I said.

"Something better than *Yellow Submarine*?"

I took a sip of iced coffee and tried to make sense of those words.

"Oh," I said slowly. "Is this what Leah Leary was trying to tell me about?"

"It's playing at that old theater on Mill, all spiffed up."

"Spiffed up?"

"You know, digitally restored or whatever."

"*Yellow*-er?" I teased.

"I don't know. So you can't come?"

"I don't even really like *Yellow Submarine* anymore."

"You don't?"

When we were in second grade Shane and I once went three weeks without talking to anyone but each other. We wrote constitutions for imaginary worlds and lived in them for months—I always played the leader, and Shane was either my right hand or my worthy opponent. We were too young to hide parts of ourselves away or to keep secrets. But now we keep having versions of the same conversation. One of us references something we used to love, like *Yellow Submarine*, and the other says, *Wait, I'm past that now. I don't care about that anymore.* Shane is the only person, aside from my mom and Dylan and a handful of cops in New Mexico, who knows about Peter.

He got wrapped up in it. Maybe that's when the split started. It's probably my fault. Shane finally saw too much of me.

"Anyway, I wouldn't want to go with you and Leah Leary and mess up all your back-of-the-theater hand-job prospects," I said, trying to keep it light.

Shane grimaced. "That's gross."

"Prude," I said, smiling.

"You have to stop calling her Leah Leary. Just call her Leah."

"I can't help it."

"Yes you can," Shane mumbled, standing, cradling Ferris in his arms. "Anyway, the movie's at midnight, if you're done with—whatever you're doing."

I watched as he went to the kitchen sink and washed his wooden chopsticks, with soap and everything, still holding Ferris. It was really endearing. I felt bad.

"Thanks for the invite," I said.

"I just thought you liked the movie, that's all."

"I do. Or I did." A thought occurred to me. "Ooh! Are you going to get stoned?"

Shane laughed. "Not with Leah."

"No hand jobs, no weed, no psycho killers . . ."

He laughed more, walking down the hallway.

"See ya, Joss," he called out.

"See ya, Shane," I called out after him.

CHAPTER 3

"Do not leave me here."

"Oh, relax. I'll be gone half a second," Rhiannon insisted, sipping her Corona.

"What if someone tries to talk to me?"

"Oh my God, how will you deal?"

"Exactly—" I mumbled, scanning the crowd. A grungy dude leaning on a pool cue across the room had his eyes fixed on Rhiannon's ass.

"Do you know him?" I asked, pointing.

Rhiannon turned around, then back, staring at her phone. "No, but cute. I'm going to see if he's on Tinder."

"He looks like his name is Justin."

"No, no, no," Rhiannon said, swiping her finger across her phone.

"You can't leave me here. I'll start screaming."

Rhiannon finished the last of her beer and handed me the empty bottle, which I propped up on a cinder-block shelf against a stack of old VHS tapes.

"Well, I was just going to go to the bathroom, but since you're being such a baby, I think I'll go introduce myself."

"No." I groaned.

"This is what people do at parties."

"I hate you."

"Be a big girl and fend for yourself," Rhiannon said. "Or just stare at your phone and pretend to text."

She left. I watched her approach the Justin, confident, electric. Everyone else in the room was aware of her presence. Before they could trace her path back to me, I ducked into a shadowy corner, to survey the room and get my bearings.

Rhiannon's older sister, Guinevere, had reluctantly invited us to the house party of her mysterious friend Edwin, who always threw parties but never appeared at them. The room was dark, with dirty shag carpeting, lit by several strands of flamingo and pineapple-shaped lights.

The only reason I agreed to go was the off chance that Kit Behr might be there. Kit Behr, real boy, caught my eye a week ago, after I started following Guinevere on Instagram. I was perusing her followers and came across his profile—it was surprisingly devoid of shirtless selfies, regurgitated memes, and pictures of beer-can towers. There were photos of him playing guitar on a rainbow-lit stage, ancient cacti formations, a road trip through Mexico with his best friend, cute videos of his toddler nephew.

I almost switched over to a fake profile to send him a message, but something stopped me. I wanted to be Rosie for him, but it was too risky since she had my face and Kit and I were only one degree of separation apart in real life. I wasn't brave enough to friend him as myself, so I watched from far away and tried to think of what I'd say if we ever met. When Rhiannon asked Guinevere if Kit would be at Edwin's party, she said, "Maybe. He doesn't really party though."

A slight buzz and the possibility of Kit's arrival were the only things keeping me from jumping onto the pool table and screaming out at the injustice of having to live in such a soulless place, where even the good parties are just outlines of what I was sure a good party could be.

I wanted rooftop garden barbecues, beach bonfires, dinners where people drink old-timey cocktails and talk about stuff they read in the *New Yorker*. Cliffside *quinceañeras* in Barcelona, ritual sacrifices, anything but Edwin's living room.

Where's Mary-Kate when I need her?

I found a seat—an orange vinyl beanbag—and checked my phone for any new texts. Nothing. I sent one to Mary-Kate.

Me: **WHERE ARE YOU. Rhiannon abandoned me. It smells.**

Waiting for her reply, I logged into a dating site app, using the username and password of someone I'd created a couple days ago when I was supposed to be working on a paper about

Madame Bovary for French lit. I scanned the profile question-naire to refresh my memory.

Thora is a twenty-seven-year-old art restorer working at a museum in Washington, DC. Her favorite movies are *Amélie* and *Roman Holiday*, she loves music but is a horrible dancer, the last book she read was—very creative—*Madame Bovary*, and she's a vegetarian who's scared of horses. She grew up in Utah (oppressive Mormon upbringing she's still recovering from) and has always wanted to be an artist. There's the slightest hint of bad ghosts of boyfriends past and fragile-girl trauma—enough to pique someone's interest—but average, nonthreatening everything else. For her face, I found a blank-eyed blonde from Kansas with the mother lode of public Facebook photo albums.

I thought about what Thora would be doing on a Friday night. Cocktails with the girls? *Tiresome.* Making pizza with her bestie, drinking wine and bitching about her boss? *Too prosaic.* Maybe she was on a date, the first in a long time—it wouldn't go well, of course, but it could be something funny enough to write to a new guy about. *Save it for later.*

Or she was working late at the museum. *That's something.*

Working late in a dark room. A room cluttered with old paintings, dusty and mildewed, waiting for Thora to bring them back to life. She's made the workspace her own because she spends so many nights there. Cinder-block shelves, a beanbag, a strand of pink flamingo lights. There's one of those high-up basement windows that she's able to crack open slightly, and the room is full with the scent of night-blooming jasmine, which grows just outside. Thora has a big desk with bright lamps and giant magnifying glasses and jars full of tiny paintbrushes.

Thora stands up straight for the first time in hours. She stretches her arms and neck, using the Pilates techniques from the DVD she watches halfheartedly while she eats gummy bears for lunch. She sets down her—

I Googled "art restoration tools," and avoided looking around for Rhiannon, scared I'd make accidental eye contact with a stranger.

She sets down her heated spatula and cracks her knuckles. She needs a break. She's a hard worker, to a fault, but it's not because she desires praise. She likes what she does, even though she feels guilty that she isn't doing something that will change the world. She loves to give paintings a second chance. Secretly, she feels like all the paintings she restores are hers. After all, without her, they'd be lost.

Suddenly, someone plopped down next to me on the beanbag. The phone flew out of my hands, landing somewhere, camouflaged in the thick carpet. I reached for it immediately, then froze when I realized who it was.

"Woah, sorry about that," said Kit Behr.

It was bizarre, seeing him in motion after scrutinizing his photos. Like meeting someone famous. His physical presence was overwhelming—I shifted, putting a few more inches between us.

Smiling, he reached across my body and picked up my phone. I grabbed it from him before he could see Thora's profile on the screen.

In Arizona, even if a guy looks like an advanced creature, cute and new, he usually turns out to be another mouth breather. You find yourself bracing for the moment he inevitably says something disappointing, like "seriously, you believe all that evolution crap?"

"It's fine," I managed. My mouth had gone completely dry.

"I'm Kit," he said, smiling again, holding out his hand.

I shook it and said, "I know."

How do you know? No!

"Uh, I mean, I know of you—from Guinevere." I was grateful for the dim light, sure I was blushing. "You're in Vesta, right? Guitar?"

He's smiling again—am I making him smile?

He leaned back. The beanbag crunched. Something about his belt and the way it interacted with the bottom of his T-shirt made me feel embarrassed. I couldn't decide where to look.

"Yep. And you're Joss," he said.

I picked at the shag carpet.

"Yes?" I said, questioning. *If you say I'm Joss, I guess I must be.*

He explained. "I've seen your Instagram."

I nearly choked on my own tongue. "Heh—what?"

"You came up in the Explore section. Or, actually, a picture you took did. *The Book*, by Alan Watts? I love that book."

This was too much. Suddenly I was thinking of James. I wouldn't want him to talk to a girl on a beanbag. We didn't have the right to be possessive of each other, but I felt guilty. I pushed the thought away.

Kit Behr has seen your Instagram. What's on there? Friends. Plants. Bueller. Books, records, collages. Oh God, Mom's comments—

"I thought my profile was private," I said, remembering to breathe.

"Nicely *curated*," Kit said, using the word but obviously making fun of it. This calmed me. He had a sense of humor.

I ran my thumb across my phone's screen, stroking it like a kid ruffling the silky edge of her security blanket, still unable to look directly at Kit.

As I locked and unlocked the phone, it started ringing.

MAX IS CALLING

I pressed ignore and opened Instagram instead.

"What's your name?"

"kittredgebehr," he answered, spelling it out.

"You don't look like a Kittredge Behr," I said, typing, bringing up his profile.

"Half-Japanese. My middle name is Hiraku."

Thanks to my light stalking, I already knew both of those delicious factoids. *And your mom was a model for a Japanese makeup brand in the seventies, and your older brother got a DUI in 2012. . . .*

I scrolled through his feed, pretending I was seeing all the photos for the first time, pretending to react to each one. When I looked up again he had his eyes closed, hands folded on his chest, rising with each steady breath. Framed by flamingos and pineapples, pink and yellow spotlights.

Without thinking, I held up my phone and took his picture. He opened one eye when the shutter sound clicked.

"Hey," he said.

"We're friends now," I said, worshipping myself, posting the picture to my profile. As I was tagging him in it, the phone rang again.

MAX IS CALLING

He won't stop. He's freaking out. Anna's been gone too long. She's fading. She can't fade.

"Uh," I said, looking at Kit, who was opening and closing one eye at a time, staring up at the lights. "Excuse me for one second."

Ten thirty p.m. in Phoenix is seven thirty a.m. in Paris. Anna's asleep in the hotel.

I answered the phone. Someone turned the music up.

It's too loud for a hotel morning—

"Hello?" I said, standing.

Max's voice. Always so jarring, with a New York accent. *Too real.*

"Anna?" he said, and it came out sharp.

"Hey, Max!" I said, walking away from the beanbag, watching

Kit Behr closely. He had no idea. The phone was a portal. On one end was Max's world, his lab and the empty apartment he always said was so lonely, his anxiety medication, his hockey team. On the other end, a split in the wires. Anna bouncing wild off a satellite.

I was staring at Kit and forgot to listen to Max. I could barely hear him. I pressed my head against the phone, plugging my free ear.

"—I just wanted to make sure you were okay."

Max, the kind of guy who will pine forever over a girl he's never met.

She distracts him. He loves it.

"Yeah! I crashed as soon as I got back to the hotel. Then I got a call about an hour ago. I heard I got that Ibiza shoot! I was just about to write you—it's going to be lightning-round travel the whole day—"

"What's going on?" Max was saying, still sharp, accusatory, picking up on the discrepancies. I was being lazy with the lie. He knew it. He was thinking of all the times he'd ever suspected—

"It's Helena. She has this awful music blasting and she brought five other girls back to the hotel. They've been partying since last night. I've barely had a moment. She totally hates me—"

Anna sighed. Max heard it, digested what she'd just told him. Thought of her perfect face, holding it large in his mind's eye, a floating vision before him.

Anna in her trashed hotel room with a bunch of Czech models who've been tripping since sunrise. Earplugs around her neck. Eye bags. Silk pajamas. Max sees her, reaches out.

"I wish you were here," *Anna says, reaching back.* "You'd keep me calm. You'd help me deal with this."

"Oh, baby," *Max coos to her. That's what he needs, to be her man.*

"I have to go," *Anna says sadly, pulling back the heavy curtain at the window, looking out at Paris. Blinking against the bright, the city drenched in morning sun.*

"Write me a letter?" *Anna asks.*

"Okay."

Max's words aren't sharp anymore. They've dulled. He's satisfied.

Anna shuts the curtain, and the whole room disappears.

When I went back to the beanbag, I sat closer to Kit, pretending I didn't mean to.

He slid the phone out of my hand—I tensed, almost slapped him. Forced myself to relax, let him have it.

The screen still read **CALL WITH MAX ENDED 10:43:11 PM.**

"Max," Kit said, matter-of-fact. He started typing, holding the phone close, so I couldn't see.

"Boyfriend?" he asked.

"No," I said, uncomfortable, unsure what to do.

"Okay," Kit said, handing the phone back.

I snatched it away from him.

"I have to go."

"Oh," I said, betraying my disappointment.

Kit stood, towering over me, something kind of other-worldly about him, like he should be levitating. A lazy grace. Beneath his gaze, I felt like a peasant being scrutinized by a royal.

"Joss," he said, a statement.

"Kittredge?"

He nodded and walked away.

My hands were clammy. I felt faint. I felt like reciting the Lord's Prayer for some reason. I felt sick and ecstatic.

I was scrolling through my contacts list, searching desperately for whatever Kit had typed, when Mary-Kate finally walked up.

"Well, this is terrible," she said, looking around.

"It's brilliant. I love it. Everything is perfect."

"What's wrong with you?"

"So much," I said.

No new entries under **K**. I kept looking.

"Can we leave?"

"Rhiannon's talking to a Justin," I mumbled.

There he is. Under *I*.

INSTAGRAM BEANBAG (KIT)

His phone number. Like he'd etched it into a tree.

CHAPTER 4

Rosie: poly roommate. Ex-boyf asks her to go
to Chile with him as just friends (use Dylan's pics)

Thora: ex-fiancé Mormon cop slightly threatening, family cut her off because he made something up

Anna: gets sick in Ibiza . . . shady photographer

"Who's this?" Shane's voice.

Joss: went from the party to Mill Avenue, because Rhiannon
didn't want to go home yet. Remembered Shane said something
about Yellow Submarine playing at midnight. He was there, with
Leah Leary. Watched movie, felt nostalgic, wondered if I'd feel
nostalgic for this moment someday. Now the movie's over, and

Rhiannon and the Justin, whose name isn't really Justin—what was it? Travis?—are making out in her car. Mary-Kate's talking to Leah Leary, and Shane just walked up. He probably has that new look on his face, all earnestness and disappointment.

"Uh," I fumbled, saving the draft with my notes, looking up at Shane. He was holding his phone out, showing the picture I'd taken of Kit at the party.

"This guy Kit. He's in Guin's band."

Joss: got Kit Behr's phone number

Shane was watching the horizon, staring at the purple outline of the mountains in the early-morning dark, at the eastern place where, in a few hours, the sun would rise.

I hopped up to sit on the hood of Leah Leary's car. It was still warm with the day's heat, searing though my jeans at the backs of my thighs. A small silver cross dangled from the rearview mirror.

Along Mill Avenue, the college bars were just beginning to close, but the parking lot behind the theater was deserted except for Rhiannon and Leah's cars, separated by a clutch of gnarled cacti living on a traffic island beneath a fluorescent streetlamp.

"I did like it, by the way," I said.

"What?" Shane asked, turning around to check on Mary-Kate and Leah Leary. "The party?"

"No, the movie."

Shane kept watching—Mary-Kate was looking at something on Leah's phone.

"Shane," I said loudly. "Focus."

"Sorry," he said, facing me again. "Yeah. It's great, right? Just like I remember."

"Except now you don't have to hide behind a pillow and have your mom fast-forward past the Blue Meanie parts."

More silence, new silence, where there never used to be any.

"Bet you can't guess my favorite part," I said.

"Probably not."

A police helicopter crossed the sky overhead, rumbling out of the desert and back into it, searchlight trailing aimlessly.

"Uh-oh," I whispered. "They're coming for us."

"It was only a matter of time," Shane whispered back.

I knew he was remembering our game—we used to play that the helicopters were after us, two little kids pretending to be spies or assassins or newly sentient robots leading a rebellion.

BZZZT, went my phone, rattling against the car.

George: **What's up, girlie?**

Oh yeah, George. Emma's husband is so close to finding out about you. That won't be good. Things will have to end.

It's 2:11 a.m., so it's just past 5 in Savannah. Emma's asleep.

I slid off the car, scrolling through my contacts again, making sure Kit's number was still there.

"Was that James?" Shane asked.

Hearing Shane say the name James so casually knocked the axis off-balance. I was worried that Shane's knowledge of James's existence might make bad things happen, move things that shouldn't be moved.

BZZZT went the phone.

I already knew what it would say.

A crack, worlds colliding.

New message from BLOCKED NUMBER

Be anyone else, please.

But it wasn't.

XXX: **LIAR.**

Another text, immediately—

XXX: **I SEE YOU.**

My hand stung. It was in pain, the phone a vibrating shock. Somewhere, someone was typing "LIAR," typing "I SEE YOU." That person knew my name, my phone number, and exactly what to say to make me freeze and wrench inward.

From the corner of the parking lot came an animal motion. A trembling of coarse brown fur. I looked—it was a flash, that's all. The lamplight flickering.

Shane was looking at me, waiting for something. *James,* said my brain. *Shane asked if that was James.*

"No," I went on, deleting the texts, dropping the phone into my bag. "That was nobody."

"Aren't they all nobodies?" Shane said.

If he'd been smiling when he said it, or if I hadn't been

picturing faceless monsters lurking in parking lots and whole worlds fracturing like glass shards, I probably would have let the comment slide. But I could tell he said it just to piss me off.

"Fuck off, Shane. You know they aren't," I said, glaring at him, lining my face up with his.

"Look—" he started, glancing back again at Leah and Mary-Kate. "Don't freak out. I just want to say something without you freaking out."

"You don't get to tell me not to freak out," I snapped.

I'd raised my voice; Shane lowered his.

"I should get some credit for waiting so long to confront you about it, considering everything that happened."

"Credit?" I asked, outraged more by his martyr's tone than by what he was going to say. I knew he'd been holding it back for a while. He was bad at hiding his judgment. What made it even worse was that I knew he wasn't wrong.

"I know you didn't stop after Peter. Like you told your mom and dad you did. And I haven't said anything. I've wanted to, but I haven't. But now—"

I crossed my arms, dared him to go on.

"I don't know." He sighed. "But you just got a text and looked terrified. I've seen that before."

I grabbed his arm and pulled him into the dark at the edge of the parking lot.

"Since when are you the arbiter of health and good decisions? You've been hanging out with Leah Leary too much.

Now you're all holier-than-thou, judging evil Joss for stringing along unsuspecting innocents."

There was that look, the disappointed look, clouded over with fresh anger.

"That isn't how I see myself, and that's not how I see you," he said. "But you have a weird blind spot when it comes to these people's actual, real-life feelings. You don't get it. If you keep doing this, someone is going to find you again. Something like Peter is going to happen again."

"I'm sick of your condescending shit," I shout-whispered, loud enough to catch Mary-Kate's attention.

Shane, you're so stupid. You cracked it open. You let the texts come in. You invited a jinx.

I wanted to say something mean, but now Mary-Kate and Leah Leary were watching us.

"Forget this," I said instead. "I don't have to explain anything to you."

"I'm sorry me worrying about you makes you so angry." Shane sighed, watching the mountains again, like he was waiting for something.

I walked away from him, rubbing the base of my neck with both hands, turning my face up to the sky. From somewhere on the avenue, a drunken voice shouted, "Woo! Sun Devils rock, baby!"

"Ugh," I groaned, to the stars and the streak-white Milky Way.

"What's up?" asked Rhiannon, appearing before me, glancing toward Shane.

"Nothing," I said as we walked over to Mary-Kate, Leah, and Shane. "Where's the Justin? I want to leave."

"Trevor," Rhiannon said, emphasizing, "is in the car. I have to give him a ride to his grandma's house."

"His *grandma*—"

"I'll drive your car," Mary-Kate interrupted, looking disapprovingly at Rhiannon, who did seem to be weaving a bit, pupils as big as quarters. "But only if I can sleep over."

"Cool," Rhiannon said. "Joss, you in?"

Shane and Leah had separated from the group and were whispering together.

"Can you drop me off?" I asked, keeping my eyes on them, wondering what they were talking about. "I told my mom I'd come home."

"Really?" Mary-Kate asked.

"But you live so far," Rhiannon whined.

Across the parking lot, Trevor opened the car door and tumbled out of it.

"Fuck!" he yelled as he arranged himself on the asphalt, leaning against the rear tire. He took a drag on his vape and brushed the hair out of his eyes, noticing all five of us staring at him. He waved.

"Gotta go, go, go," Rhiannon said. "Shane, take Joss home."

"It's not my car—" Shane protested, but it was too late.

And that's how I ended up driving the fifteen minutes north to my house with my two most favorite people in the whole world.

Leah insisted I sit up front with her, and I watched the silver cross dangling all the way to my house as she chattered on about how much she loved the movie, and was that Ryan Gonzales's brother Trevor who Rhiannon was with, and, most distressingly, how nice and cool Mary-Kate was.

"I feel like we'd never really talked before," she was saying. "And I've known her since kindergarten."

"She can be kind of quiet," I said, taking out my phone, sending Mary-Kate a text.

Me: **I miss you, Mary-K. Let's do something tomorrow, xoxo**

Leah drove and talked, Shane stayed silent, and I watched the silver cross. It caught the traffic lights in a way that made me remember driving home from parties with my parents when I was little, how I used to sit in the back and squint my eyes, turning my head from side to side to make the lights dance, red and green. One good thing about living your whole life in the same place is that you don't have to go far to visit your memories. They just live around you, everywhere.

When we got to my house, Shane came out from the backseat to sit up front with Leah. For a moment we were outside the car, alone.

"I think I got it—your favorite part," Shane said.

I smiled.

"The Beatles house, with all the doors leading to different worlds?"

"Yep."

"I knew it," Shane said, happy he'd guessed correctly. "All those mysterious possibilities."

The motion-sensor lights in the driveway flicked on, casting a mask of brightness and shadow across Shane's face. He looked older, tired.

"I'm sorry," I said. "I know I suck."

"You don't suck," Shane replied, automatic.

"What do you think it'll feel like to be eighty?" I asked.

He thought for a moment. "Great?"

"I think it'll be awful. Like all that time weighs your body down, fills it up, and you get heavier and heavier with it until you finally just die."

"And on that note," he said, opening the car door. When I leaned down to say good-bye, he was kissing Leah's cheek.

So they touch.

"Thanks for the ride, Leah Leary," I said.

I stood there for a while after they left, unable to go inside and face the three closed doors of my dead dad and missing-in-action brother and sad mom or the bright all-knowing stare of the cat who hates me. I wanted to walk into another dimension and inhabit the world of Rosie, Anna, Emma, or Thora for the rest of the night.

I must have been standing there a long time, because the

driveway lights went off and I was left in darkness.

I hurried to the gate and let myself in, ignoring the scurrying footsteps behind me, the animal in the atmosphere, his cold eyes narrowing.

I told you we could do this.

James and I are in the Dream Palace, in Rosie's room. It can be her dorm, the school library, the hillside where she smokes with her friends, but right now it's her art studio. A version of my dad's, a version of something I saw in a movie. Elements of my bedroom. Bueller the lizard is here, opalescent scales shining in the new dimension. When I was creating Rosie, I looked at pictures of freshman studios on the college website. I took the name Rose Dahlgren from the school blog, a post with photos from the incoming student show.

The Dream Palace is a dilapidated motel in the middle of an endless luminous desert—the astral plane. Each room in the motel belongs to a different girl. Some are closed forever, and some are waiting to be filled. In the cement courtyard, my fake personalities lounge around the empty pool like Barbie dolls. When I need one, she animates.

It started with Amelia. I was with my dad, dragged along on some obscure errand that I've forgotten, driving through the industrial badlands surrounding the Phoenix airport, when I saw a sign: THE DREAM PALACE. A GENTLEMAN'S CLUB. The "GENTLEMAN" underlined in pink neon. We were going to get the truck's windows tinted, maybe? And I wrote Amelia's back-story, bored in the waiting area.

She was the first one I could move into. I could bring her out, put her away, be her, leave myself whenever I wanted.

Somewhere in the Dream Palace, Amelia's door is now locked. She is still there, glowing. But I can't let her out. She is raging. I don't control her anymore. She is angry about lost Peter.

Back to James.

I was in my bed with my body curled around my phone, watching his texts appear. He was wishing we were together, cursing a world that set us a continent apart.

Come here, I said. *Come. At least try.*

I went there first. I called to him. Thought of his face, skin, his warm breath. I pictured his teeth, each of them, and the beds of his fingernails. Then he walked in. Uncomfortable at first, then easing into it. The air thick so things could morph around. Power shooting through unpredictable points like jets in a hot tub. Our bodies pulsing moodily.

Are we dreaming? James asked.

No. It's better than that.

I touched his arm, brought him close, and kissed him. Looking like Joss, feeling like Rosie. His warmth poured out, his happiness.

CHAPTER 5

"Before you leave, please make sure to write the names of everyone in your group on every page, and put your worksheets in the turn-in folder. And remember, on Thursday we move on to plant structure and photosynthesis."

Mr. Lauren sat down at his desk as the early-dismissal bell rang and everyone rushed out the door, eager to head over to the gym at the boys' school for a coeducational pep rally, that horror of horrors. I waited until the last person was gone before handing in my assignment, walking slowly past the teacher's desk at the front of the classroom, trying to sneak a peek at the notebook he was hunched over.

"Not in a hurry to get to the pep rally?" Mr. Lauren asked, without looking up. The way he said it implied air quotes around the words "pep" and "rally."

He was drawing something, shielding it with his arm.

"I totally am," I said. "I hope they hand out those little pro-life fetus-feet pins again."

He laughed. "Still going on about that?"

"It made an impression. I'm scarred for life."

"Pity."

I've given a few fake personalities flings-with-teacher stories. It's classic flirt bait. It says all the right things, like "I'm precocious, but not a prude," and "I'm a little bit of a bad girl, but only if you're in a position of authority."

"Do you have my iPod?" I asked. "I think I left it here on Friday."

"Oh yes, it's here somewhere," he said, dropping his pencil, brushing some papers over the open notebook.

"Did you see that Conor Oberst's coming to the Marquee this weekend?" I asked.

"Really?" Mr. Lauren said, searching around on his messy desk.

"Yeah. I think I'm going to go," I said.

Mr. Lauren moved his chair back and disappeared beneath the desk, banging around.

Carefully, I leaned over and pushed away the papers covering the notebook.

He'd drawn a woman—it was a nice sketch—and she was pretty.

"Found it!" he said, coming up. He unplugged the aux cable connecting my iPod to the classroom sound system. Our fingers touched as he handed it to me, and he let go immediately, straightening his glasses.

"Who's she?" I asked, pointing at the drawing.

He blushed.

"Mr. Lauren," I teased. "Do you have a girlfriend? Finally?"

I couldn't wait to tell Rhiannon and Mary-Kate. When we all had him for freshman biology, he'd worn a wedding band. One day Rhiannon dared me to ask about his wife. He said he wasn't married, and the next day the ring was gone.

He closed the notebook and stood up. I watched him shut down his computer and start to pack his bag. He tried to hide his grin.

"Oh my God. You do," I said.

"She's not my girlfriend," he muttered.

"I want to know everything. Does she have good taste in music? Are your genes compatible? Did you meet her at that robotics club thing in Yuma? Mary-Kate said she saw you with someone."

My phone vibrated in the pocket of my uniform skirt and I quickly checked the message.

Rhiannon: **w/ Shane, back row, all the way on the left**

Mr. Lauren walked to the door and turned the lights off.

"Hey," I protested. "Answer my questions."

"Shouldn't you get going?"

I approached the doorway. "Are you ashamed? Did you meet her on Craigslist?"

He cleared his throat. Standing next to him, I felt a kind of energy pass between us, the kind of energy that exists between any two humans, the kind that has neutral on one end of the spectrum and electric on the other.

You're just imagining it, I thought. *You're desperate for a way to make school less boring.*

Just in case it was real, though, I gave him a little knowing smile as I walked away, texting Rhiannon.

Me: **On my way. Big news re: Mr. Lauren**

> To Jimmy Grace,
>
> I have astral plane jet lag. Are you affected? It's a low-sitting heaviness right above my eyebrows, pressing down. Worse when I turn my head too quickly. I'm going through the motions, but everything has dulled. Colors, sounds, movements, all covered with a grey transparency. The astral plane felt right. Being here feels wrong. I'm just vamping now, but what if the world is the projection and where we were, together, was real?
>
> After we said good night, I fell asleep and dreamed I was at a high school pep rally. What were you like in high school? Did you get laid? I slept with my English teacher at the end of senior year. I had three friends and hated

everybody else. I don't know if I wasted my
time or not. Probably.

There were more scary texts this morning.
I've thought about trying to trace the number,
but I don't know how. Guess I could look it up.
Or text back.

I wanted to write you a letter. Texting is
thrilling in its immediacy, but we started out
with letters, and I miss them. Has it really been
a year? Here's a secret: When I get a letter
from you I pretend that I'm a Brontë sister
receiving a soft paper envelope sealed with
wax, written on by her beloved's hand.

Do you sometimes see things that
aren't there? Now that you've successfully
experienced the Dream Palace/Astral
Plane Rosie Experience I feel comfortable
confessing. I see things—animals, mostly. Lately
a jackrabbit, but he's turning into something
else. A coyote, I think. And he isn't really an
animal. He's a trickster. I'm not schizophrenic
or anything, I know this is my imagination.
Daydreams bleeding into the scenery. I only
mention it because it's happening a lot lately.
The texts are bringing it on.

Tell me what I would be if I were an article

of clothing. You, my constant James, would be
an Old Jacket.

Where are you right now?

xx

My finger hovered over the J key for a brief moment before
shifting up and over to press *R* very precisely.

xx Rosie

I have a recurring nightmare where I sign all the letters
with my real name. It didn't help that Rosie had begun borrowing thoughts and experiences from my actual life.

"No, it's cute! He likes this girl so much he spends all day
sketching her in his little notebook," Rhiannon was saying. She
and Shane were deconstructing the gossip I'd fed them about
Mr. Lauren and his mystery woman.

"Yeah," Shane said incredulously. "I don't know how not-
creepy that is."

"It's not creepy," I said, casting the deciding vote. "And even
if it is, it adds to his mystique."

"Mr. Lauren has mystique?" Shane asked.

"Why do you think we're even talking about him?" Rhiannon
teased.

"Shrug," Shane said, watching as I finished typing the letter to
James. When I caught him, he pretended like he was looking past

me, across the bleachers, down at the gleaming basketball court.

I pushed send, launching the words into the void, where they would ride the aether as shimmering particles before reassembling, full of light, to find James—my electronic offering. I was taking a chance, telling him so much, but I had to. I could always backtrack.

"Joss would do bad things to Mr. Lauren if she wasn't so busy with her imaginary friends," Rhiannon said.

The doors at the far side of the gym opened, revealing a line of uniformed flag team members holding a banner: CONGRATS ON A GREAT SEASON BROPHY BRONCOS / XAVIER PANTHERS. The sound of stray cymbals and last-minute practice drum reps leaked into the gymnasium, heralding the start of the pep rally.

"In what world does this make sense?" I asked. "How is this part of my education?"

"At least this one's coed," Shane said. "You don't want to know what an all-guy pep rally is like."

I thought for a minute. "Ha! Yes I do."

Rhiannon said, "Girls bring the pep. That's why they invite us."

"They put it in the drinking fountains and hot lunches," I agreed.

Rhiannon giggled. "We're laced with pep."

"So full of pep," I said, holding my stomach.

"My pep baby hurts," said Rhiannon. "I think it's angry."

Shane had to laugh.

We were sitting in the last row, as far away as possible from the actual athletes. It was just us and a few of the really hard-core Catholic girls sitting nearby—skirts droopy and below the knee, hair down to their butts like sister wives.

"I feel like I'm inside a bad cartoon version of high school," Shane said.

"They're forcing the cliché on us," I said. "And everyone here who's actually enjoying themselves is complicit."

The band started up, for real this time, and they all marched out, accompanied by the seriously demented flag team and Bronco Bill, the tumbling, manic Brophy mascot.

Bronco Bill was actually Cody Majors, who asked me out every day in eighth grade. I never said yes. I never said yes to anyone who asked me out, not that it happened very often. But saying yes seemed out of the question. I couldn't picture meeting a boy at the mall and walking around for an hour, getting boba tea or stealing from the candy store. I couldn't possibly have anything in common with an earnest, rosy-cheeked youth like Cody Majors. I hoped that was true, and not the other possibility—that we'd have tons in common, that we'd be perfectly matched, that I was just another normal girl, the sum total of years of learning to smile politely and not make anybody feel uncomfortable.

I zoned out and tried to daydream, picturing a great, thundering tidal wave crashing through the roof, washing us all away.

"Joss, you are literally grimacing," said Rhiannon.

"This is my face now."

"Where is Mary-Kate?" Rhiannon asked. "She was here this morning, but she wasn't at lunch. Did she go home sick?"

"I don't know. She wasn't in bio, either."

I checked my phone, hoping briefly that James had already responded to my e-mail. He hadn't. I sent a message to Mary-Kate.

Me: **Where aaaaaaaare youuuuu?**

A few messages down, I opened a draft I'd been working on since Friday night.

What do you say in your very first text to Kit Behr?

Me: **Hey, it's me, Joss. I'm texting you now.**

Boring.

Me: **Is Conor Oberst way too 10 years ago for you? Do you only like Japanese jam bands and vaporwave?**

Too many questions.

"And now, please stand for the Pledge of Allegiance," commanded the Brophy principal, voice booming over the loudspeaker.

Everyone stood up, leaving me and Shane and Rhiannon in a nice little enclave of anti-authoritarian peace.

"Countries aren't real!" I shouted. One of the sister wives turned around and scowled.

"I hate the way he says 'under God,'" Shane mumbled.

Swoosh—everyone sat down.

The principal announced the pep squad.

Shane waved to Leah Leary, who bounced onto the floor like a caffeinated squirrel.

Like she can even see him way back here.

"*2-4-6-8 who do we appreciate, Broooooophy!*" Leah yelled, leading the chant. Her shrill voice carried through the gym, reverberating off the wall behind my ears.

"Yep, that's my girlfriend, chant leader," Shane said.

I patted him on the back. "You are king of the cliché."

The Brophy principal's mustache hairs bristled against the microphone. He said something about the cheerleading team.

A screechy recording of steel drums started over the loud-speaker. Leah Leary and her pep squad shuffled off the gym floor as the lights dimmed and two spotlights swirled over the bleachers and basketball court.

I stared down at the blank text.

Me:

Send him something real.

Me: **I hate pep rallies.**

I pressed send before I could second-guess myself.

The cheerleading team burst out of the wrestling room to a roar of applause and catcalls.

Now, put the phone down. Don't check it for at least five minutes.

I caught Shane staring again as I slipped the phone into the front pocket of my backpack. He quickly looked away, peering down at the cheerleaders.

"Is that?" he said. "No way—"

"Holy shit." Rhiannon gasped. I followed her gaze.

It was Mary-Kate. The roving spotlight landed on her, and the cheerleading coach called out her name like she was competing at a beauty pageant. Mary-Kate raised her pom-poms over her head, shouting something that looked like *Woo-hoo!*

Rhiannon was laughing hysterically.

"Oh my God," I said, turning to her. "Did you know about this?"

Rhiannon shook her head and stood up, shouting, "Go, Mary-Kate, yeah!"

I couldn't watch. All I could think was that my friend hadn't told me. She'd kept a secret. I thought back to Friday night, when she and Leah Leary were talking by themselves.

Rhiannon sat down, and the team moved on to their next cheer.

"I didn't know she could do any of this stuff," Rhiannon said in awe.

But she could. And she looked like she fit in, not like she was in bizarro-world. She looked like a real cheerleader.

"Why didn't she tell us?" I said, not really asking Rhiannon or Shane.

Shane spoke up. "She probably thought you'd be dismissive or horrified."

"Oh, come on, like she's afraid of me? I'm her best friend," I said.

"No, Shane makes sense," Rhiannon added unhelpfully.

"Great," I said. "Now I feel horrible."

From the backpack at my feet, the chime of a new message.

Be Kit. I summoned the flexible forces of nature and karma.

Instagram Beanbag (Kit): **Hmm. This has to be Joss.**

Everything fell away like I needed it to.

Kit has entered the web.

CHAPTER 6

Instagram Beanbag (Kit): You're in high school?

Me: **Come on, you knew that**

Instagram Beanbag (Kit): **How old are you?**

Me: **16**

That was weird, saying the real answer.

I was editing his contact info, changing his name to just Kit, when Mary-Kate walked up.

"Go ahead, get it all out," she said.

The rally was over, Rhiannon and Shane were gone, and I was sitting on a picnic table outside the gym, oblivious to the activity of my fellow stragglers. And there was Mary-Kate, in her cheerleading uniform, carrying an Xavier duffel bag with her name monogrammed on it.

"I don't have anything to say," I said as she sat down next to me. "I mean, okay. It was kind of a shock. You coming out, pom-poms a'twirling—"

"Joss—"

"—since I had no idea, that's all."

A breeze sent a smattering of pollen drifting onto the table. My phone buzzed.

Kit: **I was going to ask you out. But you're jailbait.**

He's not Cody Majors. But he's not James either.

"Caroline was a cheerleader," Mary-Kate said.

Caroline is her sister. Mary-Kate and Rhiannon get these cool older sisters who pave the way for them. All I have is Dylan. Dylan isn't even on Facebook. Dylan doesn't believe in voting.

"And my mom is pretty into the idea of me being one too, for some reason. So I figured I'd try out, just to make her happy."

Me: **How old are you, 40?**

Kit: **19**

Me: **Pshhh**

"I really didn't think I'd make the team. That's why I didn't tell you at first."

"At first?" I asked.

"Well, then I started liking it."

"Shane said you didn't tell me because you thought I'd think you were stupid."

She laughed. "Aww, Shane. He's so observant."

New message from MOM.

Mom: **Where are you?**

Me: **Oh. In front of the Brophy gym—sorry.**

"I would never think you're stupid," I said.

"I know," Mary-Kate said. "You do think it's lame though."

"Mary-Kate!" someone shouted, saving me from having to answer. It was Mae Castillo, cheerleading captain. She was standing at the gym entrance with two other girls, Carmen Farrow and Nora del Toro, all in bright, crisp uniforms and identical curly ponytails.

"If those three are an alternate-universe version of us, I'm Mae," I said, scanning them carefully. "For sure."

"I think you'd probably really like each other."

"Mary-Kate!" Mae yelled, a bit more forcefully.

"Are we okay?" Mary-Kate asked, standing.

"Yeah, yeah."

She reached in for a hug and I patted her back, phone in hand.

"Just don't forget your roots," I said.

"Want to come talk to them with me?"

My mom's black Lexus rounded the corner.

"I can't. Therapy time," I said, pointing at the car.

"Text me?" Mary-Kate asked.

"Sure," I said, watching as Mary-Kate walked over to her new teammates, the girls I'd assumed we mutually disdained. She stepped up to them easily, smiling.

What else isn't she telling me?

My mom was talking to her assistant as I climbed into the

car—his nasally fry barked out from the speakerphone as she ended the call.

Kit: **What are you doing Saturday?**

I felt like I was going to throw up.

Me: **I was thinking of going to a show**

Me: **Conor Oberst**

"Joss, I said 'how was your day'?"

I rolled the window down and hauled my backpack onto my lap, searching around in it for the iPod Mr. Lauren had returned to me.

"The usual," I answered. "Flirting with the teacher, nachos for lunch, mandatory-attendance pep rally, Mary-Kate's a cheerleader."

She was wearing sunglasses, but I felt her giving me the side-eye.

"I appreciate your phrasing, by the way. Thanks," I added.

"You get so angry when I ask 'How was school?'"

"It's like instead of hearing the words, I hear this horrible screeching sound coming from your mouth."

"That's nice, honey."

Something changed recently. I mean, obviously, lots of things happened. My dad dropped dead in his studio like it was no big deal. Dylan freaked out and went to South America to trek through the jungle and blow through his insurance money. But even if they were both back home waiting for us, I think the thing between my mom and me might've evolved anyway. Maybe the bad stuff helped it along. That'd be really twisted. She's funnier now than she ever was before.

iPod plugged in to the car's stereo, I skipped through shuffle until I found the song I wanted to hear.

Kit: **Me too**

Me: **Yeah right**

"Nachos for lunch?" my mom was saying, as she sped up to race through a yellow light before deciding, at the last possible moment, to slam on the brakes.

"Maybe if I had a nice mom who packed a healthy lunch for me, I wouldn't be forced to eat delicious nachos every day."

She was horrified. "You eat them every day?"

"Only on the days I eat."

Her phone rang, saving her the trouble of trying to decide whether or not I was kidding.

"This is Nina," she said, turning the volume down. I turned it back up as soon as she looked away.

Kit: **Can I come with you?**

Kit coming to my house, picking me up. Having to consider what he'd think of how I looked, the words I said, how I acted. Having to say "I'll be right back; I have to go to the bathroom." Having to maybe eat something in front of him. Having to scratch my nose. What if I sweat? What if mascara flakes onto my cheek? What if my lip balm gives me the white crud at the corners of my lips and I don't even realize?

I slid my finger across the screen, closing Kit's chat thread, opening one between Rosie and James.

Me: I know I just wrote you, but, James—

Me: A guy just asked me out and I don't know what to do.

Me: We've avoided this. I know you must see girls, etc. . . . a year of talking, but we're not celibate. What should I say?

"One second, Tim," my mom said. We'd pulled into an office park, the kind you pass every day and never really notice, until it becomes the place where you go for acupuncture or teeth whitening—or therapy.

"Left here," I told her.

She jerked the steering wheel around. "This place is a maze."

I couldn't tell if she was talking to Tim or to me.

"Over there, two oh six," I directed.

It wasn't quite four thirty, and the sun was brighter than it seemed it should be, in an unsettling early-summer way. Cicadas screeched from the top of the palo verde tree planted in the rocks outside Dr. Judson's office.

Inside, I walked past a burbling plugged-in waterfall, signed my name on a sheet of paper attached to a clipboard, and sat down. Nobody else was there—my mom was still in the car, finishing her phone call. I pretend that I'm thirty. I pretend I am there because my marriage is slowly killing me. I pretend I am there because I'm a hoarder who keeps miscarried fetuses in jars in the freezer. I pretend I am there for many reasons, but not the real one.

I watch the women behind the check-in desk and consider changing Thora's backstory. I've done the art restoration thing before—it's easy because it was my dad's job, so I know good details. But Rosie's in art school—there might be spillover. I might get confused.

Maybe Thora manages a therapist's office. I wonder about the politics of the place, try to size up the women—this one's obviously the leader. She looks a little bitchy, like if you didn't have your insurance card ready she'd roll her eyes while you looked for it. The girl on the phone scheduling appointments seems sad.

The third girl comes out and whispers that Dr. Judson will see me now; she is like a robot moving from one doorway to the next, all day, back and forth.

She leads me to a smaller, darker room. There is another fake waterfall—this one sits on a table, and I can see where it's plugged in to the wall. When I sit down, James has texted.

James: **Ouch**

James: **I guess you should say yes**

James: **If you want to**

James: **But ouch**

A new message broke into James's lament, and I didn't notice until it was too late, until I'd sent my response to the wrong person.

Kit: **Come on, let's see Conor Oberst together**

Me: **I wish it was you**

You did a Wrong Thing. The jackrabbit-coyote beneath Dr. Judson's desk is laughing at you.

Kit sent a response, but I couldn't look. Careful, deliberate, I went back to James.

Me: **I wish it was you.**

I wished my desire for him was a physical thing, a little rubber ball I could carry around.

Dr. Judson comes in, sits down, doesn't speak. I turn off the phone.

Rosie (you would be a Soft Robe),

Sometimes this is enough, and that seems crazy to me. It's crazy that this way of knowing a person could even approach satisfying.

But tonight it's not enough and it's so deeply not enough that I'm sitting here with my arms out, helpless. I don't like that feeling. I want to help you with the person sending you those threatening texts. I want to tell you that I don't have visions of animals, and if I were your boyfriend I'd probably tell you to go talk to someone about it. Maybe I only feel like saying that because I got angry when you told me about the guy asking you out. Angry at myself for letting it get to this point.

There's too much I can't do from here.

So let me make sure you know how I feel, at least:

You can do anything. You're like a superhero to me. You should be living on the fucking frightening full moon! You should be conquering the forbidden ice castles of Jupiter's moon Callisto in the year 3010! You should be blowing up icons.

I need to say it:

I think we should meet. I think e-mail and chat and texting are hitting a critical point, and if we don't meet, I will have to stop. And then what? "Oh yeah, Rosie, we used to be pen pals, but then it fizzled out." We can't let that happen.

I'd like to build a tree house. Would you come live in it with me?

How can I miss you? I've never met you.

Old Jacket

There are steps to take when someone I'm talking to gets too uncomfortable with the unknown, and restless because of it.

After my session with Dr. Judson, my mom had to go back to the office, so she dropped me off at home.

James's e-mail came when it was past midnight in New York. I'd just gotten out of the shower. I signed on to Chat and he was there.

I dragged a video clip into our conversation.

sharkliver: **What is this?**

RosieRose: **Just open it, if you can. I don't know if it'll work. Never sent a video over this thing.**

That's a lie. I've sent videos before. I've sent the same one I was sending to James to countless other people—a thirty-second clip of me touching myself through a pair of sheer black panties. (Close-up, careful not to show any identifying marks, like the patch of freckles on my upper left thigh.)

sharkliver: **A video?**

RosieRose: **You'll like it.**

RosieRose: **I have many thoughts about your letter, and I'll write back.**

RosieRose: **(I don't feel like a superhero, though.)**

sharkliver: **You're my guru.**

RosieRose: **And you're a tree house philosopher.**

RosieRose: **Did you watch it yet?**

sharkliver: **Rosie . . .**

RosieRose: **You like?**

sharkliver: **Oh my god yes**

It turned me on, knowing that James was watching. That we weren't physically together was irrelevant. My body responded to his all the same.

I was sitting at the desk in my bedroom, wrapped in a towel. I slipped a hand beneath it—

RosieRose: **I wanted to give you something, and tell you—**

RosieRose: **Even when I'm with someone else, I think of you**

every time I come. I'm always picturing you

I typed it, and realized it was true. I was never really actually with anyone else, but it was true. I was always pretending it was James.

sharkliver: **I wish there was something I could give you in return.**

RosieRose: **You want more?**

I opened my English Reports > Tale of Two Cities subfolder, where I kept the video clips hidden, and queued up the second one. It was from the same angle as the first, but in it I push the panties aside, teasing myself with them.

I stood, keeping my eyes on the download bar as it crept forward a centimeter at a time. I dropped the towel and pulled on a pajama shirt before climbing into bed, carrying the warm laptop. Under the covers, I rested a hand on my navel.

The download finished.

He's watching.

RosieRose: **Did it get you hard?**

sharkliver: **Yes.**

RosieRose: **I can feel you.**

My hand—James's hand, I was willing it—moved between my legs—

Suddenly, sound echoed from downstairs—the garage door opening, a car door slamming, keys jangling. I jumped up and ran to turn off the light, then hurried back into bed, shoving the laptop under a pillow.

My mom's heels clicked loudly up the tiled stairs. She stopped just outside my room, took off her shoes, pushed the door open. I shut my eyes and shifted the covers a little so she'd know I was there without having to look too closely.

The door shut, she left, and except for the noise of the shower she started, the house was silent and still once again.

I uncovered the laptop and pulled it closer, dimming the harsh blue light of the screen.

sharkliver: **I'm lying in bed. About to come, thinking of you. Your eyes, your hands on my chest. You'd wear yourself out on me, then I'd lay you down.**

A new chat window popped up.

BelieverJWL: **http://www.josslies.tumblr.com**

Pulse pounding hollow against my temples, I moved the cursor over the link.

Click.

An all-black Tumblr page, blank except for four words at the top in big white letters.

JOSS WYATT TELLS LIES

Across the room, my phone, set to silent and left on my desk, lit up.

Don't look at it.

I X-ed out of the chat, and blocked BelieverJWL.

Another chat window popped up immediately.

BelieverJWL1: **http://www.josslies.tumblr.com**

I blocked it, too—but they kept coming.

BelieverJWL2: **http://www.josslies.tumblr.com**

BelieverJWL3: **http://www.josslies.tumblr.com**

No, no, no—

I clicked back to my chat with James.

sharkliver: **You want that?**

sharkliver: **Rosie?**

ROWAN MANESS

CHAPTER 7

Something is not right in Rosie's room.

One moment it's her studio, the next it's the hillside near the café. It's not a room so much as a pocket of constant flux—I can't make it stop changing. I try to ground the whole thing by focusing on the window, forcing it to stay in one place.

It's not easy, but I do it. The window, its curtains drawn, is fixed. I go to it, pull the curtains back, look over the outdoor hallway, down into the Dream Palace courtyard. Still figures lie on plastic pool loungers. The sky is a flat, starless black matte.

The room stops spinning, is stuck somewhere between the studio and a cold, photo-negative version of the hillside. One wall is peeled back and crumbling, trees bursting through it. There's a rustling in the trees. When I turn around, a turquoise glare.

It's too big to be a jackrabbit; he's decided now—the coyote *incarnation suits him best. It's a trickster, too. He is breathing. He's alive outside me, something new.*

A pounding at the door. It's James, I think. He found me here again and he will come in and make this stop.

The coyote's voice, itsnothimitsnothimitsnothim, a steady thrum. I ignore it.

But it isn't. It's Max. Why Max? His eyes are empty sockets. His hands are cut off.

And when I slam the door in Max's face and turn around, the coyote is in the middle of Rosie's room, hunched over Peter's dead body.

I slept in fits all night, following links in my sleep, waking up for good at four thirty to more texts from the blocked number, more *LIARS*. I finally read Kit's reply to my accidental text sometime around then—the dreaded **What?** followed by **Was that for someone else?**

Sunrise outlined my bedroom window with light where the blinds met the frame, and I thought of the Dream Palace and what the difference was between visiting it in a nightmare and going there consciously. Thoughts spun, floated, swam. Nothing came of them. The rectangular beam of light lengthened across the ceiling until the alarm on my phone rang. Seconds later—

"Joss!"

My mom, from the bottom of the stairs. "Are you up?"

When she yells, she makes my name two syllables—*JAW-OSS!*

Once, in the days after my dad died, when Dylan and my mom and I were all trying to win the Who's the Most Depressed? game, I said, *Why did he have to die right when summer vacation started? I don't even get to miss any school*, and it made them laugh. But I really meant it. I still hold that against him.

"I'm up. I'm up. I'm up!" I shouted, to silence the beast.

I rose, and brought the laptop to my desk. I plugged it in and began the routine morning rundown of all my active profiles and in-boxes, trying not to think about the Tumblr.

Max is two days away from losing it if Anna doesn't remind him why he's promised to marry her and tells her "I love you" even though she only ever says "I'm sorry" back. I've ignored George's last two texts. He sent Emma one of his long sex-fantasy things—I can read that in homeroom. Make those changes to Thora's profile. She works in a therapist's office. Or maybe she's the therapist—

I wrote to Max, really just to avoid writing back to James and having to confront the proposition that he and Rosie should meet.

At least leaving our chat abruptly was a good tease. He probably thought of Rosie all night, watching her videos over and over.

> Max,
> Oh my gosh, I'm so, so sorry I haven't been
> in touch. That's great about your paper getting

published. I tried to open the PDF, but it wouldn't work.

I think I am going to Turks & Caicos next, with that photographer I told you about. Remember, Rune? He seems like he's in a better place now. Not like when we were together. I'm not too worried about him—don't be jealous!

Hey, Max!

My name is Joss and I made Anna up and I'm so sorry, but I think I'm sick of her. Can I kill her off? Would you miss her much? Are you going to remember her when you're old?

I couldn't keep going.

I didn't want to check, but I had to. The Tumblr was still there, everything the same—white letters, and the sentence that had opened the door to the astral plane-coyote-Kokopelli-Max-Peter dream: **JOSS WYATT TELLS LIES.**

"Did I hear you right, yesterday? Mary-Kate's cheerleading?"

Sitting at a red light, my mom twisted the cap off her coffee mug. I grabbed it from her before she could have a sip.

"Sorry," I said, taking huge gulps. "You know the rules. If you want to have a conversation in the morning, I need coffee."

"Well, I think it's nice that Mary-Kate's doing something

82   ROWAN MANESS

social. She's always been so shy. Deb was a cheerleader—"

"You hate Mrs. Mahoney."

"I don't hate her. I dislike her. And I didn't dislike her in high school. Now, yes—"

"Because—"

"Because she gets on her high horse about church things, and every time I see her she insinuates that you're some kind of bad seed."

I laughed. "Really?"

"All she ever thinks about is who's Catholic enough, who's getting divorced, who's getting married, who's pregnant, whose kid is the most screwed up."

"Everyone knows Rhiannon's the bad seed," I said.

"Obviously."

My phone chimed.

New message from KIT

Kit: **So, Saturday?**

"Who's that?"

"Uh—" She caught me off guard. "Kit Behr?"

Me: **Why are you even awake right now?**

"Who's Kit Behr?"

I looked at my mother's face, trying to decide how much I wanted to give her.

"He's a guy."

"You're telling me something!" she exclaimed. "Should I stop the car? Are you ill?"

Kit: **I wake up early**

Kit: **To meditate**

"Does he go to Brophy?"

"God no," I said, slipping in "He's nineteen. We met at that party."

"I see," she said, narrowing her eyes.

I was glad, for once, to see the adobe facade of Xavier appear a few blocks ahead. The morning sun was already hot, cloaking the school in a glow of coral and pink. A line of cars rolled up to the front entrance, depositing one or two sleepy girls wearing headphones and hoodies before driving off to the mall or a CrossFit gym or Whole Foods.

Me: **Sorry about that text, btw. Embarrassing**

"Well, nineteen? Deb Mahoney won't be happy. But I'm so glad"—she touched my arm; it was mortifying—"that you're talking to someone—"

We pulled in to the parking lot.

"—appropriate."

Kit: **No worries**

Me: **I'm not sure about Saturday though. Not after that meditating comment**

"Okay, that's enough," I said, opening the car door.

"Will this guy come by the house sometime? So I can meet him?"

"Bye, Mom."

"Text him hello from me," she called out before driving away. "Love you!"

Kit: **You ever try it?**

Me: **No**

Kit: **Look up at the sky. Try to clear your mind**

I was near the school chapel, standing beneath the old bell tower, once part of a Spanish mission. Light shone through cut-out windows, bouncing off and around a big brass bell. Small brown birds darted in and out. One perched on a ledge, a twig in its beak. I held up my phone, snapped a picture, and sent it to Kit.

Kit: **Where's that?**

Me: **School. Xavier Prep.**

Kit: **Catholic schoolgirl. Hmm.**

Me: **Oh relax. More like militant atheist schoolgirl**

Mr. Lauren's car rumbled past and sputtered into a parking space, black smoke pouring from the exhaust pipe. He locked it, leaving the windows rolled down, and I watched as he walked up to the school.

"Something's wrong with your car," I said, catching him as he passed by.

"You think so?" he replied, with a grin and a glance at my phone. "Texting one of your many admirers?"

"Oh sure, like I have admirers," I said, watching his back as he disappeared through the door to the front office.

Me: **Okay to Saturday**

Kit: 🙌

Dear James, why do I feel like I'm cheating on you?

I propped myself up against the bell tower wall, in a triangle of shade that retreated steadily, climbing up my bare legs, as I wrote to James.

Dear Jimmy Jacket,

I like it best when we send messages to each other at the same time. Matching timestamps in Chat. Think of all the times you've texted me while I was writing one for you. Astral choreography. Not insignificant. Important.

It doesn't matter who I am. It doesn't matter who you are, or that we've never been in the same room. Our thoughts, our words have synced. In that way, we've met a thousand times already.

I'm not good with change, and I'm even worse at losing things. I fell apart when I left my favorite necklace in an Uber. You say "let's meet" and I hear "that's the end." Do you understand what I mean? It's not about you, or not wanting you. I want you. I have you. Just . . . not the way you want, I suppose. . . . I'll think about it.

Last night, after the videos, someone slipped a letter under the door. I say "someone" but I know who it was. The guy from my past—

Peter. Peter stalked me when I was thirteen. He was convinced that I was someone else, some woman he was in love with. Olivia made me call campus security. They came out and found cigarettes and binoculars in the woods below our room.

I'm really scared now. You can't get into the dorm blocks without an ID card. The door to our room was unlocked. He could have walked right in.

I don't know what to do.

xx Rosie

Twisting the real thing, enough to focus his attention off the idea of meeting. But I was looking for ways out, and each one broke my heart.

You could tell him the truth.

Never. I couldn't.

He might stay.

He doesn't want me. He wants Rosie.

I heard music, looked up. It was coming from the parking lot—

I followed it to Mr. Lauren's car. The windows were rolled down. Red leather seats marbled with white cracks. The music was coming from the floor in front of the passenger seat—accompanied by a faint buzzing sound. A phone. His phone, forgotten. I recognized the Tom Petty song, rolled my eyes at the appropriateness of it. The phone's screen was lighting up with each buzz. I stuck my head through the window.

KIRSTEN IS CALLING

A photo of a woman, similar enough to the sketch in Mr. Lauren's notebook.

"You are such a snoop."

Mary-Kate behind me, with Mae Castillo at her side.

Mae narrowed her eyes and pushed against me, looking in the car.

"Are you going to answer it?"

"I was just walking by," I said, looking at Mae but aware of Mary-Kate's crossed arms, her shifting feet.

The top half of Mae's body disappeared as she bent down into the car, retrieving the still-ringing phone. She handed it to me.

"Dare you," she said.

I held the phone. Kirsten's downcast eyes were staring right at the word "Answer."

"Don't," Mary-Kate said, right when the ringing stopped. I dropped the phone back into the car window, where the voice mail notification chimed.

"This is the hot teacher's car," Mae stated.

"I know," I said. Then my phone buzzed. I glanced at the screen—James had written back.

Nice. That was quick.

"Who's that?" Mary-Kate asked.

The way she and Mae were standing together bugged me, made me feel guilty and harassed. Mary-Kate hadn't responded to my most recent texts—I hadn't talked to her since the pep rally. I wanted to tell her about Kit and our upcoming date. Proving to her that I had some interest in the outside world was half the reason I'd decided to go to the concert with him.

And I was sure I sensed a secret, shared knowledge in Mae's demeanor. She and Mary-Kate talking after cheer practice, Mary-Kate venting about her weird friend's Internet fantasy life, Mae probing for dirt, fascinated by it but not understanding.

The bell rang, and suddenly girls were emerging from cars all around us, zombies compelled toward the church-mall-school-prison complex.

Mary-Kate and Mae were walking too—Mary-Kate turned back, motioning for me to follow. I waved her away and stayed behind, slouching against Mr. Lauren's car.

I opened Mary-Kate's Instagram—her entire social media presence consisted of a Facebook profile she'd lost the password to and the Instagram, with its eleven photos from the week I'd convinced her to download it—and scrolled through her friends list until I found Mae Castillo.

I was looking for something to hate, but there wasn't much. Pictures of the almond grove on her parents' farm, chickens and goats, a couple sunsets, cheerleading and soccer. One of the most recent featured Mary-Kate. Forty weeks deep in the feed I started seeing the same girl over and over—finally, one photo was captioned **celebrating 6m with my girl @drewzy**

That makes sense.

I friend requested Mae, knowing it would catch her off guard, and started toward school slowly, wanting to savor James's letter.

> Rosie Robe,
>
> I understand about not seeing each other, keeping it this way forever. We've been living in a land where there is no game, but there's a voice at the back of my head saying "It's a boy's job to push."
>
> And I think that as long as you're separate from my life, I'm always going to have to choose. The more I come to you, with my eyes closed, the more everything around me (apartment, friends, half-eaten sandwich, refrigerator magnets) fades, becomes contingent, unreal. My backpack blurs into the couch, the windowpanes float out of their frames and up into the sky. Everything feels paper-thin.
>
> That's why I need you here, with me. Not because it will be any better, or so we can take selfies together and post them to make our

exes jealous, but because I need you to make the world vivid again.

An interruption.

New message from BLOCKED NUMBER

XXX: http://josslies.tumblr.com

Sick with lack of control, I clicked the link.

The Tumblr page loaded, now with something extra—a new post. A familiar face. A photo of Peter, the one that was on all the local news sites when he robbed the fireworks store and stole a car to cross state lines to get to Amelia.

Peter's sad eyes, hollow cheeks. Above the picture—

RIP

Beneath it—

VICTIM #1—PETER CAPLIN

His face in the window, at the door. He knew the moment he saw me.

I was under the bell tower again. No trace of morning coolness. Cicadas starting up and a shadow figure watching.

"Hey."

Girl, Xavier uniform, not the shadow closing in but a human, someone I should know. Face hard to recognize through a dysmorphic veil. Leah Leary, friendly dinosaur.

"Hi," I coughed out.

"We're late," she said, walking past, backpack rolling behind. Every time she spoke to me it was like she needed something.

Positive feedback, a pat on the head. I couldn't stop picturing her and Shane fucking. It was gruesome and relentless.

I stared at the phone, willing my fingers to move.

Me: **Who is this? What do you want from me?**

The phone vibrated.

XXX: **I am Believer, and I want you to pay.**

CHAPTER 8

"You're being sweet," Rosie was saying.

"I mean it," James whispered to her.

On this visit to the astral plane, James built a tree house. He said he wanted to, and Rosie encouraged him. Her room at the Dream Palace was a blank slate, and James's vision colored it in—wooden slats for walls, a window open to the forest.

In the center of the room, a bed with grey linen sheets, endless mounds of white pillows, a worn flannel blanket. James held Rosie there, and the solid mass of their bodies was one true thing.

"The rain's nice." Rosie spoke into the nape of James's neck.

They both became aware of the sound of soft rain hitting the tree branches outside the window. Sunlight filtered through the leaves, suspended in the air as diffuse luminous particles.

James wanted to do something about Peter, the person stalking Rosie. He wanted her to come to New York for a while and stay with him, or for him to meet her in Los Angeles and whisk her away to a hotel while the police tracked the guy down. Rosie made fun of him for wanting to be a manly hero, but she made him feel good for it too. Her parents were dead. She had no family.

"Just telling you about it all is really helpful," she said.

"You promise to tell the police? At least file a report," James insisted.

"Okay, tomorrow," Rosie agreed.

"You don't deserve this," James said, as Rosie increased the rain, dimmed the light.

Rosie wanted to say "Sure I do," but that didn't make sense for her. Rosie didn't deserve it.

Joss does.

Shh, sit back, relax with James. He is here. That is a miracle. It's some kind of magic. You're like a witch.

It's hard to tell whose voice that is.

Rosie's arms are transparent. She tries to meet James's face, but his body is not real enough. The rain has gotten louder. They've lost it.

sharkliver: **You don't deserve this.**

I never say *I love you*, though it's been said to me. Peter, Max, George, the others—they lay the words down at the altar of an idea, at the things in their lives they wish they could change.

ROWAN MANESS

James hasn't said he loves Rosie, but sometimes he just writes her name, and they both know what it means.

sharkliver: **Rosie.**

sharkliver: **It's late.**

RosieRose: **Stay up with me? Olivia's out. I'm all alone.**

sharkliver: **I'm falling asleep. Need to be awake in a few hours.**

sharkliver: **God, I want you here.**

sharkliver: **Good night?**

There was a pause—a pause I felt him feeling.

"Good night, James," I typed and said aloud.

I really was home alone. My mom was at her weekly widows group meeting. *Widows Who Wine.* It always goes late. I say, "Drinking your sorrows away again?" And she says, "I'm a grown-up woman; I do what I please," and sometimes, if she's angry, "Would you rather I was here with you?"

The answer is mostly no, but sometimes, yes.

But she's not here, and I can put on some music, however loud I want. I'd taken Dylan's record player from his room as soon as my mom got the text saying he was at the airport in Mexico City and wasn't coming back to finish his degree in communications at Arizona State. He had a huge record collection—some of his mixed in with some of my dad's. I knew the one I wanted, with my dad's initials written on the front in blue ink. *JLW*, same as me.

Jay Louis Wyatt

I put the record on. Crackles and fizzes, the ones he used to hear.

I was thinking about how maybe some of the people I talk to online are dead people. I was thinking about how ears work. I was dancing around to the song, in my pajamas, fantasizing about dying in James's arms. I was forgetting about the Tumblr with Peter's picture on it. I was singing the words to a song I knew by heart, trying to remember the first time I heard the lyrics, the first time I heard the phrase *astral plane*.

In the silence after the song ended I heard my phone buzzing on the bedside table. I approached it slowly, hoping and fearing—

New message from SHANE

Shane: **EB?** 👽

I tried to remember how we'd known to meet up with each other before we had cell phones, but couldn't.

Outside, I started walking toward the greenbelt at the end of the block.

I forgot how cool the night gets, after the temperature shifts and the pavement releases its heat. No moon, clouds moving quick and soundless, covering and uncovering the stars, carrying the far-off scent of pine and rain. I passed long, empty driveways, one after another, lined with lavender, sagebrush, prickly pear. A huge aloe vera plant stretched her octopus tentacles out from a pink pebble side yard, reaching for the bushy shadow of a towering bougainvillea.

At the greenbelt, a depressed slope of crabgrass connecting

two subdivisions, I found the "EB" Shane was talking about—a giant electrical utility box set back from the street, protected from view by a tall hedge on three sides.

I put my foot on the lip of a recessed panel with a "Danger! High Voltage!" warning sticker on it, and climbed up.

Shane was sitting cross-legged, facing away, headphones on. A puff of smoke rose into the night, and his arm bent backward to offer me a messily rolled joint. Orange embers tumbled into a pile as I inhaled, centering myself, reorienting after the encounter with James.

You're on the box with Shane, in your pajamas, like a million other times.

Music continued to leak out of Shane's headphones after he took them off, turned around.

"What's inside this thing?" I asked, knocking on the utility box. "What is it for?"

Shane thought for a moment. "Gauges? Or, I don't know, pipes?"

"It's weird that we don't know."

Shane was still guessing, like he hadn't heard what I said.

"It's something to do with the power company. I see guys checking it sometimes. They unlock all the doors. They have special keys."

"I have a theory," I said, lying down. The box was humming. It wasn't solid. It echoed if you kicked it, like it was just covering something up, something that was mostly underground.

Shane took the joint from my hand.

"Okay," I went on. "So it's some kind of monitoring device. And it's studying all the humans. Gathering information."

Shane laughed.

"What?" I asked.

"You always say 'human' like you aren't one," he answered, and I looked up at him, smiling like the Cheshire cat in the dark. With my ear against the box, I tapped my fingers, listening for reverberations I could interpret.

Shane lay down next to me.

"Blue Dream," he said.

"What?"

"That's what this strain's called," he said, exhaling.

"Seems accurate," I said. "Home life getting to you?"

"*Dancing with the Stars* on at full volume for what seems like hours, cold meat loaf, soused parents oozing stress."

"Grim, grim," I said, picturing Shane in his bedroom, silently seething.

"What about you?" he asked.

I didn't want to lie to him, to spin something out of nothing. It was too much work, and I was having a hard enough time dealing with being in my own body. The Blue Dream lifted me up on a shaky platform—I shouldn't have smoked. It made the boundaries too porous.

Oh my God, Peter. Poor man.

"I want to tell you, but you'll be weird."

"Why?"

"You're always weird."

"Okay, but why?"

I had to regain control, had to shift the conversation so the coyote wouldn't sniff us out.

"Just—look at this."

I opened the last text from the blocked number, now marked as "Believer" in my phone, and handed it to Shane.

"Open the link," I said.

He sat up quick.

"I've been getting texts," I explained. "I was ignoring them. But then—"

"It's him," Shane said softly, and then I was back there, on the day I opened my front door to find Peter standing in front of me. He and Amelia were supposed to meet. She was on her way. He was waiting at the fireworks store in New Mexico—the halfway point between them. I had to get out of it. Called him from the house land line posing as Amelia's "friend," spinning a story about a car accident. He tracked the number. I didn't know he was capable. And he drove all night through the desert to find the person who called him, and when I opened the door, he knew I was Amelia.

Shane came later. Maybe he was thinking of that part now, after Peter chased me into the backyard and I hid but he found me, dragged me out from under the covered patio table, pushed me to the ground. Shane stepped out from the kitchen, saw Peter on top of me, shouted "Joss!"

I'd never told him what was happening when he arrived, before Peter got scared and ran out the back gate. It must have looked like Peter was going to kill me—but he wasn't. He was watching my face, seeing Amelia's. He was hurt, confused. He was trembling.

"Jesus," Shane said. "I don't know if I can handle this right now."

"Yeah, that's pretty much where I'm at too," I said, reacting to Shane's reaction, trying to keep it light so he wouldn't tailspin.

"Believer?" Shane questioned.

"I can't figure it out. I mean, this Peter stuff? He's dead. Nobody knows we were"—I faltered a little—"connected, except you, my mom, Dylan. Maybe one of the cops?"

The cops who found him. The gun he'd bought just before he met Amelia, when he was released from prison after ten years and the world seemed wrong, when he was going to end it anyway. The cops read my name in the suicide note. My dad answered when they called.

Amelia saved him. Joss killed him.

"You're fucked," Shane said.

"No, no, no," I begged. "Come on, be helpful. Have ideas."

The look on Dad's face when the cops explained what they'd read in Peter's letter. He remembered coming home three days before, finding you and Shane and the broken window by the front door. Shane saying he rode his bike into it. He thought it seemed like a lie. Now he knew for sure. A man had broken in, a stranger in his home, after his baby daughter.

I couldn't see the coyote, but I sensed him, circling the perimeter of the utility box. I turned onto my side and inched my body toward the edge. I wanted to lay eyes on him, to show that I wasn't intimidated.

"Do you think it could be him?" I asked, since Shane wasn't talking. "Maybe he can reach out from—"

"He's not a ghost. Shut up."

I didn't really think this Believer was Peter. I'd recognize his voice. Peter couldn't hide like that. He was stoic but raw, uncovered. That's what drew me to him, his bare wounds.

But I wanted to make Shane talk, and I knew he'd hate the idea of believing in ghosts.

"I mean, anything's possible," I said.

"He's dead, Joss. He killed himself. You know that."

"Maybe he faked it."

"It was on the news."

At the edge of the box. Slowly, I looked over.

The coyote looked tired, like he'd just run a great distance. He rested on his haunches, front paws splayed out at an angle, each panting breath creating a sucking concavity between the skinny ribs. Eyes trained on me, a satisfied snarl.

"What are you doing?" Shane asked sharply. I snapped my head back, but not before I saw the coyote disappear, blinking back into the night.

"I need water," I said, prying my sticky sandpaper tongue from the roof of my mouth.

"Why didn't you just stop?" Shane asked.

I was supposed to stop. After Peter, responsible parents Jay and Nina Wyatt confiscated my laptop and phone. I promised them. I promised the first therapist. I promised the New Mexico police, in a letter the first therapist made me write. I promised Peter, whom I pictured as a fallen angel even before he was dead. I promised myself. And I did stop, for a while.

But then Jay Wyatt died. He and my mom were arguing about me, and he dropped dead. When Nina separated herself to grieve, I found that the second death gave back the freedoms the first one took away. She didn't have the energy to discipline me, or do much of anything except bury herself in work. Then there was Max, George, James, all new, all full of promise and possibility, stories I could disappear into, ways I could ignore the crushing guilt.

It was the only thing that helped.

Shane and I sat in the dark, both unable to refer to our shared lexicon of inside jokes and half-formed memories, but also unable to say anything new.

A car drove by, its headlights briefly illuminating Shane's face and the hedge behind him.

"Your mom's home," he said, moving to jump down from the box. He was mad. I didn't think he should be, but I was afraid I'd warn him about the coyote if I opened my mouth.

When I jumped down after Shane, he was already heading toward his house on the opposite side of the block. My shoes squished into soft mud, dirtying the hem of my pajama pants. I hurried along the street, not noticing the dreaming plants or the houses flattened into one dimension by the clear cool night, like the facade of an Old West town.

Dear Max,

Things are not good. It's Rune. Did I tell you we dated? Before I knew you, obviously. He's always been so obsessive about me. When we met, I didn't want anything to do with him—the surfer guy thing is so not my type. But he kept asking, saying "You're going to say yes eventually, so just say yes now." I finally gave in. It was 2 months of negativity and possessiveness. But he's so respected as a photographer, and I couldn't pass up this job. Big mistake.

He tried to get in my room last night. I think he was high on something, whatever. I told my manager, but I signed a contract and he didn't actually *do* anything. . . .

Sorry I'm such a baddie not writing more to you. I am thinking of you all the time. If only things were different.

Love, Anna

George: Finally, there u are

Emma: Hey baby

George: Guess what?

Emma: Just tell me. I have to be quick. Ron's in the shower

George: He hurt you again?

Emma: I don't want to talk about him

George: Aww, babe

George: Well, the thing is, I finally got leave.

George: I'm gonna be in Atlanta for 6 weeks

Emma: Oh, wow

George: You excited, girl? Your soldier's coming home

Emma: When?

CHAPTER 9

Anna and Emma putting out feelers, flares arcing out of the
Dream Palace, off the astral plane, into the worlds of Max and
George. Max in the lab, never at home. George in the rec room
in Afghanistan. I hadn't noticed the similarities in their stories—
abusive exes and husbands. Even Rosie had a disfigured avatar
of Peter lurking in her past. I made up dangerous men to make
other men feel useful, needed, necessary, protective.

Emma's husband was pseudo-real. I'd taken the name Ron
Marchand from a story on a blog about Atlanta high society.
It listed him as a self-made multimillionaire who'd gotten rich
buying barges on the Ohio River, and the idea of both barges
and the Ohio River were so completely foreign to me I found
it irresistible. The article mentioned his wife, Emma, a former
beauty queen. Something about the way she gripped Ron's arm
in photographs from galas and charity benefits spoke to me,

seemed to say, *Take me; give me a different life.* I kept their names the same, so if George searched he'd be able to find Ron, put a face to the monster Emma told him about.

When I got home from the utility box, my mom's car was hot in the garage, its body cracking and settling. She was already in her room. I wondered if she'd checked on me, found the Modern Lovers record still spinning soundlessly, the bed empty.

Then, a little Max and George nightcap. They comforted me, lulled me to sleep, where I roamed the halls of the Dream Palace like a guard on patrol, looking into corners, daring the coyote to appear.

"What is he wearing?" Mary-Kate whispered as Mr. Lauren flicked on an ancient overhead projector. We were sitting at our usual table in the first row. Directly in front of us, the classroom wall was lit up with a white square covered in Mr. Lauren's messy handwriting.

I watched as he licked a tissue and wiped at the scrawl, then squirted it with a bottle of cleaner he kept on the tray below. I liked how deliberately he erased, making a concentric square around the glass.

"It's his favorite sweater," I said, sending off the latest text in an exchange between George and Emma, focusing on Mary-Kate. "He wears it all the time."

"It looks like amoebas."

"Wait until he turns around. There's a blob on the back that looks like a dinosaur."

"A dinosaur?"

"The one with the crested head. . . ." I trailed off as Mr. Lauren began describing the differences between meiosis and mitosis. Some mental block prevented me from remembering the dinosaur's name.

George: **We have to get rid of him**

George: **Just say the word**

George, newly stateside and in tantalizingly close proximity to Emma, was indulging in a fantasy with a murderous tinge. He would be the one to rescue Emma, to help her get away from Ron for good, "whatever it takes."

George thought he was special. Nobody else was like him, not his fellow soldiers, not his small-town friends. Emma understood what he meant when he said he was uncomfortable being labeled an American hero. He'd only signed up for the army because he missed the enrollment deadline at the community college and didn't want his overbearing mother to be angry. Emma was smart, older, sophisticated. The fact that she loved George was more evidence of his specialness.

I knew, though, that George was dumb. I would have cut him off long ago if it weren't for the novelty of his soldierhood and his proclivity toward violence.

Emma: **Let me think about it.**

The classroom lights flicked on and I jolted, ready to hide my phone from Mr. Lauren. He wasn't looking though, at me or anyone else. He pushed the projector into a corner, pausing to unstick one squeaky, rusted wheel. He checked himself out in the mirror above the emergency eyewash station before sitting back at his desk.

George: **It's the only way.**

George: **If you want to be with me I don't want you with some other guy.**

Emma: **I'm married, George.**

"Never mind," Mary-Kate was saying.

I'd missed something.

"What?"

"Never mind."

She stood up and walked to the back of the classroom, taking a seat next to Mae Castillo, looking at me with apparent disgust.

"Who's your partner?" I looked up. Leah Leary, standing with an armful of worksheets.

I wished I could sic rabid George on Leah instead of the version of Ron Marchand I'd concocted.

"Everyone's paired up, I think," she said, sliding a worksheet toward me.

"Okay," I said slowly.

"You can work with me and Zoey if you want," Leah added.

"No," I mumbled, shaking my head.

Leah shuffled off and I caught Mr. Lauren staring at me, sitting at his desk.

"Nobody wants to be my partner," I said, lowering my voice so only he could hear me.

"Leah offered," he noted, so evenly and without inflection that I was sure he had an opinion but was being careful to hide it.

"Nobody," I repeated.

"It will be twice the work if you do it yourself, but—"

"There's a splotch on the back of your sweater that looks like a dinosaur," I blurted out, enjoying his flinch as he stopped himself from twisting around to look at it.

"And it's bugging me that I can't remember the name—the one with the crested head?"

He didn't know either.

I went on. "I used to know the names of all the dinosaurs, plus all kinds of facts, like whether or not they were carnivores or herbivores and what time period they lived in and everything. I was obsessed with them when I was a kid. My parents used to make me recite facts for their friends, to show off. And now I don't remember anything."

Mr. Lauren leaned back in his chair, just letting me go on.

"In that way, I'm dumber than I was when I was four. That's depressing."

I could tell Mr. Lauren agreed that this was, in fact, depressing.

"Think about this three-dimensionally," I said. "Pretty much all kids are into dinosaurs, right? But only, like, one of them actually becomes a paleontologist. Why do we lose interest? Dinosaurs are insane. That they ever existed is insane. They roamed the earth for hundreds of millions of years."

Mr. Lauren was smiling, but I could feel eyes on the back of my head—Mary-Kate's, or everyone's.

"This earth," I added quietly, like it needed clarification, before putting my head down and penciling my name at the top of the worksheet.

what is the name of the dinosaur with a crested head

I didn't have to remember—I could just ask the Internet to remember it for me.

Dilophosaurus

Parasaurolophus

More than one, of course, and neither rang a bell. I kept scrolling through the search results.

"'Corythosaurus'!" I said, reading the Wikipedia entry. "'Upper Cretaceous, also has a duckbill.'"

Mr. Lauren and I were standing in the doorway of the classroom. I'd stopped to show him the dinosaur and also to avoid looking too desperate to catch up with Mary-Kate, who'd ignored my "Hey—" as she left with Mae.

"Childhood amnesia," he said. "That's why you don't remember."

To my puzzled look, he added, "Google it."

"No, tell me," I whined.

"So, you don't like my sweater?" he said, looking down, holding it out at the bottom, pretending to be sad.

I could hear him breathing. He smelled like shaving cream and he didn't seem to notice how close we were standing.

"I didn't say that."

"Sorry, Mr. Lauren—" Leah Leary interrupted, breezing through the doorway, forcing us apart, her little muscular legs spinning beneath her like a running cartoon animal.

"I forgot my water bottle," she chirped, grabbing it off a desk, speeding back toward us.

I reached out and grabbed the water bottle as she passed.

"Are you sure this is yours?" I said, holding it back from her grasp.

"My name's on it," Leah Leary said, flustered.

It was, written in Wite-Out bubble letters.

"I don't know, maybe there's a different Leah Leary?" I said, shaking the bottle. A chunk of melty ice sloshed around inside.

"Joss, come on—"

Mr. Lauren grabbed the bottle and handed it to Leah. She left, hurrying away, anxious to beat the tardy bell. Mr. Lauren lingered, pretending to watch Leah go. He didn't turn to look, but I felt his eyes on me, sideways and stealthy.

What if he was someone I was chatting with? One of the first people I ever talked to was a high school English teacher with a dominatrix fetish. What would Mr. Lauren confess, if he could? I imagined him reaching out, grabbing me, pulling me into the classroom. *We'd slip into another dimension—*

He shifted and opened his mouth like he was going to say something.

Dinosaurs roaming a jungle, outside time—

But he stopped himself, changed his mind. Bit his bottom lip and shrugged, returning to his desk without a word.

Halfway to world religions class I remembered it was meeting in the chapel, so I turned and crossed campus in the opposite direction, walking outside, through the courtyard, past the cafeteria, rounding the corner of the front office, where the newer school buildings met the crumbling walls of the old mission.

The tardy bell rang, and since I was already late, I slowed down more, lingering in the fresh-cut grass.

Two figures were standing in a thin line of shade outside the chapel, facing each other, talking closely. It took a moment before I recognized one as Mary-Kate, the other as Mae.

I held my phone up and took a photo—framing them in the bottom right corner, tiny shadowed forms against the gleaming structure. I posted the picture to Instagram.

idiotblush caught you tardy loiterers @mkmaho @maebsc

They hugged before they went inside—I couldn't tell who initiated.

When I pushed through the wooden doors of the chapel, I staggered a bit as my eyes adjusted to the dark. The entryway vestibule was damp and lightless, lined with brown tile as soft and lumpy as mounds of dirt.

Muffled voices came from farther inside and reluctantly I went toward them, my eyes just able to discern the inner door, the rough stone walls sliced with bejeweled light from stained-glass windows.

I found Mary-Kate and Mae in a corner, sitting cross-legged among a pile of mismatched pillows in the designated pan-denominational meditation space.

"I'm sorry," I whispered, sitting next to them.

"For?" Mary-Kate said.

"For whatever I did."

Mary-Kate looked at Mae in a way that said *Can you believe her?*

The meditation area made me think of Kit, the nebulous real boy.

I texted him, one eye on the teacher, Mrs. Braddock, who was absorbed in a prayer circle and hadn't noticed my late entrance.

Me: **You'll be glad to know I'm in a meditation space right now**

"That's why I'm mad," Mary-Kate said, her voice almost maternally angry, with a tight-lipped Deb Mahoney razor's edge vibe.

"Because I'm texting," I said, not a question but an accusation flung right back at her. *What a stupid reason to be mad, Mary-Kate.*

"Because you're always texting. I was telling you something

important back there and you couldn't tear yourself away to listen for one second. You'd rather be lying to some random guy—"

I should have asked what was so important, just insisted I cared until she gave in and told me, but I felt betrayed—she'd just alluded to my secret life in front of a girl who wasn't part of our circle. I was sure she'd already confided in Mae, finding in her what she couldn't find in me—a receptive ear.

"God, Mary-Kate!" I said, swimmy with anger. "I'm texting Kit—the guy from Guin's band. I'm supposed to go on a date with him. My first real date. But you wouldn't know because I haven't been able to tell you because you've been busy with cheerleading and"–I paused to indicate Mae–"whatever else."

Mary-Kate and I had been fighting and making up for years, but I couldn't tell whether or not she knew or cared that she almost always lost.

"Oh," she said softly. "Sorry."

"You're apologizing to her?" Mae said under her breath.

"So you like him?" Mary-Kate asked, ignoring Mae, shifting away from her to face me. *Ha!*

"I guess so. What is liking someone, anyway?"

Mrs. Braddock walked up and handed Mary-Kate a slip of paper.

"Your group community service assignment."

I grabbed the paper and read it—

Arrowhead Nursing Home

"Noooo," I groaned.

Mrs. Braddock frowned and walked away.

"Can't we just pick up litter or something?" I whined.

"You hate helping people so much," Mary-Kate said.

"No I don't," I said. "I went to that homeless shelter last year. That was fine. But old people are scary. Nursing homes are pits of despair."

"My nana's in one," Mae said. "It's not that bad. She has a boyfriend and does Pilates."

"If it depresses you, imagine how they must feel," Mary-Kate said. I was comforted by the familiar rhythm of her gentle attempt at helping me empathize with other humans.

"That's the problem," I said. "I feel their depression too much. Then I can't stop thinking about toddlers with terminal cancer or whole cities getting sarin gassed in Syria. Health and youth are shameful things I should hide—"

"Force yourself to help and maybe you'll get out of your shame spiral," Mary-Kate said, back to normal now, helpful and smart, like she should be.

"What could I possibly say to anyone to help them in any way?" I asked, standing, compelled toward the flickering orange glow coming from an alcove beneath a Station of the Cross painting—station number six, Veronica wiping the face of Jesus as he marched toward Golgotha.

The alcove was filled with tea light candles, some with clear pools of hot wax at their bases, some empty and burned out, the marks of sooty ghosts on the wall behind them. A longer, unlit candle rested on the lip of a metal donation box.

I picked it up, touching it to a flame. I wanted to light one for nostalgia and old people and Peter and my dad, and for not knowing what to do with all the life I had in front of me, even though I'd seen how a second can return it.

As the flame caught on a fresh wick, I wished for an incantation I could believe in.

"What's it like at your parents' house?" Emma asks George, leading him into her room at the Dream Palace. It's made up differently now, updated for his homecoming, altered by his allusions to confronting Ron, the Bad Husband.

Candles line the room's edges, burning down to flat white disks, cluttering the stone ledge beneath a stained-glass window.

George, out of his army uniform for the first time in Emma's imaginings. In jeans his mother bought for his return, too big in the waist, not stylish. A forest-green sweater seems too plain, like it had a logo that was removed in Photoshop.

"I don't know. It's just normal," George says, and the waves of Emma's attraction recede from him. She prefers him in Afghanistan, imagining the base under a roiling cloud of boredom and agitation. At home, he's just a twenty-one-year-old kid with a chip on his shoulder and a thing for older women.

"Ron's home," Emma says, and the room storms. The window hasn't settled on a design—the jeweled glass shards are in a state of constant rearrangement. At the mention of Ron the

pieces shift, depicting a man's face, surrounded by jewel-tone daggers.

I leave them there.

Down the hall. In another room, a man is reciting a poem.

Not a poem, a love letter.

James.

"Soft Robe, new thing," he is saying. He never bores. He is never dull. "Come here, witchy girl. Sit by me. This is where you belong."

CHAPTER 10

I started to change my mind. Changing my mind would make more sense. That's the kind of thing I would do. Just make up an excuse, bow out at the last minute. Or I could tell him it was too much. That would be being honest. He couldn't hold that against me.

I moisturized. Put on three different outfits. Took a thousand photos of myself in Photo Booth, trying to get my face to settle into a casual, chill expression. I was having flashbacks to going to the movies with Zack Matthews in seventh grade because he threatened to cut himself with his Swiss Army knife key chain if I said no.

But Kit texted, said he was on his way. It was going to happen.

Me: **I'm nervous, just so you know. Fidgety**

I went outside to wait for him, as ready as I could be in black jeans and a gauzy white shirt, wearing scuffed boots and lots of eye makeup. I sat on the curb and turned a topaz bracelet around and around on my wrist, rereading James's last e-mail.

> Dear flower, dear Rose,
> Are you still considering it? Meeting?
> What we have? Our thing? We have to
> protect it. It isn't normal and it isn't strong, not
> yet. It exists in what you call the ether. I love
> how you call it that.
> How do you always know the right words? How
> are your thoughts so new and yet so familiar to me?

A text interrupted.

Believer: **Anna.**

Believer: **Hey, Anna!**

Believer: **http://www.josslies.tumblr.com**

There was a feeling like a car just gone. A new warmth in the air, an invisible oily cloud. Heat on my cheek, a humid mark.

One new post. A picture of Anna—or "Olesya V.," the Estonian girl she really was—was on the Tumblr. Freckles, sharp features, wide green eyes. I'd chosen her for her eyes. Max projected his affection onto them like a movie screen.

Below the photo, in all caps—

VICTIM #2—MAX BLUMSTEIN

mblum2@pri.edu

His work e-mail. He used a Gmail address with Anna—the work e-mail was monitored.

Believer was letting me know that Max could be reached.

But then Kit was there, the car rounding the block, looming larger in my peripheral vision as I stared helplessly at my phone. When I stood to meet the car, I realized I'd been digging my nails into my ankle, scratching four red tracks into the skin.

Kit's serene face. I put my phone on silent and got in next to him, pushing Believer and the Tumblr onto the curb, resisting the urge to do it physically—pushing the air, making some kind of effort. Enough of the dread fell away, I felt lighter, sure of this direction. I would ignore the texts. I would go to the concert with a boy who was as close to James as I could find. This at least would all play out predictably, easily. No lies except lies of politeness. If I could get through it, it would be like ammunition, proving to the trickster god and the faceless yet familiar shadow that they hadn't scared me.

The car was his brother's. It smelled like moldy towels. He kept the windows down and the radio on a classical music station, driving with his seat pushed back impossibly far from the steering wheel.

"Did you get my text?" I asked.

He fished his phone out of the cup holder.

"Nervous?" he read, looking at me. "Fidgety?"

"Mhmm."

"Don't be. This is gonna be fun."

"Is it?"

The streets were different from his passenger seat. Everything enhanced, good and bad. We left the suburbs and entered what passed for a metro downtown. Neighborhoods I'd never seen before, so strange to me they might as well be in another country. Families were out walking—chubby kids on scooters and babies in rickety strollers. I felt very warm toward them all, and wondered if it was a side effect of being near Kit.

We pulled up to the Marquee, Kit dealing with the parking lot attendant who took his money and taped a ticket to the windshield. He seemed capable of dealing with anyone, any situation.

The guy at the door knew him, and with a nod of acknowledgment, we were given 21+ wristbands and ushered inside. I followed Kit through the dark club and out to a patio, where a few people were smoking and drinking. Kit asked if I wanted anything.

"Uh, whatever you're having," I said, unable to remember the names of any drinks.

I watched him order at the bar, handing over his card, making small effortless movements to say "Keep the tab open, please" and "Two whisky sodas." He tipped the bartender, smiling at her.

If I squinted a bit I could turn him into James. I knew it wasn't fair to Kit, but it helped with my nerves. If he was James, I could be Rosie. Like practicing. I took my phone out of my purse.

Me: **How's your date going?**

James told Rosie that she should say yes to the guy who

asked her out. But he'd bristled at it, like he'd been cornered. His proposition that they meet was putting pressure on everything, too—I couldn't keep distracting him with stalker stories. Rosie told him, hey, if you don't like it, why don't you ask a girl out? We can go on dates at the same time. Trade stories. Somehow he'd agreed to it.

Me: **Mine looks like you if I squint.**

"You know, I went to a party of his once," said Kit, handing me a tiny plastic cup wrapped in a paper napkin.

"Who?"

"Conor Oberst."

"No you didn't."

"We were doing a show in LA and somehow got invited. I think Eli's cousin's friend is their manager—anyway, we go to this mansion in Calabasas and it turns out Bright Eyes was working on their album there or something. I met Jenny Lewis, too."

"Oh my God," I said, sipping my drink too fast. "What was it like?"

"Space cakes and air hockey," said Kit cryptically. "They were all really obsessed with air hockey."

"Wow."

"So," said Kit, stepping closer. "Do you like me more now?"

"A little bit," I said.

"Good," he said. "I told that story to impress you."

I laughed.

"I just thought you should know who you're dealing with here."

We were standing in a corner of the patio, watching the sun set slowly between two peaked mountains. Behind the Marquee, the mountains were colorless, a minefield of half-rotted saguaro, but the sky was marbled fuchsia and almost heartbreaking. Stripes of orange wicked out from the horizon where the last rays of sun broke into dusty, golden haze.

"Beautiful," I said as the haze disappeared and bright, pale dusk took its place.

Kit put his arm around me and produced a tin from his pocket. I ate two chocolate-covered coffee beans that left the taste of weed in between my teeth.

Inside, the room was full. Kit weaved through the crowd as the opening band started playing, and I followed in his wake, holding on to his hand, one part happy to be the girl he was leading—aware I was being looked at by others, quick apprais-als in the dim light—and one part removed from the entire scene, wondering what James was doing, who he might be attaching himself to.

In the front row, Kit and I swayed in our own few feet of space—nobody pressing, nobody forcing into our bubble.

"Hey, man," someone shouted when the music stopped. A guy I might have recognized from another of Guinevere's parties made his way toward us, greeting Kit with a hug. Kit introduced me, and I took the opportunity to step away, excus-ing myself to the bathroom.

I followed a group of sorority girls to the back of the club, and when I turned a corner after them, they'd disappeared.

I stood still in the velvet curtain-lined hallway, trying to listen for their voices.

Then, movement from behind one of the curtains—and Mr. Lauren appeared. I jumped, startled, expecting Ms. Carey or Mrs. Braddock to appear too, like I was trapped in a teacher-filled funhouse.

I recognized him a second before he recognized me, and I saw the recognition cross his face, saw what it did to his expression, how his body tensed and responded. He grinned.

"You're here," I said finally. "You showed up."

"Funny thing," he said. "I had tickets to go before you mentioned it." He was weaving a bit on his feet, unsteady.

"You're *wasted*," I teased. He was wearing things I'd never seen him wear before—jeans, a Grateful Dead T-shirt.

He noticed my wristband.

"Twenty-one?"

"Umm—"

"*Tsk-tsk.*"

The sorority girls reappeared, moving down the hallway as a solid mass, forcing Mr. Lauren to step closer to me.

"I've been thinking about something," he said, waiting until I shook my head *What?* before going on.

"Why do you enjoy torturing Leah Leary?"

I laughed. Mr. Lauren seemed pleased with himself.

"I don't torture her," I said.

"Oh yes, yes, you do," he replied, and somehow he was even closer to me, close like Kit had been minutes ago, closer than we'd ever been.

"You don't even realize it, do you?" he said.

I looked down at the floor, sticky with layers of spill and old wristbands.

When I looked up, his eyes were right there, gold flecks in light brown irises.

I don't know if a line was drawn or crossed then, because his gaze flicked away and he moved, reaching his arm toward a woman who'd just walked up. She nuzzled into his side, rubbing his back.

I recognized her from the sketch and Mr. Lauren's phone.

"Kirsten," he said. "This is Joss Wyatt, one of my students."

Some acknowledgment passed between us.

"How awkward," Kirsten said happily. "Seeing your teacher out in public!"

I nodded.

"Perils of having generationally confused taste in music," Mr. Lauren said, suddenly less drunk.

They left, and I regrouped, finally locating the bathroom behind one of the heavy curtains.

Inside, I texted Mary-Kate and Rhiannon.

Me: **Mr. Lauren is here**

Me: **WITH A LADY**

Rhiannon, immediately.

Rhiannon: **Pic or it didn't happen**

Rhiannon: **Maybe kill her?**

Rhiannon: **& how's the dreamboat Kit?**

The coffee bean started to kick in and I washed my hands twice by accident, then grabbed my phone with wet hands as the text chime sounded.

James: **Mine doesn't look like you**

He sent me a screenshot of a Tinder profile—a dark-haired woman posing in front of a bank of lava lamps: **Gia, 27**

James: **She's nice. We're getting donuts**

James: **In this experiment, do we take our dates home?**

In the gilded mirror above the sink, Rosie's face stared back at me. The bathroom's red walls turned her skin a dusky purple. I knew, looking at her pained expression, that I could not allow James to go on another date. And I knew that the only way I could say that to him and have any ground to stand on was if I—if Rosie—agreed to meet him, once and for all. In person, as each other. To say hello, to connect two dots with a straight line, to answer a question.

Me: **I can't do this.**

I dropped the phone back into my bag and hurried out of the restroom to find Kit before the show started.

I found him, still talking to his friend, just as the room went dark and the stage lit up. Lazy spotlights roamed, passing over a sea of faces. The crowd seemed to have doubled, necks craning up toward Conor and his band as they stumbled out from backstage, took their places, and started to play.

With the amps at ear level, I pressed into Kit, using his arm to block one ear, still looking around, searching the room—there he was—

Mr. Lauren, staring right at me, a strange stillness around him just for a moment before the chorus of the first song rang out and the whole room surged, blocking my view.

I let Kit shield me from the strangers brushing up against us. I put my brain on silent and tried to forget about James, though asking that of myself was like asking my body to forget a broken arm.

For their encore, the band played an old Bright Eyes song, and I sang along with the rest of the happy humans. A burst of black confetti and pink strobe lights made us roar, and every hand held up a phone—

I took mine out, snapping a series of blurry photos, sideways blobs of color, backlit backs of heads, trying to capture a feeling that would never translate in an Instagram picture, that was only special because it was fleeting.

Across the screen—

MAX IS CALLING

I ignored the call, swiped him away, only to find Anna's in-box overflowing with e-mails—

ANNA, WHAT THE FUCK

ANNA, I CAN EXPLAIN

ANNA, PLEASE DON'T TELL MY WIFE

ANNA, WHO IS JOSS WYATT?

The music swelled to a deafening crescendo—

At the back of my head, a bass thrum—

Not from the amps.

From deep within the Dream Palace, Max pounding on Anna's door.

The song ended, the lights went up, and the crowd started to come down and disperse, returning to themselves, individuals once more.

Kit found my hand, moving so swiftly that we were the first people outside. I gasped in the chill, surprised to find that the sun was gone.

Of course it is. You watched it set.

"See, that was fun, wasn't it?" Kit was saying as we walked through rows of cars in the parking lot. Canine nails scraped the gravel somewhere out of sight.

The coyote, summoned by Max's freakout—

His wife?

Max said don't tell his wife.

Time moved in stuttering increments. One moment I was taking a picture of Conor Oberst, the next I was cowering in a corner with Anna, watching her room in the Dream Palace start to quake and disintegrate. Somehow Kit was already driving down my street.

And I'd opened the Tumblr again—there was a new photo.

Max, with a woman I'd never seen before at his side. The woman with a pregnant belly, Max pushing a double stroller holding two grim-faced children, shielding their eyes from the sun, dangling plastic Baggies filled with Cheerios.

A caption with a link to Meg Cahill Blumstein's Facebook page:

VICTIMS #3, 4 & 5—MEG, MASON, NOAH

I turned the phone off as Kit pulled up to my house. Movement came from the shadowy far side of the driveway, and the motion-sensor light turned on, revealing Shane, standing there holding a pink-and-white-striped Hula-Hoop. He held his hand up in a lame greeting.

After our talk on the utility box, he'd asked for the Tumblr address. I could tell he'd seen the update, Max's wife, the new element in play. I wondered if he was thinking what I was thinking—that Believer might be her. She'd discovered Max's secret. She'd suspected something was up. And somehow she'd found out that, cherry on the sundae, Anna was not even real. Her husband was cheating on her with a phantom.

"Who's that?"

I couldn't possibly have been acting normal during the car ride home, but Kit seemed as relaxed as ever, not even turning to me to ask the question.

"Shane," I said, clicking the car door open.

"What's he doing?" Kit asked, watching as Shane took the

Hula-Hoop, passing it back and forth in his hands, and walked up to the nearest streetlamp.

"Driving me crazy," I mumbled, out of the car, walking after Shane, Kit following.

Shane held the Hula-Hoop back like a discus thrower, and hurled it into the air—it ricocheted off the streetlamp and shot down. I grabbed it as it rolled toward me.

"It's never going to happen," I said, handing it back to him.

"Joss doesn't think it's physically possible to get this"—Shane held up the hoop—"around that," he told Kit, pointing up.

All three of us stared into the light.

"Sure it's possible," Kit decided.

"I've done it before, but she missed it."

I explained. "I bet him ten dollars that he couldn't do it—and we were twelve, so he was like two feet shorter than he is now—and he tried all day and made me sit there watching so I could witness it. I went inside for one minute, and when I came back it was around the pole."

"Yeah, because I did it," Shane said.

"I told you to wait! You probably cut it and stuck it back together."

"What, with my magical Hula-Hoop glue?"

"You don't trust him?" Kit said, voice like a placid yogi.

I didn't answer, just sat down on the curb, unable to process the situation. Shane and Kit talking. Outside my house. Anna trapped beneath rubble. Max a liar too.

"Can I try?" Kit asked.

Shane handed him the Hula-Hoop and Kit threw it, missing. It landed soundlessly in the neighbor's grass and he brought it back to Shane. Shane took another turn. The Hula-Hoop wobbled through the air, clipping the light, casting a spinning shadow across the street.

The boys kept taking turns, throwing harder and getting more careless with each miss, until Kit admitted, "It's harder than it looks."

"It's easier during the day," Shane said, trying once more.

We all sat together on the curb. I asked Shane if he had any Blue Dream. He produced a joint and lit it, handing it to me first.

"Is your mom home?" Kit asked.

Shane thought that was funny.

"No," I said.

"I want to meet her," Kit said.

"Why?"

"I like moms."

"Oh my God," I said.

"Is she cool?" Kit asked Shane. "I bet she is."

"Nina?" Shane said, making a face like he was really thinking hard. "Yes," he decided. "Intense, but cool."

"She is not cool, and she's not intense," I said, the head rush from the pot making me feel a little edgy. I stood up, wanting to see past the houses to the mountains. The sparkling black asphalt under my feet was a pool of diamonds.

The front gate shuddered in the breeze, the lock clanging. I spun around at the sound and caught the coyote there—white reflecting off the back of his shining eyes. He paused for a moment before vanishing, as if to say—

This will not go away without hurting.

CHAPTER 11

Anna and Max are standing in the ruins of her room at the Dream
Palace. It's not really a room anymore. It's a bit of solid ground, a
lighted-up square. Around it, the matte black suck of outer space.

The cold and impossible realm of Max and Anna.

Max's eyes are ringed red from crying.

"She's not going to let me back in the house," he said. "My
boys. They're going to notice something's wrong."

Anna's arms are covered in scrapes and she's bleeding from
a gash across her left cheek. Beyond that, there's a disturbing
blur surrounding her. The line where her skin meets the air is
being depleted, erased.

"You lied to me," she's saying. "You're just like everyone else."

Believer had exposed Anna as Olesya, but the reveal of
Max's secrets was huge. Anna could remain hidden behind
them, using his frantic guilt to evade interrogation.

Max's wife was taking a tray of fish sticks out of the toaster oven when she got a Facebook message from Believer saying, "Look at what your husband is doing." Transcripts of chats. Pictures of Max.

"Meg searched this name," Max is saying.

The name at the top of the Tumblr—JOSS WYATT—appears huge in the black space, letters like floating red barbs.

"A teenage girl in Arizona." Max's voice trembles. "On the debate team at some Catholic school?"

"I'm just as confused as you are," Anna replies, a little too defensive. Her skin is see-through now. She's melting like an ice cube, from the outside in.

This is the last time she and Max will ever talk.

I closed Chat and began changing passwords—e-mail addresses, Facebook log-ins, every screen name I could remember. I deleted Anna's profile on the dating site where she'd met Max. I deleted three others from the same site, including Emma's, though George would be sure to notice its disappearance.

I put a piece of washi tape over my laptop's camera. The clock said MONDAY 2:55 A.M. and my room was completely dark except for the lights of the laptop and the lizard's heat lamp. I'd left Shane and Kit outside hours ago, and responded to Max's urgent calls.

At first I'd tried to placate him. I layered new excuses on top of old ones. But Believer had done it, contacted Max's wife.

I couldn't believe he was married. Even harder to believe was the fact that I'd missed it.

I stared at a file, hidden in my English Reports > A Tale of Two Cities folder. It contained everything Max and Anna had ever said to each other. Downloaded e-mails, chat transcripts. All the mementos I'd saved in neat, organized batches. A Word document with Anna's backstory obsessively outlined.

Like a fucking serial killer, Joss, keeping souvenirs from dead people.

Reluctantly, I dragged the file to the trash and lifted my finger.

It felt like burning a diary. As soon as she was gone, I wanted her back.

Good-bye, Anna.

After, I looked back at the Tumblr. For the first time, I noticed an ASK BELIEVER button at the top of the page. I clicked it. The screen showed an empty text box.

What do I say?

I've already considered the possibility that this whole thing is a great karmic retribution orchestrated by the forces that control the give and take of the universe. That I deserve the public unveiling of all my secrets.

You say I have victims. I don't agree. Eventually Anna would have turned into a ghost. She would've slipped away from Max's

life easily. He'd have gotten over her. His wife
would never have found out. (Unless you're
her, in which case, okay, sorry. You see, I didn't
know. . . .)

You didn't have to ruin his life. That's
sadistic. That's more fucked than what I do.

You know more than me (right now), but
you underestimate the level to which I am
connected to this beyond the files on my
laptop.

Can we have a fucking dialogue at least?
—Joss

I pressed the submit button before I could think of anything better, and closed the laptop. Bueller scurried in her
tank, performing her nocturnal ritual of endless laps around
the glass perimeter. I slid beneath my bedspread and logged
into Rosie's in-box with the new password.

Dear James, I typed, after reading a while.

Dear Jimmy Grace, my Old Jacket,
Remember that Henry Miller I sent you, at
the very beginning of this?

My filaments are sensitive.

There's a lot I haven't told you about my
life, about what's happening. Worse than the

stalker guy, or ghosts, or you dating Gia age 27
who poses in front of lava lamps for her Tinder
profile.

I liked the guy tonight. He surprised me a
couple of times, impressed me, made me feel
good.

But if you were waiting for me to realize
how much I wanted you, the plan worked.

I want to put a claim on you, to take you
out of the world and keep you for myself. I
want Our Thing to be where we live. I know it
could protect us and make us stronger.

I guess we have to meet for that to happen.

So. Let's meet.

xx Rosie

"I can't drive you to school today."

My mother handed me a cup of coffee, a preemptive peace
offering.

"But . . . who . . . ?" I managed, blinking the morning blear
out of my eyes. "How?"

"I've got to go the opposite direction, and I'm already late,"
she said, stuffing her purse full of protein bars.

"Who's gonna drive me?" I asked her. Rhiannon and Mary-
Kate lived too far away.

"Why don't you ask Shane?"

"No, please," I moaned.

"Dare I ask: Why not?"

"He's so annoying in the morning. And all the other times. Why can't you just drop me off?"

"Deposition, honey," she said firmly. "Eight thirty. Queen Creek. I should be on the freeway already."

"Mom, what if there was an earthquake right now?"

"There aren't any earthquakes in Arizona."

"Mom, what if there was a hurricane right now?"

She ignored me, zooming around the kitchen and through to the dining room, where the table was covered with her work paraphernalia.

"What would you do?" I shouted. "What if an airplane fell out of the sky and crashed into the house? Would you save me? Or would you just freak out? Remember when you made me and Dylan get into the bathtub because there was a tornado warning? You said tornados don't happen in Arizona, too, but there was one."

She gathered her things and acted annoyed, but I knew she liked this game. When Dylan and my dad were around, we'd gang up on her until she ran into the garage to escape.

I wondered if Rhiannon could save me.

Me: **Please say you can give me a ride**

Rhiannon: **oof sorry, it's Guin's day for the car, my dad's dropping me off**

Me: **ughhhh x infinity**

"Oh, and don't forget, I'm leaving for Tucson tomorrow."

"What?"

"I told you yesterday," she started, grabbing her keys from a dish full of unopened bills on the counter. "I'll be gone until Thursday. Two nights."

"But what about the earthquake!"

She smiled, and came over and hugged me. Her perfume and the roughness of her curly hair against my face brought on a sudden sense memory—waiting for her to come back from a weekend away with my dad, trying to be brave in front of the babysitter but almost crying, wanting desperately to touch my palm against her cool cheek. I used to do that every night before I went to sleep.

I hugged her back, giving it a little more oomph than the usual stiff-armed squeeze, because I could see in the way she'd shuffled her papers and piled the dishes in the sink that it was a bad morning. She wasn't feeling it. She wasn't remembering that anybody cared about her. She didn't say it ever, but I could tell. She was used to a level of affection that was suddenly, irrevocably altered.

"You better leave me, like, at least two hundred dollars though, just in case the apocalypse comes while you're gone."

There was a visible post-hug burst of energy to her movements now.

"The apocalypse will not come."

"Mom! Please do not jinx it."

"There's no such thing as a jinx, Joss," she said, smiling.

"It's your fault I believe in it. You're the one who sent me to Catholic school, where we drink blood wine and learn about plagues. You pray to Saint Anthony every time you can't find your keys."

"That's different," she protested.

"I don't see how," I said in a singsong voice.

"See you later," she said, disappearing through the door to the garage. I walked over to lock it, and before I could, she stuck her head back in.

"How was your date? I'm dying to know and trying to seem casual."

"Not terrible."

"Ooh!"

"Nope, too eager," I said, pushing the door shut.

Now I had to text Shane.

Me: **Ride please?**

Shane: 😎 🚗 😈 💯

Shane: **You're the devil**

Outside, the droning cicadas, the unrelenting sun, the cacophony of Monday-morning leaf blowers—I felt each one like a jab at my armor as I walked around the block to Shane's house, moving slowly so I wouldn't start to sweat.

There are four different house models in my neighborhood. As I walked, I counted six of the same medium-size kind, seven of the other medium-size kind, three of the biggest, and one of the smallest. Shane's house was almost directly behind mine, just a few lots down, and was one of the small ones. The yard was a little too unkempt, like always, and bikes lay scattered around a faded, netless basketball hoop.

Shane was in the driveway, waiting with the engine running.

At least I don't have to say hi to his weird mom.

"Hey," he said when I got in.

"Hey."

"Let's do this."

We drove in silence, coasting through the exit gate, passing the first of a chain of strip malls.

Sometimes it seems like changing my actual physical form is the only way I could ever really leave Arizona. Cars or planes wouldn't get me far enough away. In these moods, I was sure that the world was the same everywhere, that no matter where I went, I would always be finding new arrangements of the same old things.

Shane's ten-year-old Ford Focus only had a cassette player. When he bought the car on his sixteenth birthday, I'd gone in search of tapes as a present—I looked at a zillion different places before finally finding a bin full of them for twenty-five cents each at the back of a Radio Shack.

"I don't care who knows it, and I am not being triple-reverse ironic, either, so don't complain. But I love this song," I said, turning up Green Day's "Worry Rock," the tape so worn that the vocals came out sideways.

"It's a fucking good song," Shane agreed.

We stopped at a red light and Shane air guitared the whole solo perfectly. I took a photo of him, eyes closed behind sunglasses, his Brophy tie loose around the neck of his rumpled uniform shirt, and posted it to Instagram.

idiotblush worry rock with #ShaneTatumdoesnothaveinstagram

"I could listen to that song a thousand times right now," I said when it ended.

We got on the highway and into some traffic. "Carpool lane, carpool lane!" I urged, and Shane moved the car cautiously, nosing through four lanes of giant SUVs.

"Green Day got bad, though," Shane said, like he'd just evaluated the entirety of Green Day's catalog in his head.

My phone chimed with a new text as I was scrolling through my Instagram feed, noting that Mae Castillo had started following me.

Believer: **No dialogue**

Believer: **Look who's next**

I couldn't bear to.

"Shane?" I asked.

He kept his eyes on the road while I filled him in on what happened with Max. I was right. He'd already seen the Tumblr, had wondered what the photo of Max's family meant.

"I didn't know he was married," I said before he could respond to any of it.

We pulled into the Brophy parking lot. I felt out of place. I was dealing with too many boys, being driven around by Kit and Shane, taunted by Believer, who seemed indisputably masculine, in love with James and unable to stop thinking about what Max might be doing. I needed Mary-Kate or Rhiannon, fast.

"Of course he's married," Shane said, turning the car off, cracking a window so we wouldn't cook ourselves.

"Why 'of course'?"

"Because." Shane sighed. "Everyone is lying on the Internet. Not to the extent you do it, but yeah. Of course the guy is married. Are you that surprised?"

"That's really not the point."

Shane scanned the parking lot, shifting uncomfortably.

"Right," he went on. "So this person—"

"Believer."

"Believer," Shane repeated, like the word disgusted him. "Whoever. They obviously have access to your computer. Or your phone."

"Does that happen? Is that a real thing?"

"I bet it's the guy's wife."

"I thought of that. But Max said she was shocked. She needed to go to the doctor because her blood pressure was so high."

"Jesus," Shane said. "You're definitely going to hell."

He was joking, but I didn't like it.

"Maybe you're Believer," I said.

"*Chh*," Shane hissed, taking his sunglasses off. They left a little red dent on the bridge of his nose. He straightened and tied his tie, tucked in his shirt. A pile of cassette tapes fell off his lap, clattering around his feet.

"Look," he said. "I can probably figure out how to unblock the phone number."

"No," I said.

"I could trace the IP address from the e-mail—"

"No," I repeated. "Please don't go all intrepid investigator on me like goddamn Tintin with a little pencil behind your ear."

Shane, answering the door with a Tintin comic book dangling from his hand every time I came over to ask him to come out and play.

"You don't want to find out who's doing this?"

"No. I mean, yeah, I do, obviously—"

"Come on. Why are you telling me all this, then? If you don't want my help?"

He was looking out the window. I followed his gaze to Leah Leary, waving, walking toward us.

"There's something new on the Tumblr," I said. "I haven't looked at it yet. Could you look at it first?"

"You don't want my help."

"Shane," I whined.

"Nope. Sorry. I'm out." He climbed out of the car, greeting Leah with a hug, wrapping the crook of his elbow around her neck. She pushed him away, giggling.

When I got out of the car, Leah mentioned something about

how she was joining my community service group in world religions. I couldn't stop staring at a zit on her chin, covered with a pale pancake of concealer.

"Oh, right," I said. "Next week?"

Leah laughed. I stared at her.

"Oh," she said, perkier than ever. "No. It's today."

CHAPTER 12

Dream Girl,

I'm better in person.

My friends say you aren't real—yes, I've told my friends about you. Shown them your pictures. Read bits of your letters to them. Sung the praises of your beautiful face and your darling brain. They've seen me get lost on ideas before, but they thought you'd never agree to meet.

So happy to throw it in their faces.

Do you want me to come out to California? I could stay with friends. No pressure. Tectonic plates crashing against each other, that's all. . . .

Dream girl, muse. Thanks for saying yes. I know you think it might be better to remain here, like this. What if some molecule of a chemical I inadvertently exude triggers a fight-or-flight response in some corner of your biology that you don't consciously control?

I don't get the 3-D either. It's my enemy, the opposition to my animal desire for immortality, the corruptor of everything I love. I don't know how or why these buildings stand, all over Brooklyn, thrusting up, asserting their solidity even though all their strength and height is just a tragic harbinger of their inevitable decay . . . !?!?!

I'm rambling. Sorry, I'm excited.

Does it feel like you're not experiencing anything fully, lately?

That a part of you is missing?

Tell me when and where. I'll book a flight.

Yours,

James

I read the letter over and over, sometimes separating the words and savoring them individually, sometimes racing to each new sentence.

He already knows my face. I can step into Rosie and maybe there won't even be a difference. No more Believer. No more Joss Wyatt.

"So was it fun?" Mary-Kate was asking. "Your date?"

Mary-Kate, Mae Castillo, and I were driving to the nursing home in Leah Leary's car, meandering through a part of the valley I'd never seen, a labyrinth of golf courses and senior communities, a sprawling geriatric oasis. Every car a Cadillac going ten below the speed limit.

"I texted you," I said, remembering just then that she hadn't responded when I sent the SOS about seeing Mr. Lauren.

"I don't think I got it."

I twisted around to look at her in the backseat. Mae sat next to her with headphones on, apparently listening to a linguistics podcast, a bit of information I had yet to fully process.

"We got twenty-one-plus wristbands. I felt like a complete adult."

"Isn't Kit, like, twenty-six?" Mary-Kate snapped. She'd started the day annoyed with me—for forgetting both the trip and my paragraph of the written proposal we were supposed to have ready to give the nursing home coordinator. My brain was mushy, full of holes. How could I remember the birthdays of thirty fake personalities perfectly but forget one little assignment?

"He's nineteen," I said.

"That's still old. But at least he's real," Mary-Kate said, typing rapidly on her phone. I wondered how angry she would be if I told her to stop staring at the screen and listen to me.

"Trapped by my own hypocrisy," I mumbled, turning around.

"What?"

"I'm very mature for my age," I said loudly.

"People have been telling you that since kindergarten. I think it's given you a complex."

I slouched down, training my gaze on the watery shimmer on the horizon.

When it gets really hot, you can actually see the heat rising from the ground, and on a road long and uninterrupted enough, it turns into a mirage. When you're driving, it looks like you're going to go right into it, but you never do. The mirage stays the same distance away.

I wondered what it would feel like to be inside a mirage.

Like being in cool water. Like being strong glass.

> Dear James,
>
> Planning a meeting feels forced. It seems so cheesy to say, "Okay, this is the time and place. We'll meet. You'll be holding a rose, and I'll be wearing a blue dress."
>
> I want it to feel like fate. I wish we could accidentally run in to each other. That's sort of what I thought would happen anyway, eventually. One day you'd be at the Getty Museum in LA and turn a corner and there I'd be. And we'd both know.
>
> And nothing seems an appropriate backdrop. I don't want to meet here, in my usual places, school and the dorm. Restaurant or bar, no, absolutely no. Hotel, maybe, but I'd feel like a hooker.

The moon? An Antarctic glacier? The caves

at Lascaux? On top of a pyramid?

Build a tree house, invite me over?

I'll keep looking.

I am reaching for you in the dark.

xx Rosie

A cold thought came to me. Could Believer find James? Exposing Anna was one thing, but the idea that Rosie might fall, too, taking James down with her, was unacceptable. I amended my letter, adding:

PS—The sooner the better. Next week?

Leah Leary's phone barked out a command in a stilted Australian accent.

"In five hundred feet, turn royt on Joymz Street."

"What street?" I asked, goose bumps thrilling across my arms.

"James," Leah said, turning.

Before I could properly marvel at this sure sign, a large rectangular building came into view.

ARROWHEAD NURSING HOME: A MEMORY CARE FACILITY. The building was designed to look like a Colonial house, but the dimensions were supersized. The effect was revolting—a quaint cottage on steroids in the middle of the desert. Two ambulances were parked out front.

Dread settled in. *Memory care.* It sounded like science fiction. I pictured rows of elderly people, bodies gelatinous with gravity, bald heads covered with sensors, wires everywhere.

"This terrible guy took us on a tour. He showed us around. And I got lost."

"You got lost?"

Mr. Lauren and I were sitting outside the chapel, where he'd found me avoiding going to lunch after the ride back from Arrowhead.

"I was texting someone—Kit, the guy I went to the concert with—and I sort of lagged behind. But something so incredibly weird happened."

"What?"

"I met this woman. She grabbed my arm and took me into her room."

"Did she really?"

"It was amazing."

Kit: **What you up to?**

    Me: **I'm at a nursing home, volunteering**

    Kit: **For real**

    Me: **Really. School thing**

    Kit: **Let's hang out again soon**

    Me: **My mom's gone tomorrow night**

When I looked up, the hallway was empty. I couldn't

remember where we were supposed to go next on our tour of Arrowhead—the pool, the cafeteria, the Zen garden.

Mary-Kate's going to be pissed.

I crept toward a bank of elevators, sounds of coughing fits and daytime television leaking out from behind each closed door.

"Rosie." An energetic whisper. I felt dizzy. A hand on my arm, papery skin, a large ruby ring on the middle finger.

"Come here, Rosie."

An old woman led me into a narrow room.

"I'm just here on a tour. I have to get back to my friends—" I tried to explain.

"Sit down, Rosie."

"I'm not Rosie. My name is Joss. Do you want me to get a nurse for you?"

"Just sit down."

I sat on an overstuffed chair. On the wall opposite, a huge, intricate dream catcher was hanging, threaded through with shells and stones and feathers.

There was something about the room. A big window with white lace curtains and a wide windowsill with a strange assortment of things displayed on it—an array of grocery store candles with Our Lady of Guadalupe on them, a rosary with faux ivory beads, a dozen potted plants.

I calmed down. It felt like I'd been there before. Like some version of my bedroom. A room in the Dream Palace. Each

ROWAN MANESS

object was a symbol. I wanted to rearrange them, play a game I sometimes played with my own things—arrange them the right way, to grant a wish, to make something happen.

The woman's name was Irene. She thought I was her sister, Rosie. I tried again to explain who I was, but she didn't hear it.

She asked if I remembered when her father came home from the war in the Pacific and gave us both what he said were shark's teeth, as big as bananas.

She said, "Rosie, you kept yours with you everywhere you went, until you used it to cut that boy who teased you for your freckles, so Mother took it away."

She wanted to go over what was left of her memories, I think, to keep them close. I played along. I shared one of my own.

"Do you remember when we went to the Grand Canyon and wandered off and nobody could find us? They had a big search party, with police. We'd gone beyond the railings. You saw a nest you said was abandoned by an eagle or a hawk. We sat by it and pretended it was ours. It was dark when they finally found us. We got in so much trouble."

Shane and me.

Irene laughed. "How dangerous! It was so high up!"

"It didn't seem too high," I said. "But it must have been."

MK: **Where are you?**

MK: **We're in the lobby, hurry up**

"Oh, Rosie."

Irene sat on the edge of her neat twin bed, stroking a corner of a crocheted blanket.

"Oh, Rosie," she repeated. "Do you remember when you died?"

I didn't say anything.

"I put the shark tooth with you, in the hospital. Then you died."

"I'm sorry," I said.

"I really didn't think you ever would."

I wondered, at chance and parallels. I knew that many things were always lining up and falling apart. I sensed, however irrationally, that Irene had access to a different world, just like I did.

"I'm three hundred years old," she said, looking at the space in front of my face, onto which she was projecting someone else.

On the drive back to school there was a moment. On the freeway, the Kokopelli whizzed past, a curved flash on the side of a big mud-colored retaining wall. The car and everything in it—the girls, my own body—was unfamiliar.

I looked at Leah Leary's face and could not remember her name or how I felt about her. I tried to place her, and doing so made me realize that I didn't know who I was, either.

On the Tumblr, two new entries.

The first was a series of screenshots, captured chat conversations. George and Emma.

ROWAN MANESS

George: **We have to get rid of him**

George: **Just say the word**

Below the screenshots was a photo. The Marchands—the real Ron and Emma, whose faces I'd taken and used.

VICTIMS #6 & 7—RON & EMMA

458 EDGEWORTH COURT

ATLANTA, GA 30301

And the latest entry. Another photo. George, smiling in fatigues. A picture he'd sent to Emma when she'd asked him for one. Holding a piece of paper—*George <3 Emma*

VICTIM #8—GEORGE

George is next.

Before I met James on the astral plane, I told him how to get there.

You're in bed and you make your body light.

You think of another person. You let your body long for them. It's like digging a hole in sand until you hit water, and the water fills the space, collapsing it. You push up through the collapse and then your body is vibrating with longing.

Your skin is hot and fizzing with energy. Your eyes are closed. You have to work very hard to keep still.

Then go.

"Wow," Mr. Lauren said.

"I think she saw into my soul," I said, watching him tug at his right earlobe, at a small scar that looked like it could be from an old piercing.

Invisible cicadas buzzed, the constant background drone of all my summers.

How do you know they really exist? Have you ever seen one up close?

The land where Xavier was built was once an orange grove, and the tough-skinned trees still dotted the campus, their trunks painted white to reflect the sun.

"Why'd you become a teacher?" I asked, moving closer to the nearest tree, scanning its branches, finding them empty. Mr. Lauren followed, frowning at my question.

"I wasn't a teacher in England. I worked in research."

"Why'd you move here?"

"Wasn't my choice," he said, and I remembered the way I'd caught him staring hungrily at me, his face bright in the stage lights of the Marquee.

"Why were you really at the concert?"

He moved to walk away, then stopped.

"You left this in class again," he said, reaching into his pocket and pulling out my iPod, handing it to me.

He left, and I listened to the cicadas. The sound wasn't stationary. It was tidal. It echoed internally, doing sonic tricks, bouncing off walls. I still couldn't see any actual insects. I looked at more trees. Nothing.

I liked to tell Shane that I believed airplane contrails were poisoning the atmosphere with drugs to keep us complacent consumers. I didn't really, but conspiracy theories drove him nuts and I liked to see him get all worked up.

But cicadas, maybe. Their sound pumped in. It did have a mechanical strain. What were they poisoning us with? Or was it a message, to be decoded?

Mr. Lauren is lying too.

CHAPTER 13

The receptionist in Dr. Judson's office looked like someone I could pretend to be. Maybe she was married to someone I was talking to online. I watched her as my appointment time ticked closer. We'd arrived early, my mom speeding through side streets like a madwoman.

She was upset. Dylan hadn't written in two weeks. He usually sent an e-mail every few days. He can barely put a sentence together, but she reads them like they're Dostoevsky.

She flipped the pages of a magazine at regular intervals, but I knew she wasn't reading it. Just flipping. *Here I am, taking crazy Joss to the psychiatrist again while Dylan's probably dead in a ditch somewhere.* She hadn't even asked how my day went. I tried to tell her about "church, mall, school, prison," but she just interrupted me.

"There aren't any prisons around."

"Yeah, but if I took out 'prison' it would ruin the effect—"

"I get it, Joss," she said, annoyed. "You hate living here. I'm sorry."

I guessed that her bad mood was compounded by having to leave me at home by myself while she was gone on her work trip. Maybe she was missing my dad more than usual, wishing he was alive and could stay with me.

Rhiannon and I were texting.

Me: **Mary-Kate hates me**

Rhiannon: **She's uptight. She needs a boyfriend**

Me: **That's your solution to everything**

Rhiannon: **She hasn't really been talking to me, either, and I didn't do anything to piss her off**

Rhiannon: **Is Kit coming over tonight?**

Me: **. . . maybe**

Rhiannon: **omg you need to stream updates constantly**

Me: **He's weirdly asexual**

Rhiannon: **Not for long**

I'd sent Mary-Kate a text hours ago. I tried again.

Me: **I'm sorry about this morning. I finished my part of the proposal thingie and sent it to Braddock, ok?**

Me: **Come over tonight and swim and chill?**

I told myself that if she said yes, I'd cancel things with Kit. But when I checked my phone after my session with Dr. Judson, I could see she'd read the text and hadn't bothered to respond.

* * *

James: **Weird question. Have you ever been to Phoenix?**

James: **I just got roped into doing some work out there. I've never been.**

James: **But I thought, LA isn't too far . . . maybe you could drive out?**

James saying *Phoenix*. Another sign.

Church, mall, school, prison, James.

The streets turned golden with his arrival. Walking toward Rosie, desert wildflowers sprouting in his footsteps. The ground would quake and swallow vacant exurb McMansions, golf courses leeched of color, Xavier and Brophy and Dr. Judson's office.

I wouldn't have to go anywhere. He would come to me. Whatever I had to do to preserve the lie would be of secondary importance once we touched.

Me: **Pick a day. I can't handle the responsibility.**

Me: **But okay.**

Me: **Send a song to calm me down?**

Fifteen minutes after my mom left for Tucson, Kit knocked at the front door.

"Show me around," he said, looking up at the vaulted foyer ceiling. I took him through the living room, cool and dark, wooden blinds shut tight. The unused dining room, table stacked with papers, bankers' boxes towering on top of the buffet.

In the kitchen, he looked at a row of photographs lining a windowsill.

"You look just like your mom," he said, pointing to her.

"I know."

Ferris the cat met us in the hallway, mewing for treats, wrapping herself around Kit's legs, pawing his jeans, begging him instead of me. He stumbled over her as I opened the door to the den/studio.

"Your dad was a painter?" he asked, looking around at the old canvases.

"Yeah," I said. "He didn't make any money off it though. So he restored stuff sometimes. None of that's here now."

Now his ashes are in the corner.

"Do you draw or anything?"

"I write stories," I said, without thinking, embarrassed immediately. "And make collages sometimes."

"Where are those?"

"In my room."

Ferris followed us upstairs, attached to the new male.

I sat on the bed while Kit surveyed, tapping Bueller's tank lightly, brushing the leaves of my plants.

"This one's really nice," he said, pointing to the mandala on the wall, the one I'd used as inspiration for Rosie's art show.

Kit came over and sat next to me.

So this is what it feels like to have a boy in your bed.

I was surprised at how easy it was to kiss him. The shock of connection. A little bit of guilt, a rush of pride. I didn't want to stop, but Kit pulled back and led me downstairs.

I plugged my iPod into the patio speakers, and we went outside to the backyard, where the sun had just set, leaving a pretty indigo sky behind, crisscrossed with lavender contrails, speckled with early stars.

On top of the nearest mountain, jutting up just beyond the neighborhood, a cluster of radio transmission towers blinked red.

We uncovered the pool and sat with our legs in the water. Kit pulled out a green prescription bottle full of neatly-rolled joints. He lit one and passed it to me.

"Do you get stoned a lot?" I asked, exhaling.

He shrugged. "I go in phases. I was on Ritalin and Adderall from like third grade till halfway through high school. Weed seemed like a miracle compared to that. It's good for creativity. I do it more often when I'm writing songs."

"Are you writing a song now?" I asked.

"No," he said shyly, with a smile.

"Dylan—my brother—he told me not to smoke pot until I was in college. Because my brain's too open already."

Kit laughed.

Dylan really said that because he knows it widens the cracks.

I imagined the drug spreading through my bloodstream and tried to catch a floating leaf with my toes. Kit was so cute it was hard to look at him.

"I wish I could write songs," I said, listening to a cricket chirping along to the song playing in the background.

"Anyone can," Kit said.

"I don't think that's true."

"Maybe you could be a muse?"

We played footsie in the water, and everywhere we touched was a meeting point of currents.

"I'm more of a guru," I went on, remembering something James had written.

Kit coughed. "A guru?" he asked. "What kind of guru?"

"Umm." I thought. "Like, one who guides your ideas and helps shape them. I'd have all these musicians looking to me to give them validation and lead them to the truth."

"Oh," said Kit. "You mean like a cult leader."

"You know," I said, "I can never think of anything to say when people ask me what I want to do with my life, but you've figured it out. Cult leader. Perfect."

I lifted my legs out of the water and leaned back on the grass.

"Venus," I said, pointing at the brightest spot in the sky. "You can tell it's a planet because they don't twinkle. And it's not reddish, so it's not Mars."

"I would join your cult," Kit said.

"If someone came up to you and said, 'Hey, Kit, want to go to Mars? I'll take you right now,' would you go?" I asked.

"Absolutely," Kit said, and his answer excited me.

"Oh God," I said, seeing the stars flat, points on a plane, glitter on a sheet of paper. "What if Venus used to be like Earth, but now it's burning up? And Mars will be the new Earth, after we burn up? And it keeps going all the way to Neptune?"

"Yes, cult leader," Kit said robotically.

"I'm serious," I said, ready to make my case.

I was interrupted by the doorbell ringing in the distance. At the same time, Kit's phone vibrated between us. I jumped—

"Who's that?"

"I ordered pizza," Kit said, putting a hand on my shoulder to lever himself up.

At the front door, Kit paid the delivery guy. I peered over his shoulder.

"How'd you get in?" I asked. The guy looked at me incredulously, sliding the pizza box out of its warming sleeve.

"Gates were open," he mumbled, walking away.

We took the pizza to the backyard and sat in the grass in the middle of a circle of tiki torches.

More stars were out. From the bare brown hills beyond the subdivision came the howl of a lone coyote. I saw Kit react to the sound, so I knew it was a real one. Not my coyote, the shape-shifting trickster god. Believer's minion.

Stay away.

We ate, and Kit told me about how he decided to follow his brother and move from Chicago to Phoenix. He made an allusion to a girl he'd broken up with recently. He talked about meditation and I did not make any jokes about it.

He said people kept telling him he needed to move the band to LA, and he knew they were right, but he didn't know if he was brave enough. He said every time he thought about getting a manager or recording an album he froze up.

"Just fake it," I said. "Pretend you're a brave person."

"Huh," Kit said.

"That's as good as being one."

We went inside, and Kit waited on the couch while I went upstairs. I stopped by my room to brush my hair and dab jasmine oil on my wrists.

This is what girls do. This is all normal. You're doing normal girl stuff.

I grabbed Dylan's guitar from his bedroom and brought it down so Kit could play it for me.

But when I crawled over to him on the couch and kissed him again, he pulled away.

"Joss—"

Something had changed.

"I don't think this is a good idea."

"Wait. Seriously?"

"I don't think we should."

"Seriously?" I repeated.

He cleared his throat. "Not because I don't want to. It's just that—I can tell you're not telling me something."

"What? Are you psychic?"

"I have this thing about honesty."

I stood up, folding my arms, angry now and confused.

"I mean," he went on. "Like when I met you at that party. You were cagey on your phone. Then you sent me a text that was clearly meant for someone else. And at the concert it was almost like you weren't even there. I don't know. I just—"

He sighed. "I really like you. And I'm cool with just hanging out. But if we're going to do more, then I'll need total honesty."

I couldn't help laughing a little.

"That's funny?" Kit asked.

"You like honesty, meditating, moms, you don't want to fuck me—is this some kind of performance art?"

He stood up.

"I'm just saying. I'd want it to be just you and me."

I was glad the room was dark. I was blushing, all at once ashamed and angry for being made to feel that way by someone I barely knew. That Kit's instincts were spot-on made it even worse.

He got up to leave. "Think about it."

But I was thinking about Max, how he'd wanted to send Anna a birthday present once. I figured out how to have the package routed to a mailbox place down the street from Xavier, and picked it up there. Lingerie, the kind he imagined a girl like Anna wore. Peter sent flowers to Amelia twice, bouquets delivered to an apartment address I made up. He'd even put money down on an engagement ring for her. There were many other gifts. I told myself I was accepting them as a kind of experiment.

I stood still as marble while Kit put on his jacket. At the front door he stopped and looked back.

"I'll text you," he said, and was gone. I wanted to yell *Don't bother!* or *What's the point?* but a sound echoed from the kitchen.

My phone, rattling against the counter.

I went to it, knowing.

George: **I'm outside your house**

George: **Emma**

George: **Hello?!**

George: **HELLO?**

George: **I'm ready just tell me when to do it**

I ran to the front door and locked it.

A barrage of new texts, loud as bullets—

Believer: **You're going to have to learn how to deal with the consequences of your actions.**

Believer: **I'd suggest calling the Atlanta PD.**

Believer: **But it might already be too late.**

Believer: **More blood on Joss Wyatt's hands.**

There were two long floor-to-ceiling windows on either side of the door. I wanted to check to see that the gate was shut, but I was sure that if I looked out, someone would be standing there. George, in two places at once—outside the innocent real Marchands' house and outside mine. Or Peter, reincarnated.

Not them.

"You," I said.

Me.

I looked out.

The gate was open.

The coyote was standing just beyond it.

Come down from the mountains. Not lost, not hungry.

He stepped closer, and I watched him materialize. I miraged him. He walked into the porch light and stood on his hind legs. He saw me. I ran.

I ran into the Dream Palace.

CHAPTER 14

A low-resolution Google Street View image of 458 Edgeworth Court is projected on the walls of Emma's room. I recognize it. I looked it up once. The biggest house in the neighborhood, the cleaning lady's car parked in the driveway.

It's night. If it's 10 p.m. in Arizona, it's midnight in Georgia. Ron's asleep in his bed. And Emma? Emma is here. In a grainy, two-dimensional facsimile of the middle of her street, watching George's truck pull up to her house.

He steps out, stuffs a gun in the baggy waistband of his jeans.

"No, George!" Emma calls. He doesn't turn to look. He moves along the surface of Edgeworth Court, outlined against the picture like a fly on a window screen.

Emma tries to reach him again, screaming.

"It wasn't me!"

George turns.

"I didn't text you. I didn't tell you to come kill Ron. That was someone else."

"But you want to be with me?"

"No! I mean, it's complicated—"

He raises the gun.

Like Peter. He's going to shoot himself like Peter.

"Please go home, George. Promise me. I'll explain everything in the morning."

George isn't pointing the gun at himself. He is pointing it at Emma.

"You don't love me?"

At first I think the sound is radio static.

It's cicadas. George's voice is thrumming with them.

The whole scene fractures, skipping into horizontal bars–

I back away, slamming the door shut on Emma's room. Running again, down the hallway this time, past doors with lights shining through the cracks, shadows crossing. Impatient shadows.

Make us real. Make us real. Make us real.

All my women are arranged around the pool in the courtyard. Motionless on lounge chairs. There's murky water in the pool now. It looks like tar, and at first I think that's where the smell is coming from.

Then I notice their bodies. Soured, rotting.

I look at the face of the one nearest to me.

Rosie.

James's Soft Robe, the dream girl with my face.

A lizard scurries past and slithers into the pool.

When I came to, I was barefoot, standing on the six-foot wall that separates my backyard from everyone else's. I looked around and determined I was halfway to Shane's house, teetering precariously on a cinder-block ridge five inches wide.

I stepped forward carefully, clutching my phone in one hand, arms extended for balance. Trying not to think about what might have happened if I'd fallen. I felt deeply seen, like I'd spent the blackout being strung up and inspected. Touched without knowing it.

Where had the time gone? I could picture myself climbing on top of the covered Jacuzzi, scraping my knees against the rough wall. But I was watching from across the backyard, one body in the midst of a silent, angry crowd.

Was there, at this very moment, an army of avengers, a legion of the lied-to, marching toward Silver Creek Road? Moving invisible through the resolute night, like the cicadas with their white-noise screeching?

Moving along the grid of backyards, through parcels with varying arrangements of swing sets, pools, and barbecue pits until I got to Shane's. Plastic toy detritus created angular hills in the dark. I jumped down onto the soft grass behind a sun-bleached playhouse.

Me: I'm in your backyard come out immediately

There was a text conversation between George and Emma on my phone, time-stamped ten minutes earlier.

Ten minutes?

The things they were saying in the Dream Palace. George persuaded into ending his mission. Emma telling him not to respond to any texts that came from a blocked number. The real George and Emma would never know how close he came to hurting them.

"Oh God," I said out loud, reeling, drooping, letting my head loll between my legs. I felt a tickle at my ankle and jerked away from a cricket hopping out of some bushes. I remembered Shane was always careful with bugs, stopping his bike to move caterpillars off the sidewalk.

Then he was there, groggy and puffy from sleep. I hugged him, so tight it was more like a cling.

I didn't have to tell Shane that sometimes I felt with Catholic sureness that I'd brought on my dad's death by manifesting doom, by dwelling, like a witch, in the world of jinxes and lies and letting them control me until, finally, they crossed over into real life.

Shane helped. I knew he would. I told him everything that happened after Kit left my house. Instead of a bug on the sidewalk I was a girl on a wall. He got me down. He took me inside. His parents and all the noisy siblings were asleep.

I hadn't been to his house in ages, but it was still familiar.

Same posters and furniture, new books and bedspread.

Shane sat at his computer and looked around for a while, while I sat there not saying anything, occasionally glancing at my phone to make sure there weren't any new texts.

"Do you think I'm responsible for Peter?" I said.

"No," he replied immediately, which I thought betrayed his real opinion.

"I've asked that before, huh?"

"Yep," he said.

"Why aren't you saying anything?"

"I'm checking police feeds to see if anyone got murdered in Atlanta," he said, not seriously, but not kidding, either.

"Don't joke," I said, stomach all acid, suddenly thirsty. I gulped down the glass of water Shane had poured for me.

"I'm waiting for you to go to sleep on the couch so I can pass out."

"I'm losing time," I said, cryptic on purpose.

"Joss." Shane sighed. "Just go to sleep. I put blankets in the living room."

My phone buzzed.

I looked at it—a new e-mail, from James. I scanned the first sentence and relaxed when I was certain he hadn't been contacted by Believer too.

"Who is it?" Shane asked.

"It's okay," I said, leaving his room. "You're right. I'll go to sleep."

Rosie,

We found each other. That's the hardest part.

Now I get to put my arm around you, go with you to a party, walk with you on the beach. I want us in Our Bed together, naked, deciding where we're going to go for breakfast, or what movie to see, or where to play miniature golf. (Do you like miniature golf? Is that what it's called?)

How does Sunday sound?

Sending a song, like you asked.

—James

He linked to a song, and it was perfect. I listened to it on repeat, phone pressed against my ear, cocooned on Shane's couch, until I fell asleep between the lyrics, each word a symbol, a salve, a sign.

"Joss, wake up," said a little voice.

I grumbled.

"Jossie, you have to wake up."

I was already awake. My sleep was fraught with nightmares, and the clanging of pots and pans had started at five thirty.

"Ella," I said. "Joss is awake. But Joss needs sleepy time for a little bit, okay?"

Giggling.

"It's Eden!"

Shane's youngest siblings are five-year-old twins.

"Eden," I said. "You gotta leave me alone, kiddo. I'm not well."

"You're mean! Mean Joss!" But she gave up.

A few minutes later, Shane's dad shouted, "Bacon, eggs, pancakes!" A stampede charged through the living room—the twins and the two other boys. I covered my head with a pillow and tried to stay as still as possible.

I must have dozed off, because the next thing I heard was Shane's voice. He was on his phone, pacing around.

"No. She heard a noise at her house, so she came over."

Leah Leary.

"She was alone—yeah—no—I guess not."

He laughed. "Okay, yeah. See you later. Yeah, you too."

I wondered if Leah Leary had just said *I love you.*

I folded the blankets and left them in a neat stack on the couch, then found Shane in the kitchen, dressed and ready to go.

"Oh," he said, looking at my wrinkled dress. "Right. I guess we need to stop by your house."

"Yeah, sorry."

We picked at the leftover breakfast spread. Pancakes cut into squares and soaked with syrup, microwaved sausages, cold scrambled eggs on cartoon-character trays.

"Thanks for letting me sleep here," I said, getting it out quickly.

He mumbled "Sure," and poured himself a glass of orange juice.

I rifled through a basket on the kitchen table—loose playing cards, My Little Pony figurines, old copies of *People* magazine addressed to Brenda Tatum, a remote control with the batteries missing. And a book, all the way at the bottom.

Vonnegut—must be Shane.

"Is this a good one?" I asked, holding it up for him to see.

"Yes," he said. "You'd like it."

"I don't know about Vonnegut," I said.

"What have you read?"

"Nothing. I just don't know about him."

Shane scoffed and drank the orange juice all in one sip. He slammed the cup down on the counter and made an exaggerated *ahh* sound.

I opened the book—*The Sirens of Titan*—to a random page and skimmed a few paragraphs until the name of one of the characters caught my eye.

Waltham Kittredge

"What's your opinion of portents?" I asked.

"You mean like auguries?"

"It's really more like omens, specifically," I said.

"So you're talking about presages?"

"Signs." I nodded.

"Prognosti—" Shane stumbled. "Prognosticats? That can't be right."

I laughed, feeling relaxed for the first time in a long while, despite the chaos surrounding me.

The gate was open at my house, and the neighbor's wind chime played a few creepy notes as Shane and I walked through to the front door.

It was locked, and I didn't have the keys.

"Shit," I said, cupping a hand against one of the big windows, looking inside. The cat walked by, then came back and sat down, staring at me with tranquil, unblinking eyes.

"*Psst, psst,*" I called to her. "You want food?"

She padded closer.

"Open the door, Ferris," I urged her. "You can do it. Use your tiny little paws."

"You want food, you open the door." I started a chant. "Open, kitten; open, kitten; open, kitten."

Ferris yawned and licked the fur on her chest.

I turned around to see where Shane had gone, and while I wasn't looking, the dead bolt turned.

It worked!

But it was just Shane, holding the cat.

"Patio door was wide open," he said disapprovingly.

I nudged past him and went upstairs. I wiped off old makeup and rinsed my legs and feet in the bathtub. I brushed my teeth, changed into my uniform, stuffed various papers and folders into my backpack.

My laptop was in the closet, screen saver swirling. I tapped the keyboard, waking it. The Tumblr. It must have been the last thing I'd looked at. Nothing new posted since last night. I checked its history and didn't see anything out of the ordinary. When I minimized the browser window, Emma's folder was gone, deleted like Anna's. All that digital ephemera delivered back to the aether as charred sacrifices.

I met Shane in the kitchen. He'd fed the cat and taken the pizza box in from the backyard. He was holding a green prescription bottle.

"Oh," I said. "Kit must have left that."

"He was over last night," I explained, off Shane's confused look. "Before everything. You can keep it, I guess. Whatever."

The house phone rang.

"You get it," I instructed Shane, scared of who it might be.

He picked it up.

"Hello?" He listened for a while, then smiled. "Hey, man!

"It's Dylan," he whispered to me.

"Dylan!" I said, ripping the phone away from Shane.

"Hey," said my brother. I hadn't heard his voice in months. We never talked on the phone.

The connection was bad.

"This is probably costing a bunch," he said. "I couldn't get Mom's cell."

"She's in Tucson," I said.

"Tell her?"

"Tell her what?"

"I'm coming back," he said, like I should have known.

"When?" I asked.

"Soon. I'm trying to get a flight. . . ." He trailed off, vague as always.

"Okay."

There was a pause.

"Everything good?" Dylan asked.

"Yeah," I said. "I'll tell Mom."

"Cool."

"Dylan," I said, before he could hang up. "I'm really glad you're coming home."

CHAPTER 15

"Marco? Marco!"

Trevor crept toward the deep end of the pool with his eyes shut, arms outstretched, bumping against a floating inflatable doughnut.

Rhiannon tiptoed behind where I was sitting at the pool's edge, dripping wet.

"Polo!" she called out. Trevor changed directions, groping toward the sound of her voice.

I'd invited them over after school, unable to face a second night at home alone. Shane and Leah were there too, inside the house, Leah upset with Shane for getting everyone stoned on Kit's forgotten weed.

"Do you remember when we were obsessed with giving ourselves heat stroke?" I asked Rhiannon. She shushed me but nodded, continuing to exchange Marcos and Polos with Trevor.

Intentional heat stroke had been my discovery. I'd fallen asleep on a pool raft on a 115-degree day, and when I woke, my vision was burned out. I stumbled into the bathroom off the patio, sure I'd gone blind, and climbed into the shower, turning on the cold water, slumping onto the tile.

I passed out and came to for a few seconds before passing out again. The effect was hallucinatory. I still couldn't see, but my ears rang with a complex melody of muffled voices, stringed instruments, and pounding drumbeats. As soon as my vision returned and I realized I wasn't going to die, I wanted to do it again. When I told Rhiannon about it, she went through the process too—lying in the sun until she couldn't take it any longer, sitting under ice-cold water. It was addictive.

James: **Are you serious?**

I'd just told James that I thought maybe we shouldn't meet after all.

Me: **I don't want to ruin what we have.**

James: **It's been long enough, Rosie.**

Me: **What if you don't like me?**

James: **Not possible**

Me: **The pics I've sent are the prettiest version of me**

James: **I don't care**

Me: **One thousand discarded selfies**

Me: **There are so many ways to dislike people IRL**

"Marco!"

"Polo!" Rhiannon screamed, cannonballing right next to Trevor, landing with a huge splash.

"Hey!" I yelled, wiping water off my phone.

Shane and Leah came out onto the patio. I squinted at them. Leah looked angry.

"Joss, tell Trevor that story you told us about Conor Oberst baking pot brownies for Kit," Rhiannon said.

"No," I refused. "I'm frying my brain."

"Please," Rhiannon insisted. "He wants to hear. Don't you, Trevor?"

"Brain, brain, what is brain?" Trevor shouted, lifting Rhiannon onto his shoulders.

"Kit is stupid," I said, standing. "I don't want to talk about him."

"So sad." Rhiannon pouted.

Rosie: **Can you get back to the astral plane?**

If James and Rosie could go there again, maybe the Dream Palace could be saved. Or, if it couldn't, if it was too far gone, James and I could build a new one, together. Deleting Anna and Emma left me grasping. I felt helpless, waiting for Believer's next move, all the idols on my altar set to crumble.

I closed my eyes and focused on James, bringing his face to the front of my mind.

Leah Leary's voice cut through my daydream. She was saying she'd heard there was going to be a "teacher dunk tank" at field day on Friday.

"I'm going to sneak Trevor in," Rhiannon said, then, asking Shane, "Do you have an extra Brophy shirt he could wear?"

"No problem."

"Are you sure?" Leah objected. "They plan these events based on a head count—"

I groaned, standing up, the backs of my thighs peeling off the flagstone deck.

"Trevor has to come," Rhiannon explained. "He's my emotional support animal."

Trevor barked like a dog, wrestling Rhiannon under the water.

I was standing in front of the mirror in my bedroom when I heard the crash.

Pretending the reflection was Rosie, wondering if she carried herself differently. She probably stood up straighter—I pulled my shoulders back. I never smiled with my teeth, but she might. I tried that, too. Then the sound interrupted—the blinds at my window suddenly askew, jangling, something landing with a heavy *thud* on the floor.

The house alarm blared—

"INTRUDER, INTRUDER, INTRUDER"

Footsteps on the stairs. Trevor, rummaging around in the kitchen, heard me scream.

He ran to the window and yanked up the blinds. I stood, frozen, as he looked from the shattered pane to a large rock on the carpet, comprehending the situation, a wild grin spreading across his face.

"Punks!" he shouted, and ran out of the room. The alarm kept shouting *"INTRUDER,"* and above it I could hear more commotion downstairs—the others, wondering what was happening.

Heart pounding, I approached the window.

I put my hand through the hole. There was a force passing through it, a subtle sucking wind, like the house's armor had been pierced and now something was leaking out into the night.

Something moved across the street. A rustling in the hedge separating two houses. A figure, trying to stay hidden. I could make out hiking boots and, higher up, a baseball cap.

I jerked my hand back, scraping it badly on the jagged glass. The man stepped into view. I recognized him.

It's the neighbor. Just the neighbor.

The alarm finally shut off. In the eerie silence I heard the faint jingle of a bell coming from down the street. My dad was always worried about the cat escaping. He got the bell after she bolted out the front door and almost got hit by a car.

Ferris.

The coyote will get her.

I ran downstairs, flying past Shane, Leah, and Rhiannon in the foyer, out the door Trevor had left open, nearly running into him on the sidewalk.

"I didn't see anyone!" he shouted after me.

At the end of the block, I slowed down and stayed very

still, listening for Ferris's bell. A light breeze whipped my hair across my face and carried the bell sound deceptively close one way, deceptively far the other.

I crossed through to the greenbelt, forcing myself to look carefully at each dark spot, behind every rock. I checked inside a large cement water pipe that emptied there. I was looking for Ferris but also daring the coyote to show his face again. Trying to be as fearsome and intrusive as he and Believer were.

The bell sound continued, and I kept going, calling for the cat every so often.

"Ferris! *Psst, psst!*"

Then the bell, then nothing, and always a glimpse, behind or ahead, of flashing eyes, of the strange figure stalking the edge of my perception.

I walked all the way to the main entrance of the neighborhood—up to the two big gates with an empty guard-house in between. Beyond the gates a stretch of flat, mani-cured grass bordered with rows of bright flowers. Backlit iron letters spelled out the name of the neighborhood.

An entrance so much more grand than the neighborhood really was, so everyone could feel their money well spent.

There's a fence! House cats stay inside! Coyotes stay out! Bad neighborhoods don't have names like The Estates at Corazon Point. Everybody knows that!

"It wasn't Believer," Shane said, touching my shoulder. I whirled around.

We had a whole conversation without actually saying any words.

Yes it was! It's Believer, and he's here, and he's going to murder me in my sleep tonight.

That's really unlikely. It was probably just some idiot kid. Calm down.

Don't tell me to calm down.

You're bleeding.

I know.

The cat's bell tinkled. Shane heard it too.

We walked toward the sound together.

"Are you seeing things again?" Shane blurted out, finally asking the question that was following him like a cloud.

Right, he guessed.

"It's not a problem."

Shane sighed. "This is the second time in two days you've been out roaming the streets barefoot."

"The cat got out!" I said. "What was I supposed to do?"

"Put shoes on? Bring a flashlight and a bag of cat treats?"

My phone buzzed.

Rhiannon: **Trev wants to know where's the duct tape?**

"Rhiannon," I said to Shane, who clearly wanted to know.

I stopped walking and looked at him, with his new long hair and his crossed arms. Regarding me with something too much like pity.

"You used to see what I saw."

"In my imagination, yeah," he said.

"No," I said. "For real."

"We were kids. Playing pretend."

"Don't say that."

"I can't say anything to you," Shane said. "You're bleeding and hallucinating and being stalked and still I can't say anything to you."

We were in front of the electrical box. I hoisted myself up, leaving Shane in the street.

The cat was lying there, completely relaxed, belly down on the warm, humming metal.

"Found her!" I shouted. The adrenaline in my system was wearing off and my hand hurt. I sat next to Ferris and pressed my palm against the box while I wrote out a text and sent it to Believer.

Me: **Was that you just now?**

Shane climbed up—the cat flopped over onto her back, purring for him to pet her.

"You can say shit to me," I mumbled.

"What?"

"You can say shit to me," I repeated, louder. "You're the only one I've told about any of this. I wouldn't tell you if I didn't trust you to know what to do with it."

"Okay," he said. "First step, tell Nina."

I started to say *No*, but held back. If Shane heard me say no to something he suggested one more time, he'd probably push me off the box.

"Give me some time?" I asked. "Like a couple weeks?"

I'll be gone. I'll be Rosie. I'll be new.

Shane looked skeptical.

"I just want to see if I can figure this out on my own," I said, not even convincing myself. I didn't want to figure it out. I just wanted to get out from under it.

"What is it?" Shane asked, meaning, *What are you seeing this time, Joss? The same old ghost? A new one?*

A louche coyote who walks like a human and teases you when you make mistakes?

"Let's go," I said, deflecting, not wanting to share that even with Shane.

Later, after Shane and Leah left and Rhiannon and Trevor settled in to watch a movie before sleeping over, I locked the door to my bedroom, crossed into the attached bathroom that separated my room from Dylan's, and drew myself a bath.

While the tub filled, I searched for my iPod, finally finding it in the front pocket of my backpack. I synced it to a pair of Bluetooth speakers and set everything on the side of the tub.

I eased myself in to the scalding-hot water, wincing as it washed over the scrapes on my legs and the cut on my hand. Even though Believer hadn't responded to my text asking if he was responsible for the rock throwing, I blamed him for all of my injuries. They were physical signs, proof of his growing presence in my life. I hid the cuts beneath bubbles and lay back in the tub, listening to the music.

I believe in the sentience of shuffle—that if you let it, the random string of songs will tell you something. Provide the answer to a question or clues about new paths. I hoped it would clarify some things.

After a couple old favorites, shuffle chose a song I'd never heard before. I was sure I hadn't downloaded it. I reached for the iPod and looked at the screen.

The artist and track names had been deleted. The album artwork was blank. The only identifying information was a phone number in the place where the song's title should have been.

Fear gripped me. Believer, outside my house. Believer's hand wrapping around my iPod—

Then I remembered who had it last. It had been in my backpack ever since.

I took my phone from the lip of the tub and typed in the phone number.

Me: **So, that's your move?**

A second later.

4805559516: **Who is this?**

Me: **iPod**

4805559516: **Oh.**

4805559516: **Hello.**

Me: **Who's saying hello?**

Me: I already know. . . .

4805559516: It's Miles.

Me: So, Miles. This is your move?

Miles: I didn't think it would actually work

Me: You regret it?

Miles: I'm afraid I don't.

Me: Where are you? What do you do on Wednesday nights?

Miles: I'm at home.

Me: Alone?

Miles: Yes. And you?

Me: I'm taking a bath.

Miles: Really?

I held the phone up high and angled it down, snapping a photo of my knees and toes sticking out of the bubbles.

I sent it and watched the ellipses indicating that he was typing a response flash on, off, on, off as he was deciding what to say.

Miles: Oh my.

Me: It's been a crazy night. This kind of makes perfect sense.

Miles: I'm glad it makes sense.

Me: Why'd you leave your phone number where you knew I'd find it?

Miles: So we could talk.

Me: Talk?

Me: You want another picture?

Miles: What do you think?

Me: **I think you're dying for one.**

Miles: **You're right.**

This time I pointed the phone at my face and shoulders. After a few tries, I turned my head, so the photo would capture my profile from the nose down. I finally got one I liked, and sent it.

In it, my eyes were downcast, and bubbles came up low on my chest. Wet strands of hair stuck to my collarbone. I'd dimmed the lights in the bathroom, and the water made my skin shine.

Miles: **Lovely.**

Miles: **Did you suspect? That I was capable of this?**

Me: **I could tell.**

Miles: **I've been trying very hard to hide it.**

Me: **Not that hard.**

My fingers were wrinkled. The water had gone cold.

Me: **I have to get out of this tub.**

Miles: **Okay.**

Me: **I should go to sleep.**

Miles: **Yes.**

Me: **Is that going to be enough?**

Miles: **I don't know.**

Me: **Good night, Miles.**

The hole in the window was covered with a piece of cardboard. Rhiannon and Trevor had taped it there while Shane and I were out looking for the cat. When I lay down in bed it was right above me.

I reached up and started peeling off the tape, meaning to do just a corner, but continuing until the cardboard fell, skidding down the wall behind my headboard.

Air came in—watery and wet. For the first time in the year, I sensed impending rain.

I was trying to remember a word.

The phone buzzed.

Believer: **Yes, it was me.**

Western wind is called a zephyr. I'd read that somewhere. The zephyr made a warning out of its molecules and told me to watch for the drawing up of a storm.

CHAPTER 16

I woke to the sounds of the garage door rumbling open at five o'clock. I wandered downstairs, bleary-eyed, passing the intertwined mound of Rhiannon and Trevor asleep on the living room couch.

My mom was in the kitchen, in full manic Nina power mode, doing a thousand things at once—making toast, loading the blender with frozen fruit and almond milk, brewing coffee, typing on her phone at warp speed. A news channel blared from the TV mounted on the wall.

She barely registered my entrance.

"I thought you were going to be back in the afternoon," I said, sitting at the counter, wondering how angry she'd be about Rhiannon and Trevor.

"Dylan's coming home!" she trilled.

"Have you been driving since, like, three in the morning?" I asked.

"He's coming home today!" Every sentence was a more offensive exclamation.

I searched for and found the TV remote, using it to mute the awful news chatter.

"Isn't this great?"

I decided to use her happiness against her.

"Rhiannon's asleep in the living room," I said. She continued her whirl of activity, saying nothing. I added, "With her boyfriend, Trevor."

"I thought her boyfriend's name was Justin?"

"That was the last one," I answered. "The last three, actually."

She started the blender, still typing on her phone.

"Um, and someone threw a rock through the window in my bedroom."

That got her attention.

"What! Who?" she said, focusing on me as her smoothie sloshed to the bottom of the blender.

"Probably some guys from Brophy," I mumbled.

"Who? We should have them pay for the repair—"

"Well, I don't know for sure—"

"Why would anyone do that?"

"Guys are idiots," I said. She nodded. "So—that's why Rhiannon stayed. I was scared."

"Oh," she cooed, sidling up to me, squeezing my shoulders. "Poor baby. I missed your face. Your cute little face."

She squished my face against her neck.

"Mom," I whined, pushing away. "You know, the only reason you think I'm cute is because you're genetically invested in me being cute."

"I'm what?"

"Genetically invested," I repeated. "I learned it in AP bio. The survival of your genes depends on me. And Dylan. That's why you love us."

"I'm depending on you two for what? Immortality?"

"Yep."

"Well, if I'd known that, I would have had a few more children. Maybe then I would've gotten a good one."

She chuckled at her own burn and went back to buzzing around the kitchen. I poured myself a cup of coffee and zoned out, staring at the TV screen.

A group of solemn people with huge, expressive faces were arranged at a semicircular desk in a room lit like a spaceship. From the cutaways to footage of bloodied women and children, I gathered they were talking about a misguided drone bombing. A scroll running across the bottom of the screen showed tweets about a celebrity couple breaking up.

The closed captions lagged and backed up, then spit out at once in an incomprehensible block of text.

~#@af mol bar wed:

normal war

I held up my phone and zoomed in on "normal war" with the camera, snapping a shot of the drone graphic as it zoomed across a flat blue background toward a cartoon desert oasis. I uploaded it to Instagram.

"Why'd I have to be born now?" I said out loud. My mom sipped her smoothie. She'd been watching as I took the picture.

"This is so primitive," I said, meaning the news and the war and the boring flatness of my place in it all, me sitting there taking pictures of a screen, sharing it on another screen, doing nothing to stop any of it, just perpetuating. Robot weapons? Sure. Perfectly acceptable.

My mom reached out and tucked a strand of my hair back behind my ear.

"I love you." She smiled.

When the thing with Peter was happening, my mom had known somehow. We kept getting in fights because she knew I was keeping something from her, and I kept denying it.

When she said she loved me I almost spit it all out. How I was hallucinating, losing time, James and the plans we were making. The urge to confess all my secrets came from somewhere outside myself. The coyote, making a push.

Shouldn't she know? Why doesn't she know?

* * *

Shane and I got roped in to meeting Dylan's flight after school. I complained when Shane found me in the Xavier parking lot and told me the plan, but he reminded me that I used to love the airport. We'd beg our dads to take us there to eat gift shop snacks and people-watch.

We were sitting in the international terminal, watching people exit customs through a bank of mirrored sliding doors. Dylan's flight was delayed, and Shane and I passed the time by making up elaborate backstories for each person as they walked by, guessing where they came from, what their secrets were.

"She's just escaped a doomsday cult and is meeting her estranged sister at baggage claim," I said, about a woman in ill-fitting clothes who looked exhausted and overwhelmed. "He's a hugely famous stage actor in Spain, but here he's nobody," Shane said, of a short, handsome guy in designer sweatpants. "She's a bartender in São Paolo." "He's a clone slash assassin. Oh my God, he is so obviously a clone slash assassin."

After a steady stream of professional-looking Japanese people in business suits, there was a lull. I checked my phone and noticed that Kit had liked my normal war Instagram post from that morning.

"Are you going to do the driver's ed thing next weekend?" Shane asked. "At school?"

"No," I said, stretching my legs out across the armrests of the empty chairs next to us.

"Why not?"

I pictured James and myself-as-Rosie walking through this same airport the Monday after meeting. Legitimate, breathless, walking hand in hand with synchronized steps. The two most in-love people in the security line. I had access to money, an account with a debit card I never used because it felt like acknowledging my dad's death as something positive. Maybe we wouldn't go back to his place in New York right away. After I explained that I'd been using an assumed name—*because of the stalker. I'm sorry. I wanted to wait to tell you in person*—I could make it up to him by buying us tickets to wherever he wanted.

"I don't know," I answered Shane. "I guess I'm not really in a hurry."

"So you're never going to drive?"

"Someday, yeah."

The doors slid open and a big group came out.

"This is our boy," I said, glancing up at the arrivals screen.

I thought Dylan would be the last one out. He never tried to get to the front of any line, never hurried, never rushed. Finding him gone without any warning was such a shock I thought he'd been kidnapped until he called and told us where he was.

But he burst through the doors at the front of the pack, in the center of the chaos, a huge smile on his face.

"Well, yeah, but his epilepsy, that's what sets him apart. It's like, from his brain to his fingers is all this weird wiring—that's why, personally, I think he can't be touched. There's absolutely no comparison—"

I slid down onto the floor like liquid. The underside of Dylan's bed was surprisingly clean. An obscure triptych of three random things—blue crayon, empty plastic water bottle with the label peeled off, one orange foam earplug.

I wondered where the crayon came from. Wondered what might happen if I moved it a centimeter to the left—James getting hit by a taxi. An end to the normal war. My mom forgetting her phone at work.

"You fancy yourself enlightened now," I said to the room, vaguely aware I was interrupting whatever Dylan was going on about. "Because you went on a vision quest."

"Shane knows what I'm talking about," Dylan said, flipping through his record collection, which he'd dramatically reclaimed from my room, along with the player.

"I know what you're talking about too," I said, though I had no idea. "I agree with you."

"You agree with me about Neil Young being God?"

"Why do you have to use that tone of voice? There's too much conviction in it. I don't like it."

"I feel like my voice is my normal tone of voice right now."

"You're not doing it consciously, duh. I know that."

"What else do you know, Joss?" Dylan asked.

"You know lots of stuff, don't you, Joss?" Shane echoed, teasing me.

We were all sitting in Dylan's room. It was alive with us, no longer a dark, closed place like my dad's studio. The window cracked open, Dylan impatiently skipping around to find songs on records, sometimes instructed by Shane, who was stuttering hypotheses about B-sides and liner notes gleaned from late-night Wikipedia spirals.

We'd left the airport, gone through a Sonic drive-through as instructed by Dylan, and come home to get extremely stoned before my mom got off work. Before we did, Dylan took me aside and asked, "Are you sure? You're okay to smoke?" and I didn't even mind because I was so pleased he was there to worry about me.

"I know that every time I'm in a group of two or more boys eventually they will end up talking about Neil Young," I said.

"Anecdotal," Shane mumbled. "That can't be true."

Dylan started telling Shane about Peru or Argentina, villages with doctors who consult ayahuasca-induced hallucinations as they would a medical textbook. I let him go on for a while before interrupting again.

"I never did like earnest young men," I announced, raising one finger in the air for emphasis. My voice seemed to echo off the walls, in the gap between songs on the album playing in the background.

Shane and Dylan laughed hysterically.

"You remember Joe Value-Pack?" Dylan asked me.

"Yes!" I said, sitting up on my elbows, excited both by the

memory and the feeling of sharing it with Dylan. I'd forgotten how nice it was just to be near someone who'd been around your whole life. If Dylan existed in the world, then so did I.

"Huh?" Shane interjected.

"He was this friend of my dad's," Dylan explained. "One of those survivalist, off-the-grid guys. He had a fallout shelter we went to once, a cabin up in Pinetop, with a million guns and a homemade solar generator. It was the raddest place ever.

"When I went down to South America I thought I was going to get off the grid too, just go way out and never have to go to a Target again, you know? I thought about that guy a lot."

I reached under the bed and retrieved the empty plastic water bottle, handing it to Dylan.

"I think this pertains," I said, "to this wonderful story you are telling."

"Pertains," Shane said, the letters of the word tumbling out of his mouth, floating up to the ceiling. He was holding Ferris, scratching hard beneath her collar, drifting tufts of her fur onto the carpet.

"Copy kitten," I told him. "Stop copy-kittening me."

"Guys," Dylan said, stopping us. "Anyway, there I am on this commune in Argentina with all these German tourists, and I realized something. There is no such thing as off-grid. A person is a point on the grid. You can never get off. Nobody can."

We all went silent, reverent in the face of such a deep truth.

"Joss knows how," Shane said, looking at me.

I shushed him.

James made the tree house even better this time. He's good at this, like I knew he would be. I haven't told him, but I'm not Rosie right now. I'm being myself, breaking that barrier.

I wonder what is beyond the Dream Palace on this plane. Is this it? Nothing else? Or are there other gateways?

Before I went to Rosie's room, I walked the halls. Peeked into rooms. Some disintegration had occurred, but the structure was sound.

James and I are together. I want to graffiti the walls with evidence. We were here. We existed. This was our place. No matter what happens when we meet in person, this can never be undone.

ROWAN MANESS

Halfway through homeroom the next day, as everyone's feet were tapping, impatient for the early dismissal, Believer texted me.

Believer: **Are you wondering who's next?**

Believer: **I can't decide. There are so many to choose from.**

I glanced around the room from my seat in the back row. The girls were colorful islands, wearing bathing suits and cover-ups for field day. Out of the usual uniform white and plaid, our differences were highlighted. Suddenly I could see that each girl's inner life must be as vivid as my own, and I winced at the overwhelming sadness of the realization. It was all so fragile, and I didn't want to feel it.

Mae Castillo scooted two desks over and sat next to me. She was eating a cup of yogurt, scraping at the last bit with a plastic spoon.

"So," she said, spying my hidden phone. "Are you going to go to prom?"

"When I look into the future, I do not see me having fun at prom."

"Mary-Kate said you'd say that."

"That exact thing?"

"Well, that you'd think it was dumb."

"I guess I'm getting predictable," I said. "At least to her."

"I can't decide if I like or hate being a teenager," said Mae as she carefully examined the nutrition label of her now-empty yogurt.

"I know exactly what you mean," I said, watching her.

"So," I went on. "Does Mary-Kate hate me?"

"She talks about you all the time," Mae said. "You know what? If the yogurt people really want me to keep buying this yogurt, they should market it to teens."

"Oh, you mean, like cool, teen yogurt you can buy with your cool, teen disposable income?"

Mae nodded. "Every day I wake up and I think to myself, 'You know, I could really go for some yogurt. But it's so uncool.'"

"You need a yogurt that fits your cooleen lifestyle."

"It should be called something really cooleen. Like . . . Yog' Jamz."

At that, I cracked, laughing loudly enough to jolt Ms. Munoz out of her nail-filing stupor at the front of the classroom. She gave us a look before going back to her happy place.

"Yog' Jamz!" Mae said, holding up the yogurt. "For coolteens only!"

The two girls in front of us turned around.

"Guys." I smiled at them. "We should jam some yog' before field day! It's gonna be awesome!"

With the specter of Believer looming over me, destroying connections and scrambling timelines, talking to Mae felt like a small victory. *See, I can keep it together.* If I pretended I was texting her, forging a tenuous alliance, it was easy to avoid thinking about the glitches sparking everywhere else.

The day started out sunny, but by the time homeroom ended, the sky was grey and the air was heavy and unusually humid for the desert in late April. My tank top clung to my skin and my toes slipped around in my sandals.

I walked over to the Brophy athletic fields with Mae, and we found Rhiannon and Mary-Kate among the exodus of bikinied girls. Halfway across the parking lot, Trevor emerged from his hiding spot in Rhiannon's car, joining us.

The fields were set up with a stage, bounce houses and inflatable waterslides, rows of carnival games, and a dunk tank being filled by a hose extending from an unmarked white van.

We met up with Shane and Leah Leary beneath a balloon archway and migrated to the outer reaches of the field, where five Slip 'N Slides were set up on the hill that separated the Brophy campus from the back of a strip mall.

I took my shoes and top off and used them to hide my phone in an out-of-the-way patch of tall grass. Everyone else did the same thing, and we passed a bottle of sunscreen between us while we waited in line.

Rhiannon, Mary-Kate, Mae, Shane, and I all got to the front of our lines at the same time. Student council members handed us inner tubes, and we stepped back to get a running start, flying down the hill in unison, sending up huge sprays of soapy water, Leah Leary and Trevor cheering us on.

We went through the line another zillion times, in different formations. Rhiannon, Trevor, and I linked inner tubes and tumbled over each other in the soggy grass. Mary-Kate and Mae went down with Nora del Toro and Carmen Farrow, cartwheeling up to the slides and missing their inner tubes completely, sliding down sideways on their stomachs. Mae and Rhiannon danced to the bad ska band that was playing on the stage—"Someone's brother," explained the student council treasurer—and we all collapsed in a heap by the first aid stand.

"Ugh, my feet are dirty. I hate dirty feet," Mary-Kate said.

I picked some grass out from between my toes.

"Don't complain, MK. You'll ruin the field day fun."

"Did you just cop to having fun?" she asked.

"So what if I did?"

"Nothing," Mary-Kate said. "I'm glad to hear it."

A group of Brophy boys came up to us, greeting Shane, apparently impressed that he was with a group of seven girls.

I knew most of their names, but the only one I'd ever had any contact with was Evan Fairbanks. When Rhiannon and I wrote record reviews for the Xavier-Brophy newspaper, he'd written a letter to the editor complaining about my analysis of one of them. He followed me on Instagram.

Somehow he wound up next to me.

"Dylan Wyatt's your brother, right?" I tried to overlook his rat teeth and his buzz cut. I really tried.

"Yeah. Why?"

"He's legendary."

"Legendary for what?"

"Stuff."

"Oh. He actually just got back from South America."

"Rad."

"Yeah," I said, looking around for help, finding everyone else absorbed in their own conversations.

Trevor said he wanted to try the sumo wrestling, so we all stood up and gathered our things. I tied my hair back and unwrapped the phone from my wadded-up tank top. Evan walked too close to me while I checked it for any new messages—I was surprised to see that the screen was unlocked and the texts from Believer were showing.

At the sumo wrestling ring, we watched Trevor and Rhiannon fight it out, waddling around in suits that made them look like they weighed five hundred pounds. Trevor kept his sunglasses on and seemed to relish being pummeled into submission by Rhiannon over and over again.

Mae and Mary-Kate went up after them, and everyone else disappeared, pairing off—Shane and Leah Leary, Rhiannon and Trevor, Nora and Carmen with their Brophy boy equivalents. I was left with Evan, and tried to avoid conversation by reading the e-mail James had sent that morning.

> Rosie,
>
> I'm looking at pictures of you. The videos.
> I'm lying in bed and it's like you're all around me.
> I know we're so far above it, but the way all the
> dirty stuff fits into our thing is so good.
> Remember, you're my guru. Making love to
> you—fucking you really well—will be like giving
> back—

"So. You going to prom?" Evan asked.

I laughed, looking up from my phone.

"Sorry," I explained. "That's just the second time someone's asked me that today."

I wondered if it would be different if Evan and I were texting—it would be easier to overlook his flaws that way.

"I know it's probably not your kind of scene," he said.

I smiled at that. "You're right," I said.

"So. Do you wanna go?"

"What?"

"With me. You want to? Clint's having an after-party at his house."

"Uh—" I stammered. "Why do you want to go with me? You don't even know me."

"Okay, never mind," he said, and I was surprised to see his face redden. I felt bad, aware that I'd misjudged his sincerity.

"It's just—I have a boyfriend," I said. Mae and Mary-Kate climbed out of the arena just at that moment.

"You do?" Mary-Kate butted in.

"Yes," I said, urging her to follow along, scared that she wouldn't get the message. "That's why I can't go to prom."

"It is?"

"Yes," I answered, through clenched teeth.

"It's not because you're antisocial and you're against doing anything normal because you think you're so edgy?"

Evan managed to slink away without saying anything. Mae stepped back, leaving me and Mary-Kate standing there.

"That was bitchy," I said to her.

"I'm a bitch?" Mary-Kate questioned, indignant. "You couldn't even force yourself to be nice to Evan for one second."

"I was going to be nice to him!" I snapped. "You interrupted!"

"You were lying to him."

"I had to, a little," I said. "I do have a boyfriend, kind of—"

I trailed off, thinking Mary-Kate would ask *Who?* and I could respond by telling her about my love for James. Mae would disappear and it would just be us, and I'd explain how

James and I were two parts of a strange whole, and she would understand completely.

But the conversation turned, and everything Mary-Kate had been holding back came raging out of her.

"You know what, I don't feel like sitting around condoning your pathological lies anymore."

"Come on," I said. "I didn't want to hurt Evan's feelings."

She wasn't hearing me.

"You don't care about his feelings. You were lying for the same reason you always lie—because you're addicted to the weird power it gives you over other people. And I'm tired of pretending I think it's cute or smart or somehow more interesting than real life."

That struck me as the most radical thing Mary-Kate had ever said. I didn't know how to reply.

"We all got to get our kicks somewhere," I mumbled.

"I'm so sick of your kicks!" Mary-Kate yelled. Rhiannon and Trevor walked up to us, holding blue clouds of cotton candy.

"Are Mommy and Daddy fighting?" Rhiannon asked, before realizing a second later how serious we were.

"Guys—" she said, trying to calm us.

"No," Mary-Kate said. "I've wanted to say this for a long time. I didn't know how, didn't want to make you feel bad. But I don't even think it's possible to make you feel bad. Nothing touches you. You think I'm lame like you think everyone else is lame."

I started to object, but something about her accusation

rang sort of true, and it made me stop. I wanted the conversation to be over, but I didn't think I could end it.

Mary-Kate could.

"I don't want to hang out with you anymore. And considering the fact that every time I voice an opinion, you either laugh at it or it annoys you, I'm guessing you're fine with that. It's not like we've actually spent much time together lately anyway."

"How surprising," I said. "It's all my fault."

"No," Mary-Kate said. "You don't get to say that. I'm just going to say it's all my fault, so you can't. It's my fault. I tried out for cheerleading. I made friends with Mae. I showed you all those chat rooms when we were in fourth grade. It's my fault because I don't agree with everything you say. It's my fault that I've accepted that yes, this is the world, and this is how things are built and bought and sold and done, and yeah, you can laugh at it all you want, but you don't instantly become some world-altering rebel just by saying 'fuck everything and everyone I don't believe in!' It's my fault because I want to be normal."

"It's my fault!" I said, angry more at her using the word "normal" twice than anything else. "And you're just as dishonest as I am, reading your stupid fashion magazines all the time, secretly in love with a girl—"

I knew I'd gone too far. Mae took Mary-Kate's arm, pulling her back. We were inches apart. I waited for Mary-Kate to dig in, to go deeper, to skewer me the way only she could. She got steely-eyed instead.

"You're making this so easy," she said.

Her face was distorted, masklike. I thought of what my mom said about what happened to Mary-Kate's mom and her other high school friends. They grew up, they changed, they became these programmed drones. Inside the moment, it seemed impossible that Mary-Kate and I were ever friends in the first place.

"Fuck you," I said. "Have fun growing up into nothing."

She had tears in her eyes—I noticed just before Mae took her arm and they walked off. Rhiannon tried to comfort me, but I wrenched away from her and she went after Mary-Kate too, with Trevor trailing behind holding her cotton candy.

The ground seemed unsteady. The footsteps of everyone around me seemed to shake through it. I worried it was all crust, hollow beneath, and would break under my feet. Mary-Kate was a magnet, and the center went with her when she left. I was alone, in the wrong, despised.

My phone buzzed.

Believer: **How's your hand, Joss?**

Believer: **Still hurting?**

As soon as I read it, I realized my hand did hurt, from the cut I'd gotten on my broken window. I'd lost the bandage covering my palm somewhere on the Slip 'N Slide, and the wound wasn't ready to be uncovered yet. It was reopening.

A bright light burst along my peripheral vision and I turned to look at it. The sun had appeared from behind cloud cover and was shining on the row of windows along Xavier's north side, far across the parking lot.

The beacon disappeared as the clouds shifted again, and then I saw him. My coyote, moving boldly through the crowd.

I followed him, keeping my eyes trained on his alert ears as he loped on all fours, zigzagging through the field day maze. Trailing him like a pack animal, I wasn't sure I could have stopped if I'd wanted to. He was pulling me by an invisible string.

He led me toward Xavier, and soon I was pushing through metal doors, glimpsing the coyote at the end of an empty hallway. I could still hear music and shouting from the fields, and see the shuddering turrets of bounce house castles through the windows that lined the corridor.

My phone kept buzzing. Each time I checked it, it seemed less important. The phone was a toy, a piece of plastic. The coyote on his mission was all-consuming.

Rhiannon: **What happened?**

Rhiannon: **btw I am on your side. I think . . .**

And from Shane.

Shane: **Do you want a corn dog?**

Shane: **nm, there's no more corn dogs. I eated them all**

The air-conditioning made my wet clothes icy, and I thought of the coyote's fur, how it might feel if I could touch it. How warm it would be.

I was very close to him now, walking faster, skin prickled all over with permanent goose bumps.

He turned a corner in front of me and I took huge strides, sure I would catch him—but when I turned, he was gone and so was the invisible string.

Why'd you go?

No answer.

I continued, passing closed classroom doors. Outside each one was a bronze plaque listing the teacher's name and the subjects they taught. I read them as I walked by.

EVELYN HEATH / FRENCH I, II, III & AP FRENCH

JENNIFER CAREY / ALGEBRA I, II & PRECALC

SR. DORCAS FRY / LATIN

I stopped at the next door and cupped my hand against it, listening. I thought I heard something. A low growl, or music? There wasn't any light coming through the gap at the floor.

He's in there.

The plaque was newer than the others, shinier.

DR. MILES LAUREN / BIOLOGY, AP BIOLOGY, AP CHEMISTRY & PHYSICS

BZZZT went my phone.

Miles: **Is that you?**

There it is. The sign you were waiting for. Everything that will ever happen to you is lined up. You can push it a little by jinxing, but this was always going to happen. You've known it since the first time you saw him.

I opened the door.

Mr. Lauren was sitting at his desk, facing the windows. Wire mesh inside the double-paned glass fractured the view of the back side of the chapel, shading it all over with tiny octagons.

The lights were off, and there was music playing—coming from his computer, curling through the air. The contents of a brown paper lunch sack were strewn across the messy desk. I knew he brought the same thing every day: an apple, a Tupperware container full of quinoa salad, a stainless-steel water bottle. I focused on the details, standing behind him, before he finally turned around.

Rosie's English teacher fell in love with her. She didn't think anything of it. She liked him too, but what are you going to do in that situation, really? What can you do? Either ignore it or . . . don't. Rosie chose not to ignore it because she's always been open and brave.

The world where I'm Rosie instead of Joss isn't too far away. It's right next door, an adjacent parallel universe.

"How'd you know it was me?" I asked.

He was still holding his phone. He looked from it to me, then set it down and met my eyes with a steady gaze.

"I didn't know," he answered. "I saw a shadow, and hoped."

I smiled.

"Eating your lunch with the lights off?"

"It's been a stressful week."

"Why?"

"Nothing interesting."

"Mine too," I said.

The sleeves of his white button-down were rolled up. He'd taken his glasses off. His dark hair was getting shaggy around his ears. I took a quick look down to check my own outfit. Blades of grass clung to my ankles. I smelled like sunscreen, but I could tell I'd burned, like I always did on overcast days. Even with the heat trapped in my skin, I was shivering, and I moved to sit on the table where I usually sat during class.

Rosie was eighteen, I think. Only two years, that's hardly anything. She didn't just let it happen, either. She had control. She came out fine. She's going to meet James. I'm going to meet James. He'll be able to see through me unless I make myself more like her.

"I can't do this," Mr. Lauren said. He hadn't moved an inch since I walked in.

Yes, you can.

"Try reading my mind," I said, closing my eyes. "I'm sending my thoughts out."

I tried to transmit, to push some mood or a clear sentence his way.

Mr. Lauren, come over here. I want you to come over here. Pretend I'm Rosie, if that helps. She's already been here, in this room, in a room like this. Maybe it had different windows though, and I guess it was in California.

Refine the message, Joss.

Come. Over. Here.

I heard him get up, leave his chair, and walk across the linoleum. I kept my eyes shut, but the black void morphed a subtle change with the presence of his body in front of my eyelids. He touched me. I opened my eyes.

"Grass," he said, wiping a stray blade off my shoulder. It stuck to his finger.

"You're doing it," I said.

"This," he said, returning his hand to my shoulder, running it slowly up and down my arm. "Is already too much. Far too much."

Touch him back, Rosie. You've done this with how many men? You know what to do. It's the simplest thing in the world.

I moved the arm he was touching and reached out to pull him closer. He was rubbing his temple with his other hand—I brushed his hand away and rubbed it for him, putting pressure there, waiting until he could look into my eyes. When he did, I saw the moment he stopped being scared. He wasn't going to turn back now unless I made him.

He was gone and so was I. I straightened my back, relaxed my mouth, kept my eyes half-lidded, did the things Rosie would do. It was easy to be her, as I knew it would be.

Rosie's movements were confident, assured.

We were kissing, and his hands were on my arms, then underneath my shirt. He untied my bikini top. I stood up, arms around his neck, as he unbuttoned my shorts.

I stopped thinking and let Rosie take over.

I went to the Dream Palace and took her place in one of the lounge chairs around the pool, watching the scene remotely, gathering details I could use later to fill in shallow outlines or deepen other lies.

CHAPTER 18

Where Rosie ended and Joss began was a time-slipping mirage. On the other side of meeting James there was another world, and on this side I was with Rhiannon somewhere. Transported somehow. Vague memories of yet another car ride. I kept getting in cars and time kept moving forward, and that was all I knew for sure.

My feet were in water. That's what I saw first, my feet in a tub of bubbling green-tinted water. Without looking up from them I sensed the rest of the room. Fluorescent, narrow, some weak natural light leaking in from a source to my right.

I was sitting up high, a padded chair undulating at my lower back.

Nail salon.

Rhiannon driving me home from school. Dropping Trevor at a Walgreens to pick up his grandma's prescription. She thought I was being quiet because I was sad about fighting with Mary-Kate.

Nail salon.

A gigantic off-brand TV was playing an episode of *Friends* subtitled in Korean. I located Rhiannon, standing in front of a wall display of nail polish bottles organized by color.

"All these reds are ugly," Rhiannon was saying. "Reds are so hard to get right, you know?"

"No," I said, though I knew the question was rhetorical. Rhiannon ignored me anyway, nodding to herself before choosing a bottle.

A woman sat at my feet and grabbed one roughly, depositing it on a folded towel. The foot gave off steam, cooked pink by the hot antiseptic water.

I looked down at the phone in my hands, an auto-saved Notes draft illuminated on the screen.

> Rosie: liked the way her teacher's eyes clouded over when she took her clothes off. Exchanging powers. This is a story I'll tell myself when I'm thirty and it will explain who I am. A lizard to a water-holding cactus, a ghost to a new dimension. Witch to a crystal circle

Joss sloughed off like a snakeskin crust. Rosie new and pink and clean beneath. I was stuck in the in-between, trying to function normally for Rhiannon.

Then I was next to her, at side-by-side manicurists' tables, with my feet in paper slippers, toenails like a row of perfect orange wedges.

I wrenched my hands way from the woman holding them. She snapped her head back, surprised.

"Never mind," I said. "Just the toes, okay?"

"You'll have to pay for a manicure. I cut and buffed already."

"Fine, sorry."

Rhiannon cutting in as I stood up. "You're done?"

"Yeah, I'm just going to wait."

I tried to make a casual expression with my face, but it was hard to move my mouth the way I wanted. Something about it belonging to Rosie.

I sat on a velvet couch in the salon's waiting area and watched the *Friends* episode fade into another one, not the one that came after it in sequence, but one from a different season.

Rhiannon's new text alert was a bomb whistling and exploding. It went off three times in quick succession before she apologized to the manicurist and clicked it to silent.

When she was done we wandered the shaded walkway that wrapped around the strip mall, heading from one end to another, to meet Trevor at the pharmacy.

Great Clips, vacuum repair, Baja Fresh, another nail place.

At the main attraction, the grocery store, misters sprayed water above the open entrance. The place where air-conditioning met hot air created a little tornado.

"Hey, Joss." Rhiannon turned to me.

"Have you ever, like, involved people you know in what you do on the Internet? Like use stories from real life? Or pictures?"

"No," I said automatically.

"You swear?"

"Yeah," I swore. "Why?"

She handed me her phone.

I watched Rhiannon and Trevor drive off. As soon as I'd comprehended what was on her phone's screen, she'd jerked away. Looked me in the eye. Shook her head once, not like she was dismissing me, but like I was something, finally, that she couldn't understand.

She'd left me there, hardly saying anything after I saw what she'd seen—a link to the Tumblr, texted to her by a blocked number.

A new post. Rhiannon's face, smiling out from a screenshot of a dating site profile. Photos I stole from her Instagram and Facebook, Snapchats she'd sent me. She looked old enough to pass as twenty-one-year-old Greta, a children's librarian in a tourist town on a picturesque island off South Carolina I'd seen in a Lifetime movie while home sick from school one day.

"I didn't even meet anyone as her," I'd tried to explain, through the new barrier between us.

VICTIM #9—RHIANNON

And the rest of the Tumblr below. Rhiannon would show

it to Mary-Kate. I pictured them browsing through Believer's roster of my so-called victims. All the people and nonentities I had ever been now pursued by a shape-shifter—the some-times-coyote, sometimes-Kokopelli, the all-time trickster god.

Rhiannon was more hurt than angry, and that made me feel worse than if she'd just started yelling. But she was stunned. She could overlook my eccentricities because they were some-times funny—dick pics to make fun of and insights into the brain of the average male. But this was different. I'd used her. Shame piled on shame.

"Who even are you?" she'd muttered. And then she was gone too.

Believer stepping closer, closer through a grid of back-yard squares. Hunting the girl with an encyclopedia's worth of names and histories in her head, in Word documents and spreadsheets created at two in the morning with twenty browser windows open to twenty different worlds.

Something was wrong with the Starbucks in the strip-mall parking lot. It was bleeding noise and light, a seeping yellow aura that competed with the heavy grey dusk outside. Thicker than an aura, more like a stain. The desert prepares for rain by turning up her tough green arms.

James: **So, surprise**
James: **I'm already in Phoenix**
James: **Got an earlier flight**

I breathed deeply; for the first time, it was the same air James was breathing.

I twisted around in my seat at the Starbucks and looked out a window at the sun drooping toward a smear of purple clouds along the western horizon. The same clouds James could see, if he were looking up.

If I listened carefully and filtered out the noise of the coffee shop, I might be able to hear his voice. Maybe he was calling one of his friends to tell them he'd landed and was going to really do it, really meet the girl he'd been chatting with for more than a year.

A new person walked in—the bored barista and I looked up at the jingling of the bell above the door. A guy the right age and build, a hat hiding what might be the right hair color and cut. He seemed to have the air of recent travel clinging to him. His clothes just slightly too stylish and expensive to belong here. Wearing trendy sunglasses at dusk.

This was James. Of course we wouldn't have to set up a meeting place. Of course we would be led to each other by outside forces, by the turning wheel that spins and decides who goes where, and when, and why. Fate put us together virtually, and now she was finishing the job.

I stood up from the couch and moved toward him as he waited at the counter—finally, my James, and just when I needed him, just when everything was falling apart. He was holding a phone, typing on it too, and when he stopped typing mine buzzed.

James: **This is a weird town.**

"James," I said, out loud, a whisper.

At the same moment, the barista spoke—

"Can I get your name?"

"Greg," said the guy. His voice was too high, too guarded and aggressive. When he turned around he took his sunglasses off and his eyes were so close together they looked permanently crossed.

He had to step around my body, and as he did I felt him check me out the way certain kinds of men do, like it's beyond their control and they don't even really want to. A lecherous scoop of a glance that leaves you taking stock of your whole existence. What did he see, when he looked? Young. A bikini under shorts and top. Sunburn setting in on my cheekbones and shoulders.

He smiled at me.

"Do you want more water?" the barista asked. I handed her my cup to refill.

Greg waited for his drink, and I watched him become less and less like James. It was like watching the color fade from a painting, leaving an outline, some negative space. I'd colored him in so easily.

Me: **No way. You're there?**

Me: **If I start driving now, Waze says I could get there by midnight**

Me: **Tonight, James**

James: **Oh my god**

James: **Please?**

Me: **I can't wait anymore**

My mom picked me up from the Starbucks on her way home from work. When she asked why I was stranded there, I explained the bare minimum without actually lying. Rhiannon was going to drop me off after school, but she wanted to get mani-pedis. We got in an argument over something stupid.

"I'm sorry, honey" was the cursory response, and then she was off about the dinner Dylan was supposed to be cooking for us that night, "Chilean specialties" he'd learned to make from the girl he was in love with.

"He's in love with someone?" I asked, squirming in my seat a bit with a nervous stomach, thinking of Rosie driving out of Los Angeles. I was planning how best to prepare myself. Bath, exfoliants, the new outfit I'd bought months ago just in case this day ever came. This night.

I didn't want to meet James at his hotel, though I knew it well from summers when my grandparents would visit and stay there. Dylan and I lived for it, the attached water park and room service and rotating restaurant.

But it wasn't right for Rosie and James. They'd been limited by electronic devices for so long, they needed space. A sky full of stars and far-off storm clouds. An epic romantic backdrop. No one else around. The thought of telling someone where I was going, just in case, crossed my mind, but it didn't stick.

There wasn't anyone to tell. The girls were gone. The boys—Shane and Dylan—would press for details and try to stop me.

Thoughts of James, knowledge of the closeness of him, kept other thoughts from seeping in, muted the coyote's warnings. The clock on the dashboard skipped minutes, the scene out the car window switched irregularly. The gates of the Dream Palace were open, creaking.

On the highway, we passed a large park. I'd been there many times, on Girl Scout campouts and school field trips to the zoo and botanical gardens.

And there was something else, a weird monument. I saw it as we zoomed by, lit up against a holy Martian-red mountain.

A white pyramid.

Some long-gone governor's burial site. In a park closed at night, but not gated or patrolled.

I linked James to the park's website.

Me: **I've found our place**

Me: **Look up "Hunt's Tomb"**

James and I would meet there on the rough sandstone path. We would hold hands and look down on the valley at night, the city a grid of stars across the desert floor.

Nina, almost at the end of her second glass of wine. Dylan on his fourth or fifth, and probably as many THC-laced gummy bears eaten over the course of the day. Joss sober but faint—not dizzy. Fading.

Dylan made salmon empanadas, so many they were heaped in a huge pile in the middle of the table. I picked at one but couldn't taste anything, all my senses dulled by anxiety.

I was half aware of the conversation between Dylan and my mom turning tense, of the desperate hitch in her voice, the exasperation in his.

I held on to James, texting him as Rosie drove closer. Telling him what she was seeing, making frantic promises.

Me: **I've passed Palm Springs**

James: **I want to take you there. Have you ever been?**

Me: **No**

James: **We'll go**

Me: **I'm driving 100mph and it feels like I'm inching toward you**

James: **This is crazy**

James: **I can't believe we're doing it**

James: **Finally**

Me: **I'll melt. I'll dissolve**

James: **Will you make me wait? To touch you?**

"Maybe that's what you can focus on when you go back to school," my mom was saying.

"When I what?" Dylan asked.

"I think CGCC has summer classes, and if you get all the basic requirements out of the way before fall, they probably have a program to shunt you into the culinary school—"

"Shunt me?" Dylan was almost yelling.

I left the table, moving upstairs to my room, again losing seconds on the stairs, going up one by one but blacking out between, phone open, nothing changed on it, no new ideas, no new feelings.

James, waiting in a hotel room. Passing the hours by writing to me and readying himself. Three miles from where I stood, where the ending of Joss was happening. I thought about packing a bag—taking my computer, clothes, things I thought I'd miss—but I was incapable of looking too far into the future. I expected that, upon meeting James, time would begin to move sideways, not forward. Maybe a version of me would stay behind, and nobody would even know I'd gone.

I fed the lizard a couple strips of red pepper I'd taken from the dinner salad and sat on my bed.

Me: **As soon as I see you I'm going to want you**

James: **It's our duty**

Believer and Mr. Lauren were texting me, too. Believer saying he knew where I was going. Mr. Lauren asking how I was.

I looked at the broken windowpane above me and tried to draw up a curse or an anti-jinx to keep Believer from following James and me to Hunt's Tomb at midnight. I said things out loud, for protection against them.

"Believer will be there."

"James won't show up."

I saw it like lining things up. All of these things leading to the sharp apex of a white pyramid.

"James isn't real and he's Believer."

That last one worried me. I talked to James far more often than anyone else, especially in the weeks since Believer had appeared. And Believer had found everyone but him. James was safe. Never even mentioned.

"James is Believer," I said. The lizard munched on her peppers and watched me.

Saying it was enough. The jinx was at work and everything would be perfect. I started the ritual of getting my body ready. Bath, lotions, makeup, outfit. And in between, I dragged files to the trash bin on my desktop. Years of creative energy, procrastinating at homework, worlds built and imploded. I purged the laptop of everything false, and when it was over I felt clean. I was ready.

A door slammed in the hallway—the final note of the argument between Dylan and my mom. I could not let myself feel guilty or bad for leaving them. They'd both left me before, in different ways. It was my turn.

The electrical box was buzzing like a cicada when I walked up to it. The thought occurred to me that it might be a sleeper spaceship. An observation pod for aliens. Maybe they were in there, inside the electricity, making the sounds and the warmth, traveling on those currents. They could be going underground from in there, too, burrowing and popping up miles away, out in the middle of the desert.

It was just kind of vibrating, the whole thing. I put my hand on it. The hot, beige metal seemed to recognize me. The aliens inside were scanning.

Oh, Silver Creek Road. We put a Kokopelli in her mind, didn't we? We talk to her from her computer.

She's lining things up.

I wish she'd just go away. This is making me uncomfortable.

Do you think she knows? Can that happen? Have we been too obvious?

I wasn't concerned with how it was possible, but I sensed that if I waited long enough by the box, eventually I would get to Papago Park and meet James.

She does know, doesn't she?

It'll be late by the time Rosie arrives at the white pyramid. She might have gotten lost in Phoenix, and the park is closed from sundown to sunrise, so she has to leave her car on the street and hike up to the point. The point where James and Rosie will each climb through a window, each open a door, and make solid a once-formless love.

He'll be the first to speak, as he was the first to reach out.

"Is it really you?"

"It's really me. Is it really you?"

"I don't know anymore."

"Yeah, that's what I meant to say."

"Do you want to go somewhere? Do you want to stay here? What should we do?"

"Maybe let's stay here, for just a minute."

They will sit next to each other, hands entwined.

"This is the right place," James will say.

"I knew it would be," Rosie will answer.

Before they kiss, they will talk about how strange it is to be real. Now that they are real, it feels like they always have been, they'll agree. They'll agree on everything. They will make shy jokes, teasing each other. And only when they can't stand it any longer will they will kiss.

CHAPTER 19

There are five man-made ponds in the park, and the trail up to Hunt's Tomb starts near the largest one. A water pump in the center of it turned off and on a few times as I shined the light from my phone onto a map posted outside a public restroom. It was hard to read, written over with Sharpied graffiti, with little brown paw prints to mark various hiking paths.

I was carrying a dented, half-empty plastic water bottle and it gave me something to do with my hands, a noise to make in the darkness. Something to focus on other than the gulping, irregular beats of my heart—hollow shudders that echoed around and out of my body, seeming to crest the valley with atomic backward gasps.

The hike to the pyramid took longer than I remembered, but I arrived well before midnight. I wanted to be there before

James, so I could make myself as calm as possible and watch him walk toward me for the first time.

The night was absolute. I'd applied a jinx to keep the rain from falling, and the air was thin and clean. The meandering trail twisted and turned. One moment I was walking along above the glowing city, and the next I was completely cut off from it.

I was guided by small blue lights designed to blend in to the rocks on either side of the path. They were meant for emergencies—lost hikers, brush fires—and I followed them, hearing every little scuttle of a lizard.

Human on the path. Human on the path. Run, run, run while I can, while it's not too hot. Where's my hole? Where's my food?

I was sure I hadn't been followed by Believer, and I'd left the coyote at the trailhead, sitting on his haunches.

You can't come.

I'm going to.

Not tonight.

Finally, I reached the pyramid. It was all lit up, as I'd hoped. I was disappointed to find it surrounded by a spiked, wrought-iron fence. I second-guessed my choice, worried that it was too ugly, that the cracked concrete benches—segmented so no homeless people could sleep comfortably on them—would bring bad vibrations. But the view made up for it.

I watched the valley and said good-bye. The oppressed valley, laid over with stars, answered with peculiar stillness.

It took a while before I was able to sit down on one of the benches. I tried to read an informational sign but couldn't get past the first three words before losing concentration, starting them over again and over again. My entire body was shivering with nerves.

To steady myself, I thought of James. I wondered about his gaze. It wouldn't be like Mr. Lauren's—eyes like a nervous dog, with a bit of sweat at the thought of being caught—or Kit's lazy stoner's grin.

I needed his eyes on me. He would complete the change-over, turn me into the person he thought I was.

I heard him. The crackle of footsteps on the path. I felt him walk up behind me and stop a few feet away. His presence washed over me as a warm wave. I thought I might fold up into nothing. He was here, my James Constant, hero of my deleted worlds, New Thing. The space around us, the peak and Hunt's Tomb, was the entire universe at that moment.

"Rosie?" he said. I thought he said that.

Moths were flocking one floodlight at the base of the pyramid. Just one light, not the others. I'd been staring at them, and when I turned around to meet James's face I couldn't see it at first, because it was covered with the negative image of a hundred frantic moths.

I blinked them away.

It wasn't him.

"Get away," I said, shocked that someone else was taking

up the space where James should be. I rose from the bench.

"What are you doing here?"

"I—"

Shane stepped toward me, the floodlight throwing his shadow onto the red rocks behind him. Shane's huge ghost.

"You have to leave." I came around the bench and took his arm, shoving him back toward the path. "I'm meeting someone."

"I know—" He moved, letting me push him.

"You have to leave before he gets here."

"It's me," he was saying. He kept saying it.

Then I knew. I could see it in him. Another face. The guy he wished he was.

"Joss. It's me."

It made sense.

"No!" I shouted, the last time I could shout because then I was just crying, a soundless cry that tore through my gut and caught in my throat.

"No, no, no." I was hitting Shane. He grabbed my wrists, held them. When I met his eyes, he looked terrified, pale and powerless.

But he also looked like someone else.

"Soft Robe," he said, letting my wrists go so he could touch my face.

James wasn't coming. He was there. He had always been there.

Desperate, I tried to make him real. I leaned in to Shane, shut my eyes against his shirt, tears streaming out helplessly.

I tried as hard as I could, but he didn't change and neither did I.

I banged on the door to Rosie's room in the Dream Palace and found that it was sealed shut. I'd swallowed her up just as Shane had taken James and disappeared him.

The tears stopped. Rage uncoiled.

"You killed him!" I said. I was liquid, disgusted. There was a hole right through the center of my body and it was a lonesome wound. The lonesomeness went out of me and wound down through the valley of nobodies.

Shane just kept saying, "I thought you knew."

"James is dead!"

"You quoted me about *Yellow Submarine*. You gave me that Henry Miller after you sent it to him. There were so many overlaps. The Green Day song. I thought, 'She's sending me hints. She knows it's me—'"

"Oh my God." I blushed down to my bones. "All the things I said to you. The pictures. The videos?"

"I'm sorry," Shane said quietly.

"You're pathetic." He took it like a blow.

"Please, Joss, okay," he said. "I fucked it up. But you—you should know how this feels more than anyone else."

He kept trying to meet my eyes again.

"Don't look at me," I snapped. "I hate you."

"Will you even try to understand?"

"Are you Believer, too?"

"What?" Shane shook his head. "No. No. I would never—"

"You are!"

"No, Joss—look. All of this was for—" He tried to come closer, but I backed away.

"I love you," he said with a shrug. "I didn't know how else to reach you."

I didn't believe him. Shane couldn't love me. How did he do it? I thought back to when James first messaged Rosie.

Hey, you look familiar

Ha-ha, really?

Shane was staring.

"I said don't look at me!" I snarled, gathering up any calm I could find, trying to keep my hands steady, stop them shaking.

"Joss," Shane said, pleading. Each time he said my name it physically hurt.

"The Dream Palace?" I questioned.

"What?"

"I was there, with him. How could that have happened if he's not real?"

"That was fantasy—"

"You're a liar! You lied to her!"

I knew it was ridiculous to say.

"We were going to disappear!" I yelled.

"Everything I own is in my car," Shane said. "I'll do whatever you want to do. We can go to Palm Springs, or anywhere—"

Beyond Shane, in his looming shadow—

The coyote. Twin white pyramids reflected in yellow pupils. I directed my thoughts his way.

You knew this would happen. Why didn't you warn me?

The coyote wouldn't answer. Brazen now, emboldened by Shane's ripping-open, he sauntered past us, around to the other side of the pyramid.

His voice was a low purr.

You can still disappear.

"I meant everything he said," Shane was saying. "I hid behind him, but my feelings were real."

"You're nothing like him," I spat out. "None of it means anything now."

"Look, I'm admitting so much shit," Shane said, finally letting himself get angry too. "Let's be real with each other. I'm sick of not being real. Aren't you?"

"I don't want to be real!" I shouted. "I want James to be real. I want him!"

I closed my eyes and pictured James's face. It was already fading.

"I'm sorry," Shane said. "I'm sorry for lying to you. But if you're going to stand there hating me, then you're a hypocrite."

"If you start calling me names, I swear to God—"

"You lie all the time! To everyone! And you excuse every lie you tell because oh, what, you're somehow doing it differently, or better? You're telling a story?"

"What did you think was going to happen, Shane? You'd do

this big reveal and I'd instantly forgive you? Love you back? You thought I knew? That's so stupid. You had to make someone up for me to love because you know it wouldn't happen any other way."

He didn't back down.

"Hey, guess what? Even though I feel like I'm dying because of what's happening right now, I'm glad the lie is over. The weight's off my shoulders. It's a relief. That's how human beings are supposed to feel."

"Now I'm inhuman?" I shrieked.

"That's not what I meant—"

My phone buzzed in my pocket.

James, I thought automatically, and it hurt that it couldn't be. That it would never be.

"I don't care what you meant," I said. "Here's something real: I never want to talk to you again. So if you need a human being to talk to, you'll have to find someone else."

"That's how it goes?" Shane asked, the bottom half of him, the part I could stand to look at, his shoes in the chalky gravel. "A lifetime of knowing each other means nothing?"

"I can't even look at you."

"Yeah, because if you hear, or see, or feel something you don't like, or can't deal with, you just shut it out. You—you're practically autistic! I'm an idiot for thinking it would be any different."

Inhuman, hypocrite, autistic. He's right.

Shane was really hurting me somehow. He never had before. I didn't think he could. He felt it too, and pulled back.

"I'm sorry," he said. "I love you. You're wonderful. You stand alone. You're my dream girl. Why won't you live with me in the light? You aren't hearing any of this, are you?"

James was coming toward me.

I mean, Shane was coming toward me.

I kept backing away. The coyote's voice came from behind the pyramid, chanting an invitation.

You can still disappear.

CHAPTER 20

On the other side of the pyramid, it was almost dawn.

The coyote was standing halfway down a slope that led away from the hiking trails and ponds and into the wilderness of the north part of the park. In the far distance, the double peak of Camelback Mountain pushed softly into the pinkish-grey sky. I focused on that landmark, used it to ground myself, and followed him.

I stayed close and watched him carefully. I didn't want to lose sight of him and get lost. The coarse coyote fur along his backbone seemed influenced by the nature around us—it made subtle changes in color and sheen, ranging from dusty purple to pale green, sometimes shining like a seashell's underside, sometimes clouded and dull.

It helped to think about what someone else would see if someone else could see him. I could imagine a person squinting their eyes, discerning easily enough the overall outline of a coyote-shaped thing. It was looking within the outline that took a certain scrutiny. There, he played his trickster games and pushed energy around. His tail appeared shorter or longer from different angles. He grew and lost inches of height with every step. He tried out the paws of bears and hooves of sheep when it suited him.

The dawn made no advances toward daylight, and it was hard to tell how long we'd been walking. Eventually, we came to the top of a butte and stopped. The coyote sat down, panting, very much an animal. I looked out, expecting to see the city, and found it was not there.

Beyond the mountains, on all four sides of the valley, I could see that it was still nighttime, and the night sky met the false dawn at an abrupt edge. I watched a blinking airplane approach the weird seam from the other side, and held my breath as it disappeared.

The coyote was curled up tightly. His belly moved up and down with breathing.

I asked him, *Why'd you bring me here?*

This is your light.

It was my light. Whatever I called it. The astral plane. A phrase stolen from a song Shane and I obsessed over, a record from my dad's collection. I'd sent it to James, very early on. Was Shane right? Had I known the truth? Had I suspected?

No. I wish I had. He fooled me.

My rage came back like rising bile, but it was tempered by

the atmosphere, kept at bay. Extreme emotion wasn't possible here. My body was heavy and numb, hard to move.

The Dream Palace was there on the astral plane. I'd never seen it from the outside. Inside, it seemed endless, but now I could see its precise limits. It was neglected, elegant. I thought of Amelia, Anna, Emma, and Rosie dead in the courtyard, my other women gathered around their dissolving bodies.

I couldn't picture going home and creating someone new, but I couldn't imagine a life without escape, either.

With effort, I brought my hand up and swiped it through the air. The Dream Palace blinked out of existence, momentarily washed away.

In its place, I put the city back where it belonged, each block even and familiar, the grid I'd been wandering my whole life. When it was done, I apologized to it.

I'm sorry for thinking you're all nobodies.

My breath synched up with the coyote's. I sat down and began to pet him. I'd wanted to touch his fur for a long time, and it was as I'd imagined. Coated with dirt, bristly and hot.

You're not sorry. You don't feel sorry for anything.

How could he say things and keep so still?

Yes, I do. I feel sorry for everything.

I simply don't believe that. Do you feel sorry for Shane?

The coyote had the upper hand—he was part of my thoughts, so he could hear them, but I didn't know what rules, if any, he followed.

I don't want to argue with a portent.

He responded to this by going to the edge of the butte and standing on his hind legs, rising to his full height.

I pulled out my phone. The buzz from earlier had been a storm of texts and e-mails. Believer, at it again. Not finished with me. If only he knew how beaten I was. A list of names had been posted to the Tumblr—dates, e-mails, and pictures for each.

VICTIMS #10–20:

Ben (Daisy)

Patrick (Grace)

Garrett (Lara)

Brian (Caitlin)

Russ (Eugenie)

Allison (Eve)

I stopped reading. The e-mails and texts were from all of them. People I hadn't spoken to in years. Some I'd talked to for a week, some months. Some I'd mostly forgotten, and maybe they'd forgotten about me. But they'd been reminded. And they were all angry. Ten people in the world, feeling some version of what I was feeling about James.

Okay, Believer, I get it! I fucking get it!

The coyote shifted at the edge of the overlook.

I held the phone up and pointed the camera at him, centering him in the frame, careful to show the patchwork sky as well.

Click. There he was, frozen enough, reduced enough. I posted the photo to Instagram.

idiotblush what is this?

What part of my brain made you?

I knew he wouldn't like the question, but I didn't expect it to make his outline tremble the way it did. There was a sound like crackling electricity, and lightning came up from the ground beneath him, shocking his body, making him glow.

The part that made up all those people.

The part that made up Believer.

There was some key element of all this that I was missing.

Think about it.

That's impossible.

You deserved it.

The coyote laughed, borrowing the mirthless cackle of a hyena. I remembered how scared I was when he first appeared, and knew I should have stayed afraid. I'd accepted that he was part of me, and now he was saying Believer was part of me too.

The electricity was giving him power. He spoke out loud, and as he did he took all my light away and left us in the vortex of his trickery and falseness, a dizzying, groundless plane of flashing color and perverted energies.

"It is you. You're doing this all to yourself."

He was using my voice.

"Stop using my voice!"

"Stop not knowing things! You're going to wind up here. This is real. Everything else isn't. If you make me go away, I'll burrow deeper. You're not special. You're like George. You're like all of them. You're a murderer, too—blood on your hands. Nobody tells the truth, not ever. I'll keep going until you realize—"

He was one thought ahead of me. I was drowning in him.

I focused. Synched my breathing with the coyote's again. I changed him—made him smaller. He resisted, twisting and growling. Slowly, my light started to return. The butte, the vista, the phone in my hand, a new message on its screen.

Dylan: **Stay where you are. We're coming**

The coyote kept diminishing.

The mountains reappeared. They were blurry, but they gave me strength.

This is the light of my creation. You don't exist outside of it. You're wrong!

The permanent dusk. Made up of the green light of youth, the purple light of sadness, the yellow light of longing, and the pink light of phantoms.

The coyote used his last bit of power to force me to look down at the ground.

Written there, one word.

BELIEVER

My finger, covered in sand.

Dylan and Shane pushed me into a sitting position, and one of them unscrewed the cap of the plastic water bottle and put it to my lips. The water was warm, and after the bottle was empty, I was able to open my eyes.

It was night again, the sky full of stars in slightly changed positions. The mountains and the cityscape were back in their places. Shane was standing near the edge of the butte, in the same spot the coyote had been in when I took his picture, and Dylan was crouched down next to me

"What did you take?" Dylan asked. I got the feeling he was repeating himself.

I glared at him. "Nothing. I think I just—fell asleep."

"In the middle of the desert?"

"This isn't the middle—"

"If you hadn't posted that Instagram, we wouldn't have been able to find you."

"Did you see him?"

Dylan shot a look over to Shane.

"See who, Joss?"

"Nobody," I said, grabbing my phone off the ground. I opened Instagram and looked at the photo.

A dark, grainy, unfiltered photo of the view from the butte. It showed the city lights just outside the scope of the automatic flash, which illuminated nothing but the dirt and a row of painted rocks that weren't visible in the dark.

"Bullshit, 'nobody,'" Shane said.

"Shut up!" I yelled at him.

There was a comment on the photo.

idiotblush what is this?

kittredgebehr hey, I know that spot

Dylan saw me looking at it.

"Shane messaged that guy," he said. "It was his idea, to ask him how to get here. And he called me. Three hours, Joss! I thought, like, a chupacabra ate you or something."

When I didn't smile or react to that, Dylan recognized the tension between me and Shane.

"What were you guys doing out here anyway?"

"Shane didn't tell you?"

Shane turned around. "Joss—don't—"

"He—" I started, then realized I didn't want to out him. Outing him would mean admitting I'd been in love with his avatar.

"He's a very good liar," I said instead. "Better than me."

Dylan left it at that, though I could tell he wanted to know more.

"Let's go home," he said, helping me stand, moving back up the slope.

Even though I felt like I'd vanquished the coyote and sent him back into his world as I successfully returned to my own, I waited for signs of falseness. I was afraid to look beyond Dylan in front of me for fear I'd see something that would let me know I was still in the fantasy, stuck there for good.

But the straps of my sandals blistered my ankles and a helicopter flew by high overhead, and Shane was radiating anger and hurt and Dylan babbled on about nothing, the way he usually did.

It was a more difficult walk than the one I'd taken following the coyote, steeper and rockier than I remembered. It took a long time before we hooked up with one of the hiking trails, and even after that it was a good ten minutes or so before we came to the parking lot.

Shane hurried into his car, and through the windows I saw suitcases waiting in the backseat. How could he have been so hopeful? He saw us together? Entwined? I knew what magical thinking could do to people—Max promising to marry Anna even though he was already married—but the Shane I knew was sensible, concrete.

The Shane I knew did not fall in love with the Joss I knew.

Dylan had driven my dad's old truck to the park. It was comforting to see it, to sit in the cab and run my finger over the quarter melted into the soft pebbled dashboard like I'd done a thousand times before. When Shane left I deflated, exhausted, and sank into the passenger seat without saying a word. Whatever combination of chemicals kept me going through the evening left my brain abruptly, and I felt sad and heavy and stupid.

CHAPTER 21

Dylan came back from South America because Believer told
him to. He explained it all the next morning, when my mom
went out for a run. He sat next to me on the couch. I was nursing my second cup of coffee, looking though my laptop for hidden files, log-in info I'd stashed somewhere. I'd already torn
through my room trying to find the phone I must have used to
send Believer's texts, but came up empty-handed.

He'd been silent on the drive back from the park, and when
we got home he let me fall into bed without providing any more
explanation for what had happened that night, but now he was
asking questions. I tried to brush him off at first.

"Nothing's going on," I said.

"Then who's Believer?"

He'd gotten an e-mail, in Chile. A link to the Tumblr and a
message:

Your sister needs you.

So the prodigal son returned.

Our conversation went around and around, me trying to downplay the significance of the Tumblr victims, Dylan bringing up Peter's intrusion into our lives, my history of compulsive lying. He was being nice, framing his questions gently. I hated having to admit how out of control things were. Saying everything out loud made my actions seem even crazier.

"You can't tell Mom any of this," I told him. "I am not going on medication again."

After Peter I made the mistake of telling the first therapist all about the Dream Palace. I told her I saw Amelia, that she'd been in the house with me when Peter barged in. That I followed her to the backyard to hide. That I was sure Peter saw her too. I was briefly put on medication that made me feel like a wretched, drooling lump.

"I didn't agree with that," Dylan said. "Remember?"

"No," I said. "But okay."

Dylan waited for me to go on.

"It's—I don't think it's really a stalker. I think it's me. I know it's me, actually. I just don't know how yet."

"So you e-mailed me? As Believer?"

I nodded.

"And you've created this Tumblr and sent yourself texts and whatever else?"

I nodded.

"Why?"

Then I told him the details about Max and George, about the messages from other long-lost flirts that were still flooding my phone. I told him about Believer saying I needed to be punished, and I admitted that I'd been blacking out and was unable to account for where I was or what I was doing at critical moments.

On the mountain, Shane said exposing himself as James made him feel lighter, free. But confessing to Dylan just made me feel depleted. I sank into the couch.

"I think this is the only way I could get myself to stop."

"Have you?" Dylan asked. "Stopped?"

"I'm done. As of last night."

"Good."

We sat there for a while. Dylan appeared deep in thought. I pictured all this new information filtering through his brain, trying to reconcile it with his experience, with what he knew of me. What kind of person I was.

"This is a really annoying thing to ask, but I want your honest opinion," I spoke up. "It would be helpful."

"Sure."

"Am I a horrible person?"

He didn't answer right away.

"Did I kill Peter and Dad?"

"What? No," Dylan said. "You can't think that."

"But I feel like I did."

"I saw him, you know," Dylan said.

"Saw who?"

"Dad."

He'd been asleep on the beach of a small island at the bottom of Chile. Dylan said it was the bottom of the world and it felt like it. He said the sky was bent; you could see it was a dome. He was going from island to island, sneaking onto ferries and hitchhiking across bridges. He wasn't even thinking about Dad much except that the insurance money felt like death, following him around.

But he woke up on the beach and Dad was next to him, looking out at the moonlit waves. Dylan thought it was a dream, but later his friends told him they'd seen him sitting there, talking to the air.

I asked what they talked about.

"I asked him why he had to die."

"What'd he say?"

"That he didn't."

They went back and forth, arguing. Dylan saying, *Dad, believe me, you are definitely dead*, and Dad just insisting *No*.

He was telling me this to let me know that I wasn't the only one who saw things, talked to people who weren't there, beyond the realm of daydream or overactive imagination. I was a little jealous of him, though. I wanted to see my dad, not a mischievous animal and a motel full of fake people.

"Anyway," Dylan continued. "I don't think you're a horrible person. I know you aren't. And honestly? I've always kind of admired what you do."

He went on. "Before you did it on the Internet, you did it

by dressing up, pretending to be some character, insisting we all call you a different name. I get why it appeals to you. You're bored. You're trying to find out who you are. You hate it here. Reacting to a passively oppressive environment."

I laughed.

"But you are hurting people," Dylan added. "So I'm glad you're stopping."

"Shane called me autistic," I said under my breath. "And inhuman."

Dylan raised an eyebrow. "Want me to beat him up?"

"No," I said.

"The word I'd use is 'sociopath.'" Dylan smiled.

I punched him hard in the arm.

"Should I ask how Shane is involved in all this?"

"Absolutely not."

Later, when my mom came home, we went swimming, all three of us, until we were wrinkly from the salt water. When we got out, Dylan made dinner, and he and my mom didn't revive their ritual argument over his future. They let me be quiet, and I listened to them talk about nothing very important.

I kept checking my phone for messages from Believer, but none came. I'd hidden the proof from myself, but Believer's sudden silence was enough to let me know the coyote was right. I did this to myself, for a reason. I needed to stop, and now that I had, maybe I'd stop seeing things too. I could take what Mary-Kate said to heart and try to see things differently. Try to be more generous, less judgmental.

I answered everyone who sent me questions, admitted I wasn't who I said I was, and typed the words "I'm sorry" more than I'd ever typed them before.

Kit texted me, wanting to know if I was okay.

Kit: **Did Shane find you?**

Me: **Yeah, just a miscommunication**

Me: **How'd you know where I was?**

Kit: **I recognized the pic you posted. The painted rocks at Papago? That's my meditation spot**

I told him that he'd been right when he'd said I was hiding something, being dishonest with him. And I told him I was done with it. He didn't say *Great, be my girlfriend; I'm coming over*, but he said *Cool*, and invited me to see his band play that Friday night.

I wanted to text Mary-Kate and Rhiannon. I needed to hear their voices and tell them about Shane. But I couldn't. I didn't know how to start, how far back to go, or if they would even care.

The weekend passed like that. Watching TV with my mom and Dylan, my phone on silent until everyone was dealt with and the messages died down. At some point I realized I hadn't gotten an e-mail or text in more than an hour, which was the longest I'd ever gone without some sort of communication.

On Sunday night the storm clouds that had been hovering over the western mountains all week finally rumbled overhead and broke. I took a bowl of ice cream out to the patio and sat in the dark watching the rain and lightning.

CHAPTER 22

Going back to school was a loss. I showed up moping, with a headache gnawing at my temples as I said good-bye to my mom.

It was still raining on and off, but the morning was dismally hot. When I arrived at Xavier, girls lounged like sloths in the yard, drooped over wet picnic benches, heaped beneath roof overhangs. Uniforms were already dingy and untucked. Nobody had bothered to do their hair or put on makeup.

I scouted around for signs of Mary-Kate or Rhiannon and saw none, then sat at the base of a palm tree. The grass around me was littered with dropped fronds and weird yellow fruit.

A few feet away, eight tiny aloe vera plants were growing in an evenly spaced two-by-four plot. Each plant had four or five pale tentacles. They were reaching out to one another, trying to touch. Like some plants grow toward the sun, they were growing toward one another. They were aware I was looking at them.

The presence of a boy on the Xavier side of the parking lot was usually enough to get a telepathic wave going, alerting all girls in the vicinity. I felt it, looked up, and was surprised to see Shane across the yard, talking with Leah Leary.

I tried to hide in plain sight by staying really still and communing with the pattern in the palm tree's bark, but Shane rolled his head away from Leah Leary and caught me. He looked away as soon as he recognized my face, but in that fraction of a second I saw that he was miserable.

It was going to be hard to keep hating him.

Miles: **It's true.**

    Me: **I don't believe you.**

    Me: **A crumpet?**

    Miles: **An evil crumpet.**

    Me: **Proof, please**

Mr. Lauren claimed he almost cut his thumb off trying to butter his morning crumpet, and the photo he sent seemed to support his claim. His entire left hand was wrapped in white gauze; shirtless, he stared into the phone's camera, dark circles beneath his eyes.

The classroom was empty—I'd arrived early and texted him when he wasn't there waiting for me, like I thought he would be.

    Me: **Who's our sub? Do you know?**

    Miles: **They'll probably have Campos do it.**

I moved from my seat in the front to a table in the back

of the classroom. Senora Campos, usually the Spanish teacher, was not a friendly.

Miles: **Are we ever going to talk about . . .**

Mae Castillo sat down next to me. A few more girls came in after her, taking their seats, chattering. My ears perked up when I heard the name "Rhiannon," but I couldn't make out what they were saying.

"What are you doing back here?" Mae asked.

"We have Campos today. I don't want to sit too close to the front or I'll pass out from perfume stink."

"But she smells so good. She smells like my auntie Patricia."

I wanted to ask Mae what she was doing, talking to me. Why she was even bothering, after what I'd said during field day.

"Mary-Kate's coming," Mae said. "Just so you know."

"Yeah, I assumed," I said.

"What happened to Mr. Lauren?"

Without thinking, I flashed my phone's screen at her. "He's home sick. He cut himself and had to go to the hospital."

If she realized I'd been texting him, she didn't seem surprised.

"I bet it was a botched suicide attempt. That guy is grim."

I was about to do it—just come out and ask what Mary-Kate's friendship meant to her. I wanted to know if they were dating, as I suspected, or moving toward it. I was going to ask if she knew how to best go about trying to get Mary-Kate back. I was done lying online, and now I needed to translate that resolution into real life. I would present myself exactly as I was, unafraid of what people might see or think.

Then I noticed the other girls in the room. Every one with a phone in her hand, looking down, thumb scrolling. Mouths open in shock. The perking up of whispers. I turned to Mae.

She was staring at her phone too.

"What—" I began.

She shoved her phone in my hand, her face an unrecognizable shade of horror and disbelief.

"Someone posted a link on the school Facebook," she explained, as I saw what she'd been looking at. What they were all looking at.

The Tumblr.

With new entries.

The photos I'd taken in the bath and sent to Mr. Lauren. Excerpts from the text exchange we'd had that night. The name "Miles" bold and highlighted.

VICTIM #21—MILES

And there was more. My body. A gallery of hundreds of nudes. Most faceless, but then—in some, I stared into the laptop webcam, the phone. Some were straight from my computer, never sent to anyone.

The videos I'd sent to James. Downloadable as an MP4 file, for anyone to take and save.

The girls around me, whispering.

Oh my God. This is so sad.

Is that Rhiannon?!

Look at all these guys.

She must be freaking out.

James's face. Victim #22. Even though I knew he wasn't there to receive an anonymous e-mail, seeing the face I loved lined up with all the other tawdry Tumblr items made me want to reach out and grab him, turn his face away.

Not only is JOSS WYATT an uncontrollable
LIAR, a HOMEWRECKER, and an unrepentant
MURDERER, but she is also a CRAZY SLUT.

SHE NEEDS TO BE MEDICATED.

Her PSYCHIATRIST is Dr. Gillian Judson and
she has been diagnosed with DELUSIONAL
DISORDER.

A picture of a piece of paper I'd never seen before. Not from Dr. Judson, from the first doctor, with the diagnosis. A note to "Mr. and Mrs. Wyatt."

Her DAD had a HEART ATTACK AND DIED
when he learned about her LIES.

VICTIMS #23–25—HER OWN FAMILY

My dad's obituary.

When I saw his face, I swallowed a crying-out.

This was not my doing. I'd last checked the Tumblr while I was sitting under the palm tree before school, and none of the new stuff was there. I could have scheduled the posts to auto publish, but I knew even in a blackout, plagued by guilt and masochistic feelings, I would never have gone this far.

Believer was still out there. He wasn't finished fucking with me. I'd deleted everything and been doubly punished by the revelation of Shane as James. I'd apologized to the faceless horde for nothing.

On Mae's phone, with the girls around now openly staring, waiting for me to do something, say something, I navigated back to the Xavier Facebook page. The Tumblr link was posted there by Believer X, along with a helpful thumbnail of a topless Joss Wyatt, available for all 1,162 members to click and follow.

I watched as likes and comments flooded the post. Names I recognized—girls I had freshman gym class with, girls who graduated last year, the girl sitting in front of me in the classroom.

Tessa Clark OMG

Phoebe Monk ^ WOAH

Fallon Pedersen nice

Marina Aguilar no is this a joke or what @Brady Nix look at this

Someone shared the post, and I knew it was now on Brophy's wall. My phone started buzzing nonstop when someone tagged me.

Brady Nix BOOBS! @Sparks Holman, @Julien Rocha, @Hassan Mendes

Carmen Farrow omg @Joss Wyatt

Brady Nix I knew she was a freak @Cairo Crombez @Evan Fairbanks @Fletcher Riggs @Jeremy Hoyer @Cody Majors

Jeremy Hoyer this is like nudes Christmas

My insides were dry, scraped out. The floor of the classroom was swaying, and from somewhere in the hallway came the coyote's dreadful howling laugh.

I looked down at my phone. Missed calls from my mom. I knew she'd gotten an e-mail too. Seen everything.

There was nowhere to hide anymore.

I ran out of the classroom, colliding with Mary-Kate as she walked through the door.

Then I was outside, holding my uniform skirt down because the wind was blowing from the ground up.

I was thirsty; that's what brought me back. For the first time ever I was glad that my untrustworthy mind was trapped inside a human body and required water to keep working. A simple, basic need that I could understand. Fake personalities don't need water. Figments don't get dry mouth.

I walked a bit, staggering into the nearest 7-Eleven, realizing I wasn't carrying any money. I wandered the empty aisles, listening to an ad for the state lottery.

I was reminded of a conversation I'd had with Peter once, when he was on his way home from work. He'd stopped at a convenience store and texted Amelia about being unable to choose what kind of canned soup to buy for dinner. There were too many choices—he'd been in jail for ten years; everything seemed foreign and overwhelming to him.

My stomach lurched. Unlike the other men, I'd seen Peter in person. I'd looked into his eyes as he tried to comprehend a teenage girl standing where he thought the love of his life would be. I'd never had to answer for any of it.

The cashier was eyeing me suspiciously, so I went back outside. I looked at my phone, ready to throw it into traffic.

Mr. Lauren's latest texts.

Miles: **Are we ever going to talk about . . .**

Miles: **What happened between us?**

I could never go back to school. That seemed obvious. I couldn't go back home, either. Believer was tracking my every move. He was probably aware I was at the 7-Eleven. Maybe he'd known that's where I'd flee, even before it happened.

Why isn't Mr. Lauren freaking out?

I texted him back.

Me: **Can you pick me up at the 7-Eleven on Indian School & 7th Ave?**

Me: **Don't ask why, just come**

Miles: **There in 10**

On the sidewalk across the busy street, a guy holding a gigantic arrow-shaped sign was staring at me. He threw the arrow in the air, spun around on one foot, and caught it behind his back, dancing to whatever music was playing through his headphones. He looked familiar. Like one of my victims.

He was pointing the sign at me. Every time he caught it, the tip of the arrow was aimed right at me. I moved from one side of the parking lot to the other and hid behind a plaster column. I wanted to yell.

What are you doing? Do you work for him? Tell me who he is!

Then Mr. Lauren pulled up in his little red car, his injured hand resting on top of the steering wheel in a permanent thumbs-up. I jumped into the car before he even came to a complete stop.

My phone was ringing nonstop, my mom and Dylan taking turns calling. There were already two hundred comments on the Facebook post, and I had unread texts from Mary-Kate, Rhiannon, and Kit.

As we turned onto the street, the guy with the sign pivoted and looked right at me. I slouched down as far as I could, but he caught my gaze and smiled, throwing the arrow again. When it came back down I could read the text on the other side:

MATTRESS LIQUIDATION 75% OFF & MORE!!!!!

I turned my phone off and closed my eyes.

At first Mr. Lauren clearly thought I asked him to pick me up so we could have sex again. But as I told him what turns to make, he realized that something was seriously wrong. I was near tears, now fetal in the passenger seat, gripping my legs to my chest, white-knuckled, wincing at every red light because I was sure Believer was watching through the windows.

"Is this your—therapist?" he asked, idling in front of Dr. Judson's office, squinting his eyes through his glasses to read the sign on the front door.

"Yes," I said, looking around, checking for coyotes, ghosts, Believers.

"Are you going to go in?"

"Yes," I said.

"You want me to wait?"

I didn't have an answer for that.

"Where were you born? What's your birthday?" I asked instead.

"I was born in Yorkshire," he stuttered. "On April tenth."

"What are your parents named?"

"John and Helen. Why are you asking?"

"Have you ever been married?"

He sighed and scratched at the skin beneath his bandage.

"Yes."

"What's her name?"

"Susannah."

"What happened to her?"

"She left me. She moved here. It was either stay in England and see our child once a year, or follow her."

"Child?"

"Rufus. He's eight."

"Okay," I said, blowing out a deep breath. "Okay. Thanks."

"It feels good to tell you all that," he said, smiling.

"I didn't ask because I care," I said. "I don't care."

"Oh. Well, that's nice—" he said, and I realized how callous I sounded.

"I just needed to make you real for a second. I needed proof."

"Proof?"

"Proof that you're not a manifestation."

I tried to explain.

"Sometimes I can make things happen just by thinking about them. I thought about you—I obsessed over this car. I obsessed over all your mysteries. And then I made you want me. I can do that. I can do it better online, but I can do it in real life, too, I guess. Um—

"Things are weird right now," I went on. "Unsteady. I asked you those questions so you could tell me something I'd never thought of before—something true, that I couldn't have made up."

Some of the color in Mr. Lauren's face paled and faded, paled and faded.

"If it helps," he started. "I wanted you. All on my own. Not as a—"

"Manifestation," I mumbled.

"Not as part of a manifestation. I think I'd know, if that were the case."

I nodded.

"And, look, I'm sorry. Really, really sorry. It wasn't me," I said.

He looked confused.

"Check your phone," I told him, moving to leave the car.

He reached into his pocket with his good hand.

I shoved the jammed door with all my weight and stepped out, quickly scanning all directions for signs of Believer before sprinting into Dr. Judson's office.

CHAPTER 23

The coyote's skin, its covering, is chameleonic not only in the way it changes color but in the way it changes texture. Lizard scales for direct sunlight, silvery gills for swimming in a mirage, and his standard tough brown fur for nighttime creeping.

He'd trailed me into Dr. Judson's office, reversing our usual roles of followed and follower, and now he was curled up tight in the corner, watching me talk. He was not his usual thin, rangy self. A bit of exposed belly gave him the air of a well-fed pup.

She knows about me?

She knows.

When I'd walked in from Mr. Lauren's car, I'd tracked muddy footprints across the grey carpet in the waiting room. The receptionist rushed out to stop me, and I started crying, blurting out everything that happened at school. She sat me down, and two minutes later Dr. Judson was there. I overheard her apologizing to someone, ushering them out the back door before coming to meet me.

"What do you think your options are?"

"I don't know. Dying? Running away? Burning down the Internet?"

"I can tell you, after we're finished here, I am obligated to bring this to the authorities. The nude photographs alone constitute child pornography. And the implication of your teacher, the inclusion of my name—these are extremely problematic."

The first thing I ever told Dr. Judson was that I judged her for having a collection of ceramic angel figurines arranged on one of her office bookshelves. She explained they were inherited from a family member and had sentimental value. They weren't really her personal style.

Now they stared at me, full of secret knowledge.

"I should have told you about Believer before," I said. "But—you see why I was being so paranoid? It wasn't based on nothing."

"Tell me more about Believer."

"I don't know how he does it. I figured it was someone I'd chatted with. But now—it has to be someone I know, right? I thought maybe it was Shane, or even Mary-Kate. Then the coyote told me I was doing it all to myself, and that seemed to explain everything. It seemed right. It should have been me."

"The coyote—the threatening figure you've described?"

"He's not a threat."

Never was.

"You have used the word 'threat' to describe it, multiple times."

"I think at first I was conflating him with Believer, this person who is real and who really is trying to hurt me. They showed up at the same time. But I think the coyote was trying to warn me."

"Is the coyote in this room right now?"

I didn't want to admit he was.

There was a gentle knock at the door, and the receptionist poked her head in. I watched Dr. Judson's face for its brief annoyed tic—she hated being interrupted.

The receptionist handed her a slip of paper—she read it quickly before handing it back.

"Joss, I want to let you know that your mother's here and has been notified that you're with me. We can continue."

I felt a mixture of relief and agitation that made it hard to sit still. My mother had always been aware, in the abstract, of how deep my lies could get, but now she'd seen the evidence. She was probably fielding passive aggressive phone calls from Deb Mahoney and Brenda Tatum out in the waiting room.

"Did you tell her I was here?" I asked, watching as the coyote began to shrink to the size of a small mouse.

"No, I didn't."

There was no use trying to tell if Dr. Judson was lying—after seeing her every week for more than a year, I knew she wasn't.

"And what about the ghost of Peter Caplin? Are you still seeing it?"

"No," I said. "Why do you bring him up?"

"He broke into your world. Like this Believer."

Dr. Judson's first name is Gillian, which suits her. The oldest of Rhiannon's sisters is named Gillian, too, but she pronounces it with a hard G, like Guinevere. I cycled through these facts in my head, things I knew to be true, objective points my jinxes had no effect on.

"When did you dissociate last? Was that Friday, on the mountain?"

"Yeah," I said. "But I'm always on the edge. The clock trick doesn't work anymore. I watch for five minutes and know it's five minutes, but it could feel like a second or an hour, and then that starts getting to me."

"What starts getting to you?"

"If it's possible for a moment to feel like forever, then what isn't possible?"

We kept talking. I let Dr. Judson push the conversation as far as she wanted. The coyote was the one who ended it. He scurried over to my chair and climbed up, perching himself on the arm, mouse-size and alert.

I'm bored. I don't like it here.

He started shrinking again. I held my palm flat and he walked onto it. Dr. Judson was asking questions.

"What do you feel like doing?"

"Making a fist."

"What do you think will happen if you make a fist?"

"I'll squish him, or he'll disappear."

"Is that what you want?"

Yes.

"He says it's what he wants."

I looked at him for the last time, and met his eyes, now tiny as pinpricks. When I closed my hand, he slipped across the seam. He didn't feel like anything. I licked a salty tear from the corner of my mouth, felt its wet trail on my cheek. I was crying not because he was gone but because he existed in the first place. I banished the coyote to the astral plane. He could live there with my made-up women and my ghosts—I wouldn't visit them anymore.

I had to live here, in the ugly, imperfect world where I was only one person and everyone knew my innermost secrets.

I had to face my mother. I had to look at her and understand that I'd collapsed her world like Believer collapsed mine. I had to repeat embarrassing things to her, my friends, the school administration, the police. There was nobody in the world in love with me anymore, no one holding on to promises I made, no one waiting for me to make them feel something.

Her face was like the calm eye of a hurricane. She hated me. Dr. Judson took her aside and they spoke while I waited in a chair and the receptionist watched me like I might start trashing the place.

Out in the parking lot, she led me to the car, walking fast

so I had to hurry to keep up. I wanted her to hug me and tell me everything was going to be okay, but she wouldn't. She kept putting space between us.

She hadn't taken the time to find a shady spot like she usually did, and the car was too hot to sit in. She started it and ran the air-conditioning while we stood on the sidewalk and waited for the leather seats to cool. The car was straddling a white line, taking up two spots. I thought of her speeding to Dr. Judson's office, mind racing with Tumblr images and their implications. I couldn't bear it.

Something caught my eye from the covered parking on the other side of the office park. Mr. Lauren's red Volvo. He'd waited after all. He was talking on the phone, distressed. He'd seen his name on the Tumblr.

When we drove past, he pulled his car out too. I didn't turn around, but in the side-view mirror I saw his bandaged thumb. He stayed behind us as we headed west toward a neon sunset piled up in the sky like a slow explosion.

My mom waited to talk until we were almost home.

"How are you feeling?" she started out.

"Is that what you really want to say, or is that what Dr. Judson suggested you say?"

"It's what I want to ask."

"Are you asking that because you want to yell at me but you want to make sure I'm not suicidal first?"

She sighed and the car went faster.

"I'm asking how you're feeling because I don't know how you're feeling. I don't know how you're feeling because you don't tell me how you're feeling. You don't tell me anything. Ever. Maybe I stopped asking, and that's why this is happening."

She looked at me. "Answer the question, if you can."

The "if you can" bothered me enough. I answered.

"I'm feeling a little blurry."

"Do you know who did it?"

"No," I said.

"You must know."

"I'm trying—"

Her voice was hoarse, on the edge of breaking. Her eyes were soft and red. Her hands gripped the steering wheel like it was the only thing holding her to the ground.

"It's not fair to you, Joss. I want you to understand I know it's not fair, and actually it's some kind of assault, and we will find out who did it and they'll be held accountable. But I can't be there for you right now, and I don't particularly care if you're upset about that."

"I get it."

"You give me nothing. I have nothing to give you at this moment. I am so deeply ashamed of myself."

"Mom, it's not your fault."

"Just—" She choked up. Her face crumpled for a moment before she regained control, flexing her jaw, holding it still. I had to look away.

"Later. Later," she managed to say, in a raspy whisper that made me feel as small as the disappearing coyote.

At home, I waited as she unlocked the garage door. I was suddenly scared, still not completely convinced I was in the correct dimension. I recited the necessary words, said the things I was afraid of so they wouldn't happen.

The coyote is waiting in the kitchen.

The coyote is waiting in the kitchen with Believer.

Peter Caplin is back from the dead.

Believer is waiting in the kitchen.

The first thing she did was take my laptop and phone, tearing my room apart, grabbing my Kindle and iPod, too, just for good measure.

She'd looked helpless, clutching them in her arms as she yelled at me.

"Why do you do this? Why do you put yourself in these situations?"

Dylan appeared. Some shared exasperation passed between them—they'd clearly already talked about everything. Dylan probably tried to calm Mom down, repeat the things she needed to hear. *You're a good mom. It's within the realm of normal teen girl behavior. She's safe.*

My mom dumped the laptop and phone into Dylan's arms and stormed out, footsteps heavy on the stairs. Cabinets slammed in the kitchen. Ice clinked in a glass. She poured herself a drink and stomped back upstairs. I saw her as she passed my door on the way to her room. Distraught, tight-mouthed Nina, her chest splotchy with hives.

"Dylan—" I started.

He was mad too.

"No way," he said, shaking his head. He knew I was going to ask him to let me back on the laptop.

"But I have to figure out who's doing this to me," I begged. "I know if I could just look, I could find them. I've written to them. They want me to respond. Each time they give me little clues, clues I've missed—"

"What good would it do, if you knew who it was?"

"Come on. I need to know what people are saying, at least."

"You don't want to know," Dylan said, more serious than I'd ever seen him. "The school took down the original post, but your pictures and"—he blushed—"videos—are all over. They're hashtagged and searchable on Tumblr. No matter what happens, they'll be out there forever."

"I know." I sat down on my bed.

"Not good," Dylan said, shaking his head.

"I know," I repeated. Then, indicating the laptop and phone, I asked, "What are you going to do with those?"

Dylan left without answering, and I imagined him tossing my devices into the swimming pool. I was defenseless, disconnected. How I would ever recover from this intrusion and public humiliation was beyond thought.

Maybe my mom would decide we had to move, to start fresh somewhere new. I could go by my middle name. Louisa Wyatt was pretty great. Totally different from Joss. I could be Lou, or Lulu. Once enough time passed, I would convince my mom to let me have a laptop again. I'd agree to some kind of keystroke-monitoring program. I'd let my mom check my history every day.

But at least I would be online. Maybe, if I swore I would be careful, I could even talk to people, as my new self. My mom always wanted to move to the Pacific Northwest. Louisa Wyatt, mysterious new girl from Arizona with shades of a traumatic past, arriving in Seattle, or Portland, or Vancouver.

I'd miss Mary-Kate and Rhiannon, but I could make new friends. I could leave behind the less savory aspects of my personality. As Louisa I would be open-minded, optimistic, sweet. I would force down my cynical side and shrink it like the coyote until it wasn't a part of me anymore. All the things I hated about myself would be eliminated.

It was a physical severing. Like my hands had been cut off at the wrists. My eyes kept darting around the room, looking for some way to transport myself, to get out. The absence of my phone was particularly disorienting. I didn't know where to look, what to do. Thoughts came and went every second. I felt like I was losing them. I needed to write them down, but there wasn't an outlet.

I could hear muffled conversation from my mom's room,

phone calls made, her voice calm one moment, tremulous and nervy the next.

I watched the neighborhood through my window. Cars pulled into driveways, unloading batches of kids in sports gear and backpacks. Families went on evening walks, toddlers stopping to investigate every crack in the sidewalk. A large black poodle stopped at the gate in my yard, sniffing until his owner had to yank him away.

Do you smell the coyote?

The cat came and checked on the lizard, resting one paw on the shelf holding the cage. She hopped up, slinked between the cage and the wall, and fell asleep immediately in the warmth of the heat lamp.

The only clocks I had were on the laptop and phone. There was no way to know what time it was. It had been dark for a while when I found *The Sirens of Titan* in the stack of books on my desk. The absence of Shane's voice in my life was a bigger gap than I expected. I'd almost called him to come get me when I was outside the 7-Eleven. He was the first one I thought to ask.

I read the whole book. Waltham Kittredge was a minor character, the name I'd seen when I flipped to a random page at Shane's house. But the main character's last name was Constant. Like James. Shane must have used it for him. Signs and portents. I'd seen what I wanted to see, just like the men I chatted with overlooked improbabilities in favor of prolonging a fantasy.

I'd been so mean. I understood that now. I could walk around the block and knock on Shane's door. He'd be there.

In bed, a watery breeze drifted across my face from the hole in the window. Kit's instructions on how to meditate floated through my brain.

Kit: **Look up at the sky. Try to clear your mind**

I laid an intention down.

Find Believer.

Somewhere in the neural network of my body there were things I'd known and forgotten. The names of thirty different dinosaurs. Facts about each one—carnivorous, upper Jurassic, duck-billed. Answers to pop quizzes. Moments passed with my dad. My whole life before age eight.

I wanted access to the full scope of my memories. I had questions, but the answers were well buried. I was so good at lying that I'd fooled myself first and best. Where did I go when I blacked out? What happened to the time I lost? Why did I do nothing to stop Believer? Why did I welcome him into my life?

Who drove me to Papago Park, to meet James?

CHAPTER 24

I woke suddenly. A dream vanished.

Slip 'N Slides. Drone attacks. Ghosts. The coyote in exile, tearing at the seam trying to get back in. Lyrics to a song: "Tonight I'm all alone in my room/ I'll go insane."

It was always going to end up like this. All the brains and hearts. I was always going to separate from them violently. It was always going to be a matter of deleting.

The air conditioner gave a cold zap and stopped working. The house creaked and settled unnaturally. The power was out, and the air was stagnant when I looked through the hole in my window. What I first thought were spaceships turned out to be bright slashes of lightning beyond the mountains.

I heard footsteps. They stopped outside my door, and I saw Dylan's bare feet, lit blue with the light of his phone. He checked the thermostat and continued downstairs.

I sprang out of bed and crossed through the bathroom to Dylan's room. Musty and lived-in now, no longer abandoned, it was darker than mine because his window faced the house next door directly. I searched quickly, looking for my phone in piles of clean laundry, underneath strewn records, at the bottom of his dresser drawers. Something caught my eye on the floor—a blue crayon, pointing under the bed. I pounced on it and reached my hand out—

My fingertips brushed against the familiar shape of my phone case. I grabbed it quickly and ran back to my room, diving beneath the covers.

I opened Facebook and logged in. I had a ton of new messages, mostly from Brophy boys wondering if there were any other videos. There was no way I was going back to school, so I knew I would never see them again, and I was able to read their words without letting shame or despair overtake me. It helped that the boys were so focused on my exposed body. They were distracted by its easy availability, so they didn't care to put together the other clues on the Tumblr—clues about not only my secret online life, but my secret inner life, too.

There were no additional posts on the Tumblr, but all the entries had new notes on them—and Dylan was right, they weren't just people from school. If I clicked on the time stamp on each entry, I could see the tags that Believer used to make the videos and photos widely searchable—there was "NSFW," "nude girl," "porn," and "girl masturbating." Believer had gotten a little creative with them, too, and perversely, I found some amusing—"teen tits," "stupid blonde bitch," and "Arizona schoolgirl."

The video and photo gallery posts were reblogged more than two hundred times each. I followed those links to new pages—most were random collections of porn GIFs, but there were weird personal blogs, too. On one, run by some guy in Russia named VladymyrXO, my naked breasts were sandwiched between a pencil drawing of Bart Simpson and a revolving, three-dimensional animation of a yin-yang.

When I couldn't look any more, I opened my text messages. Mary-Kate, from right after I left school—

MK: **Are you ok?**

Then there were two from around dinnertime—

MK: **I called your mom and asked if I could come by but she said no**

MK: **I can't believe this**

Rhiannon sent a slew of incomprehensible texts. Hours later she sent more explaining she'd stayed home from school that morning because she'd gotten all her wisdom teeth taken out and was high on painkillers.

Rhiannon: **wtf wtf wtf Joss I don't know what to say**

Rhiannon: **I'm sorry for being mad at u**

Rhiannon: **What do you need boo**

Rhiannon: **I'm telling everyone u were hacked and it's all fake**

It was stifling hot under the covers without the air conditioner running. I came out and sat by the window, opening it fully, shivering a bit in the cool draft. I was listening for something, and realized the reliable *click* of the motion-detector light in the driveway wasn't working. I craned my neck and checked: Other houses on the block still had electricity—but the only light in ours was from the curved line of solar-powered lights lining a path through the front yard.

My bedroom door creaked open. I shoved the phone into the track of the window frame and turned, using my body to hide it.

"Dylan—"

He was holding two pints of ice cream and a box of Popsicles.

"Electricity's out."

"I know," I said.

"These are going to melt, if you want one."

I hadn't eaten since breakfast, and hunger hit me all at once.

"Thanks," I said, holding my hand out, not wanting to get up and reveal the hidden phone. I thought Dylan would move on to his room, but he sat on my bed and made himself comfortable.

"You want to know something sad?" I asked.

"Sure," Dylan said. He'd finished one Popsicle and opened the ice cream, taking alternating bites from each tub.

"It's been about twelve hours since Mom took my computer and phone away, and I'm already finding it hard to believe I exist. I'm atrophying."

Dylan shrugged. "I always find it hard to believe I exist. You probably don't feel it usually because you go on your little Instagrams or whatever and pretend. You and your sub-millennial friends, just avoiding reality at all costs."

"*Subliminal* friends," I said, smiling. Dylan laughed.

"Okay, that's great," I went on. "That's a lovely vision of modern life."

"Shit's bleak," Dylan declared. "But, historically, less bleak than ever before."

"Yay," I said weakly.

Dylan stood up, gathering his snacks. Something at his neck caught the moonlight and reflected it, catching my eye. Dylan was wearing a necklace, a small silver cross.

"Where'd you get that fancy lady necklace?" I asked, meaning to make fun of him. I felt an odd pulling at the back of my head.

Dylan tugged at the chain, looking down.

"Sylvie—this girl in Chile—gave it to me," he said. "I don't actually wear it, but I was just about to Skype with her before the power went out, so I put it on. Can't escape Catholic girls, I guess—"

He trailed off, mumbled, "Good night," and walked back to his room.

The pulling feeling in my head turned into a thought. A memory. A silver cross dangling in the air. Red and green light bouncing off its shining surface. Someone talking.

"You sure you want me to do this?"

"Yes I'm sure." That was my voice. *"Just leave as soon as you drop me off, okay? And that's it. Then we're done."*

From within the boarded-up Dream Palace came the whispered breath of the coyote—

You know who it is.

Behind me, the phone rattled with the muted cut-off *thump* that meant its battery was dying. Believer, summoned by the trickster god one final time.

Believer: **Hope you don't mind, I went rogue.**

Believer: **Just couldn't stand following your orders anymore.**

I wasn't Believer. I was the coyote.

Who was I talking to? The silver cross, red and green light, a car, someone's car, the rearview mirror—

"You don't even realize it, do you?"

Mr. Lauren's voice in my head now, the conversation we had in the velvet curtain-lined hallway of the Marquee. And a new memory of what happened directly after seeing him, strange and distant but definitely my own. Texting a blocked number in the bathroom, the words on a screen, clear as day.

Me: **Send the Tumblr to Max in 5 minutes**

"I don't torture her."

"Oh yes, yes, you do."

The electricity surged to life, setting off a chain of flickering reactions. The heat lamp above the lizard's cage turned back on with a tinny click. Across the room, the shark-faced air-conditioning vent now spewed cold air and was once more bordered by a square patch of brightness cast from the motion-sensor light shining from outside.

I watched, stunned, as a shadow traversed it.

Someone moving on the street below, passing in front of the driveway lights. Lingering on the sidewalk.

I turned and looked out the window.

Leah Leary's face was a blur, her eyes slit like a serpent's. When I met her on the sidewalk nerves were sparking off of her. She was standing near a creosote bush still stinking from the weekend's storm. Its bitter fragrance wafted over us as we stood face-to-face.

I remembered everything. It was the first really hot day of the year, and the anniversary of Peter's suicide. Rhiannon and Mary-Kate had a lunchtime meeting of the Graphics Design club, and I went into the chapel to eat there so I wouldn't have to sit alone in the cafeteria. I said a jinxy prayer for Peter's life and picked at a paper tray of tortilla chips covered in congealed nacho cheese. I ingrained every recovered detail in my memory, afraid I'd lose them again and have nothing to come at Leah with.

Because she was coming at me.

"I thought I was helping you," she growled. "You said you wanted to stop. When I saw you in the chapel, you swore to God you would stop. I only agreed to do everything you said because I thought I was going to save you."

I remembered watching her walk into the chapel that day. Shane had just told me about Leah's summer program at MIT, how she'd been selected as one of ten students in the country to go mess around with computers there. She was smart. The coyote whispered the plan into my ear, and I recruited Leah Leary to hack my shit and expose me to the world.

It was her, picking me up at the utility box, driving me to the park to meet James, the silver cross dangling from the rearview mirror. I made snarky comments about how it would look ironic if she ever died in a car crash. Even in a blackout, I'm an asshole.

She followed me as I walked to Hunt's Tomb because she was worried James would murder me. But then she saw Shane. Heard him declare his love.

So even though I'd told her that was the end, she could stop being Believer, she kept going. She realized I was incapable of remorse. You can only repent if you confess your sins and agree that what you've done is deplorable. But I hadn't told her about James until that night. I'd kept him for myself because even though I'd orchestrated the punishment, I was still looking for a way out.

She'd seen things when I'd given her my passwords and

screen names. She saw the nude photos and the videos and knew that if she posted them to the Tumblr and sent them to my mom and the entire school I'd have to stop. Finally and for real.

"You're insane," I told her.

"I was just finishing what you started. I did this because you begged me to do it. And I think we both know who's the crazy one here."

She was bigger and taller than me, and though I couldn't imagine something as crazy as Leah trying to hit me, I was intimidated by her.

She clutched at her stomach suddenly, like it hurt.

"Why'd Shane even bother with me?" she asked. She'd been intent and serious before, but suddenly she was on the edge of tears. "If he loves someone like you?

"You're so evil," she said, emphasizing the last word so I'd know she wasn't throwing it around lightly. She was putting me beyond forgiveness and compassion. "At first I felt bad for you. But you showed me who you are. You're false, corrupt. You love hurting people."

"Leah—" I tried to stop her.

"He was always on his phone," she went on. "I never said anything about it. I read all the letters. All the things he was telling you while he was with me."

She choked up—her face a mess of tears.

She said Shane was still trying to help me. Even after I'd said the most hurtful things to him, he'd come home from the mountain that night and broken up with Leah via text. She couldn't tell him what she knew without exposing herself, so she'd just had to take it when he lied and said he didn't feel like they had anything in common. She asked him if there was anyone else. He insisted there wasn't.

"You have no idea," Leah said. "Every lie you told made a million other lies possible. He keeps calling me asking me to help track the blocked number, the IP addresses. He still wants you."

"Leah." I tried to appeal to her. "I'm so, so sorry about that. You saw, I had no idea. I don't have those feelings for him. That's out of my control."

She started moving toward me, and I backed away from her, tripping off the cement, into rocks. I considered yelling for Dylan or my mom but was still laboring under the assumption that she'd stop, and I'd look stupid, scared of an angelic Goody Two-shoes in Converse and a denim jumper.

"Hurting you is the only way to punish him," she said, the words not quite directed at me. Directed somewhere else, to an invisible Shane, standing there watching.

"You could be charged with distributing kiddie porn," I said, spitting out the words to try to make them as threatening as possible.

"Nobody will ever be able to connect anything to me," she spit back. "If anyone even gets close, it'll look like it was posted from your bedroom."

"And," she went on, "you're an actual murderer. I talked to Morgan—Peter's sister. Did you even know he had a sister?" Her voice was sure again, rising, and she was still coming at me with an unhinged look on her face.

"She blames you, too. She was very interested to know you hadn't stopped lying, even after your moving letter about how sorry you were for killing him. I had to talk her out of coming here with me."

Leah reached out and pushed me into the neighbor's yard, out of reach of the driveway lights. I staggered, and hit the back of my ankles on a brick planter. I couldn't back up any farther, and she blocked me every time I tried to get away.

She kept talking. "I never liked you. I thought I wasn't being gracious enough, that there must be something redeemable about you. But the more you showed me, the more I knew I was right."

"I'm sorry," I squeaked. She wasn't hearing me.

"It's shameful," she said thoughtfully, "But I started to envy the way you can hurt other people and not let it affect you."

"Leah," I said. "You hurt me. I'm hurting, a lot, I swear."

She laughed.

"Look," I continued. "You want me to beg for forgiveness? If you want to hear how deeply embarrassed I am, I'll tell you all about it—let's just take a deep breath and go up to my bedroom and you can hear how sad and sorry and depressed I am, and we can just fucking figure this out and it'll be over."

"You'd just be putting on another show. I've watched you. I see you now."

An idle wind cut between us like a roving knife, blowing strands of the neighbor's palo verde across my face. Leah was momentarily distracted by it, and I rushed her. Her arm shot out and struck my face—Leah shrieked, suddenly her normal self again, not a vengeful attacker but a heartbroken teenage girl.

That's the last thing I saw. Leah's face melting from anger to horror to helplessness as she knocked me backward hard and my feet slipped on the rocks and my legs buckled. Pain exploded at the small of my back a split second before my head hit the edge of the brick planter and everything went black.

CHAPTER 25

My mom let me stay home from school the rest of the week.
She was the one who'd answered the door when Leah knocked,
crying hysterically, repeating, "I didn't mean to kill her; I didn't
mean to kill her," over and over again. I think the few seconds
between that moment and when she found me passed out in
the neighbor's rocks, bleeding from a gash in my head, did
more to return me to her good graces than anything I could've
done on my own.

Leah's parents met us in the waiting room at the ER. I was
propped up on my mom's shoulder, dizzy and seeing double,
when they arrived, but I managed to stop Leah from confessing
absolutely everything. Yes, she'd posted the link to the Tumblr
on the Xavier Facebook page, and yes, I'd enlisted her to be
my stalker, but I insisted that the nudes were my own doing. I
swore Leah tried to convince me out of posting them.

Part of me really did want to get back at her, but I saw how pointless it would be. I'd gotten kicked in the ass and I deserved it, no matter what Dr. Judson or my mom or Dylan said. Nothing I did to Leah could change the fact that the entire populace of Xavier and Brophy had seen me naked literally and metaphorically.

A doctor led me to a windowless exam room and asked me questions while stitching me up. I had a hard time answering them. She asked if I knew the day and year, and all I could think of was something I'd heard in a documentary about Janis Joplin—"As we learned on the train, it's all the same fucking day, man." The doctor did not find it amusing, and diagnosed me with a mild concussion.

At home, the physical effects of the past few days hit me fully. I didn't get out of bed until Thursday morning, when Dylan burst into my room dragging his record player across the carpet. He hooked it up and started blasting a B-52s album. He jumped on my bed and yanked the blinds open on the newly repaired window, singing at the top of his lungs.

You're living in your own private Idaho

"Go away," I muttered, kicking at his legs.

"Mom said to get Joss out of bed," he said, out of breath.

"Go away!" I yelled.

"Dylan does what he is told!"

I kept kicking him until he jumped down and cranked the volume on the record player as high as it would go, leaving it that way so I had to crawl out of bed with the comforter wrapped around my body in order to turn it off.

I saw Dr. Judson later that day. I don't know what good it did, but I told her everything. I even told her about Shane and Leah and what I'd done to both of them. My mom came in and joined us and we talked about the measures the school was taking to protect other students from such "vicious, targeted bullying." My mom's coworker recommended an attorney who would perform the service of "expunging sensitive material" from the Tumblr and beyond.

Mr. Lauren took some quick thinking to clear up. All Leah knew, it turns out, was that I'd texted and sent photos to someone who said his name was Miles. But the phone number didn't match the phone Mr. Lauren had on him when he was called in to talk to administration. He'd decided to resign, even though I insisted nothing happened between us. All my secrets were gone. My hands were empty. I had to keep something to myself.

On Friday Mary-Kate and Rhiannon came by on their way to prom. My mom still refused to let me have access to a laptop or phone, so they surprised me just as I was about to try to tackle a mountain of makeup assignments and missed homework.

"Joss, your friends are here!" my mom yelled from downstairs.

Friends?

I pictured Anna, Emma, and Rosie at the front door, like, *Can Joss come out and play, Mrs. Wyatt? You know, we really miss her.*

Deb Mahoney's voice brought me back to reality. When I walked past her to the Hummer limousine waiting at the curb, she regarded me fearfully, like I was a condemned inmate.

At least my mom's not chaperoning prom.

Inside the limo, Mary-Kate was wearing a mint-green gown, looking at her reflection in a compact mirror, making a disgusted face, picking at her eyebrow. Mae was sitting next to her in a black minidress, and across from them Rhiannon and Trevor were arranged on the leather seat, Rhiannon lying across Trevor's lap to keep her satin dress from wrinkling.

Mae was telling Mary-Kate, "Seriously, nothing is wrong with your eyebrow."

I knelt on the limo floor, at Mary-Kate's feet, and felt a little self-conscious about my greasy hair and the pineapple-print pajamas I'd been wearing three days straight.

"You look really pretty," I told her.

We looked at each other, and I thought about how sometimes there's a kind of communication you have with another person that is so intimate it's almost banal. Maybe my friendship with Mary-Kate wouldn't survive past high school, but at that moment I was thankful she saw me, knew me enough to understand with a look that I was sorry, so sorry, for hurting her and for being a shitty friend. There is immeasurable value in being able to tell a person something without uttering a word. It's impossible to do via e-mail or text because the degree of intimacy is lost. Using words removes you a degree, separates you from the actual emotion.

Mary-Kate reached down and wrapped me in a hug and held on to me for a long time.

"My eyebrow is so messed up," Mary-Kate whined when we finally parted. "How come it's always one side of my face that looks jacked? I can do one side perfectly and then the other one looks like a sad clown. Am I crooked?"

"You are not crooked," I said. "And your eyebrows are perfectly matched."

"They're not supposed to be perfectly matched! I read that they're supposed to be like fraternal twins."

"Gross," I teased. "Where'd you read that?"

"In a terrible magazine you'd make fun of me for reading," she said, staring at her face in the mirror again. Mae reached out and yanked the compact out of her hand, throwing it out the limo's open moonroof.

"I'm not going to make fun of you for reading terrible magazines anymore," I said. "I swear. They're not terrible, anyway. I am."

"No, don't stop," Mary-Kate said. "I'd miss it. Sometimes I do Joss commentary in my head. Like, 'Mary-Kate, eyebrows are stupid anyway. What are they even for? What's their *function*?'"

I asked what was going on at school and she filled me in. Apparently everybody who'd commented on the Facebook post was given after-school detention, and some of the Brophy boys who'd been particularly lewd and shared it on their own walls were suspended. I was infamous for a couple days, but then prom excitement took over everyone's forebrains and people moved on.

"Good," I said. "I'll probably be back Monday. It's extremely difficult to be at home without the Internet. I feel like a frontierswoman. I'm dangerously close to developing hobbies."

Rhiannon made a sound—an annoyed *chh*. Like, *Yeah right.* Like, *Hey, you need to talk to me now.* I looked to Mary-Kate for direction. She shrugged. Like, *Fix what you broke, Joss.*

I turned to face Rhiannon.

"You okay?" I asked, knowing her tough heart wouldn't want to hear "I'm sorry" again.

"I'm fine," she said. "But I'm not really ready to be all cool, cool, cool."

"I get it." I nodded. "If the roles were reversed, I probably would've killed Trevor in revenge already."

"Hey," Trevor complained.

Rhiannon managed a little smile.

"Oh," she said. "Guin told me that Kit wanted to remind you to come to their show tonight. It's at Trunk Space. I told her you were grounded, but she said he really hopes you'll come."

Kit, huh. Right.

She added, "Even though I told him everything and showed him the Tumblr."

I felt a pang of rage but let it pass. Rhiannon was allowed some kind of retaliation.

"Great," I said, covering my eyes with my hands.

Trevor took a vape out of his blazer pocket and puffed on it a few times before passing it to Rhiannon, who stared out the limo's moonroof, evidently done talking.

"And what do you think of all this?" I asked, turning on Mae, who'd stayed suspiciously silent.

"Hey, I don't do drama," she said, holding up her hands. "I hate drama."

"Ugh." I groaned.

"What?" Mae asked.

"Sorry. That was an automatic reaction to someone saying 'I hate drama.'"

Mae laughed.

"Anyway, of course you like drama! Everyone does! Everything is dramatic! God, that phrase—"

"You know what I hate?" Mae said. "'It is what it is.'"

"'Love and light'!" I said.

"'Right on'!"

"'Right on' is a good one," I agreed. I hadn't believed Mary-Kate when she said Mae and I were similar, but suddenly it seemed obvious.

"Justin, please stop doing drugs—" Mary-Kate hissed at Trevor. Out the window, our moms appeared at the front gate, talking animatedly. Mine had somehow gotten ahold of a glass of wine.

"Look at them," I said, catching Nina as she rolled her eyes almost imperceptibly, nodding along to whatever Mrs. Mahoney was saying.

ROWAN MANESS

"Your mom has great eyebrows," Mary-Kate said.

"What are they talking about?" I prompted, hoping Mary-Kate would play along.

She imitated her mom's voice.

"Mary-Kate's turned into a lesbian. I don't know what I am going to tell my mother at Thanksgiving—"

I imitated my mom in response. "Would I be one of those Scottsdale bimbos if I got a little Botox? I mean, I wake up every day shocked I'm not thirty anymore. Would it be so bad, if it makes me feel more confident? Is that setting a bad example?"

"Oh, now, I don't know about plastic surgery, Nina. The Bible doesn't say anything about it."

Right when Mary-Kate said that, her mom leaned in toward my mom's face, and my mom pointed out the wrinkles at the edges of her eyes. Mary-Kate and I dissolved into laughter.

"Have fun tonight," I said, opening the car door. "And uh, I'm sorry. To you too," I added, for Rhiannon.

"We know," Mary-Kate replied. "We're sorry too. We're here for you, okay?"

"Aw, all right."

I stood with my mom and we giggled together when Mrs. Mahoney climbed into the passenger seat of the limo using a tiny ladder that extended out from a side panel with a robotic whir.

"Yeah," my mom said, draining her wineglass. "She definitely thinks you're the bad seed now."

As they drove off, I leaned in and gave my mom a hug. I hadn't touched her since the emergency room, when there'd been two of her swimming in front of me and I'd spent the long wait trying to combine the Ninas into one mega-Nina. She kissed the top of my head, and I felt her body relax.

"Do you wish that was us?" I asked.

She hmmed and started stroking my hair.

"Do you wish I was going to prom tonight? Like—like a normal person? In a normal dress with a normal date?"

She didn't answer. I separated myself from her a bit, tried to read her face.

"I'm sorry, Mom."

"No," she said firmly, wiping a tear away. "I am so, so glad you're exactly who you are. Obviously you need help, more help than I can give you. I really hope you know that everything you did was not okay."

"I know," I said.

"But all this shit, whatever energy makes you want to act out this way, I know you're going to take it and direct it toward something amazing someday. And I wouldn't want you any other way."

The foundation dropped out when my dad died. I'm not sure my mom knew how to build it back up. But she was trying.

When we went back inside, Dylan was waiting with news. Sylvie's visa had been approved and she'd be coming to Arizona to study. This meant Dylan wasn't going back to Chile and would be staying at home for the foreseeable future. My mom, already high from my show of physical affection, was ecstatic.

That's how I convinced her to let me go to Kit's band's concert. A little bit of good old-fashioned in-person emotional manipulation. She liked the idea of me doing something social, and she loved the idea of Dylan chaperoning. I begged for my phone back too, but she was a genie who granted only a single wish. A phone was one request too many.

I showered and blow-dried, careful with the stitches on my head, arranging my hair to cover up the puffy yellow bruise that surrounded them. Singing along to a Neil Young song, I thought of Shane and what he might be doing. My mom mentioned she was surprised he hadn't stopped by. As far as I knew, our time as James and Rosie hadn't come out during Leah's big reveal—she was still the only person who knew how Shane felt and what he'd done to try to show me.

I watered the plants in my room with water I saved from a bucket in the shower, and as I did, I thought I caught a glimpse of him out the window, riding his bike to my house like he'd done hundreds—probably thousands—of times. Riding through the memories that surrounded us, same old stories, same old street.

It was some other kid though—younger, lighter, happier.

CHAPTER 26

"Are you sure you want to do this?" Dylan asked as we pulled up outside Trunk Space, a roving performance venue whose current home was in the back room of a Lutheran church.

"Why wouldn't I be?"

"You have no problem attending a large gathering of people? In public? Without a phone?" Dylan said, teasing me.

"Don't remind me I don't have a phone," I said. "I have an Altoids tin in my purse, and I'm just going to hold it if I get scared."

I tried to convince Dylan to drive off and let me go to the show alone, but he insisted on playing bodyguard. I warned him it might be awkward, and told him that if Kit came up to talk to me he was to make himself disappear immediately.

Unlike the Conor Oberst show, Trunk Space was all ages and there wasn't a bar. Thirty or forty people crowded into the small room, leaving a little half circle clear at the back wall, where equipment was set up beneath a tattered tapestry depicting the Roman goddess of the hearth and the namesake of Kit's band—Vesta.

"Wow," Dylan said, eyeing the crowd's weird demographics. "Eclectic."

I scanned the room for anyone from Xavier or Brophy who might have decided to ditch prom for something better. I looked for Kit but didn't see him, and imagined him getting ready, meditating. I couldn't picture him nervous, but maybe he was.

I'd decided to go not because I was dying to see him, or sick of being cooped up in the house. I just wanted to be somewhere, in a crowd, surrounded by people who didn't know who I was. It was a kind of relief, something approximating the feeling of disappearing into a character.

Guinevere appeared, serene and breathless.

"Joss! And Dylan!" she exclaimed, hugging us both, her long hair falling over our faces. "You came!"

She said she'd tell Kit I was there, and we should try to get a spot up front for "something really special."

Before she left, she repeated, "It's going to be really special tonight, guys. Mercury just left retrograde!"

Dylan watched her back as she drifted away toward the equipment and picked her bass up. It seemed huge against her bony frame. The drummer, a guy named Paris, came out from a door marked EXIT, and he and Guin started a droning melody that skirted the edge of atonal. The lights lowered and Kit came out, hair flopping over his high, smooth forehead.

The first song was their most popular, the one they'd been getting played on the local indie radio station for the past few weeks. Dylan wormed his way toward the front, but I stayed back, unsure how to deal with Kit's liquid gaze, his searching eyes. It crossed my mind that the situation was one I'd dreamed of months ago, when I'd first stalked Kit online. This magnetic boy, looking for me as he sang.

The song ended with Kit and Guin harmonizing beautifully— singing poems to a roomful of strangers, channeling their energy.

"Hey. Thanks for coming everybody." Kit spoke into the microphone, looking at the floor, adjusting pedals with his feet. "This is new, this is Normal. Normal War."

My stomach jumped.

He sang with a smile.

> It's a normal war we're waging right here
> And in the heart a clash
> With the comedown near
> A normal war of broken treaties
> A normal war of unbreakable ties

The song worked to transport me. I couldn't take my eyes off Kit.

> These young players present electricity

To the virgin goddess who hides the supplies
Out of the daydreamer's reach
In her secret cave of impossible lies

He was standing perfectly still, but then the droning broke and he bent over the guitar and played it wild and crazy so everyone started moving. I felt absolutely sure then that he would move to Los Angeles and become a famous rock star, and someday I'd have to send him a text message reminding him who I was.

Possible lies
And impossible lies
In a normal war
It's a normal war

Everyone was dancing, except me.

After the show, most of the crowd seemed to hang around despite there being no bar or room to party. Dylan and I followed the wave up a set of wide white steps and came out onto a lawn wet from recent sprinklers.

I watched Kit talk to several people before he made his way over to me, his face shiny with an adrenaline-sheen. We hugged, only slightly awkward, and Kit said something playful about how busy I'd been. Dylan came up and I introduced them to each other—they bonded immediately, and I caught Dylan's eye and smiled at the first mention of Neil Young. *See, it's not anecdotal; it's every single time,* I wanted to say, but realized I would have been responding to something Shane said, and Shane wasn't there.

I couldn't stop thinking about him. If anyone pinned me down during the week and forced me to admit what was on my mind, chances are I'd say, "Shane and James and Rosie, and what am I going to do about it."

Before leaving, I told Kit I liked the song, and hoped he was sensitive enough to understand what I really meant.

I like the song. I can't be your girlfriend. I wouldn't know how, and even though there aren't twenty different guys talking to twenty different versions of me anymore, it still wouldn't be just us. Someone else has a claim on me.

Driving home, Dylan was unusually quiet. His phone was connected to the truck's stereo, and its sentient shuffle tarot selected a song from one of the bargain-bin cassettes I'd bought for Shane. He'd played this particular tape so often that it had deteriorated and he'd had to throw it away. I tried not to see it as a sign, but it felt like one anyway.

On the freeway, each overpass shocked the cab with a brief moment of darkness, and presented a new mosaic—Gila monster, rattlesnake, roadrunner, a stylized four-pointed sun.

The Kokopelli was next, exactly 1.5 miles ahead, guarding the exit that led to the outlet mall. When it rushed past my window, I turned back to look. The design receded quickly into a shadow, just a flat combination of square turquoise tiles pressed into cement, a bit of sad cultural appropriation decorating the side of the road.

I'd had to work hard to convince my mom I didn't need to be medicated for my hallucinations. Dr. Judson and I talked about how they might be a side effect of all my time spent immersed in fantasies—my guilt, manifested. She and I persuaded my mom to give it some time, see how I reacted to the new reality. I was supposed to be keeping a journal.

But I knew I'd never see the Kokopelli's henchman, the coyote, again. I'd locked him in the Dream Palace with the others—he was powerless, prismatic. He burned himself on my world.

"You know what Dr. Judson said?" I asked Dylan as we exited the highway and slowed to a stop at the top of an off-ramp, waiting to turn left. "She says she's never once doubted the integrity of the real world."

There wasn't any cross traffic, but the red light lasted forever.

"How can someone live like that?" I went on. "Never being skeptical, never imagining another possibility? Accepting everything around you without a second thought?"

Dylan reached over and opened the glove compartment. A square hunk of purple plastic fell out and he handed it to me.

"What is this?" I asked, turning it over in my hands like an ancient artifact.

"Your new phone," Dylan said. "It's for old people who are confused by technology."

My mother had made a concession in the name of safety and practicality. A flip phone that could only text and call preprogrammed numbers, protected by a secret password.

"This is humiliating," I said, flinching as the phone powered up, a pixilated starburst chiming across the tiny yellow screen.

There were six numbers in the contacts folder. My mom's work and cell, Dylan, Mary-Kate, Rhiannon, and Shane.

"I picked the color—'galactic fuchsia,'" Dylan said. "Thought you'd appreciate."

"Thanks?" I said, scrolling down to Shane's number, wondering why he'd made the cut.

"She pretty much put people in there who might give you rides," Dylan said, reading my mind. "And she told me to tell you that she's monitoring your texts, but I don't know if she really is."

"Why didn't you give this to me before the show?" I asked.

"I just wanted to see if you could do it without," Dylan answered.

Encouraged by the inanimate Kokopelli and the shuffle playing Shane's favorite song, I composed my first text on the old-people phone, making typo after typo on the sticky keypad as I tried to decide what to say.

Me: **Shane, it's me**

Me: **Joss**

Me: **Need to talk**

I stared at the screen, hoping for a response, until we got to the neighborhood entrance gate. Then I gave up, flipping the phone shut. Dylan laughed as it chirped good-bye.

"Shut up," I muttered.

Shane wasn't going to text me back. At the park, with his feelings exposed and laid bare before me, I'd rejected him and said I never wanted to talk again. The difference between Shane and James seemed insurmountable then. Accepting them as the same person was too big a stretch.

I remembered something George said after I'd confessed and told him Emma was a lie. He'd said he wanted to get to know me as Joss Wyatt. I told him I was a minor and I wasn't allowed to talk to people anymore, which was the line I used with everyone, but he pressed.

"Why?" I asked. "Why do you want to know me? I'm not Emma."

"Yes you are," he said. "You made her up."

As Rosie, I'd revealed more of my true self to Shane than I ever would have if we'd just been talking like we normally did, and he'd done the same. Our masks provided freedom to explore aspects of our personalities that were just beginning to form—secret hopes for our future lives, urgent desires, shades of people we wished we could be.

Dylan drove past the electrical utility box and I craned my neck to try to see the top—

A light. Some blue glow. Shane sitting there, looking at the text from my new number, not responding.

"Hey, drop me off?"

Dylan stopped the car and I got out, indicating the box,

pointing up at the now-visible form—Shane, encircled by the striped pink Hula-Hoop he was holding upright in his lap.

When Dylan was gone, I sat at the base of the box, propped against the warm metal, legs stretched out in the dirt, and texted Shane. I heard his phone indicate he'd received the message. I was trying a new tactic.

Me: **Hi, James.**

Me: **It was so good meeting you in Arizona.**

Somewhere across the greenbelt, a dog barked, and a few seconds later another one responded with a lonely, paranoid howl.

My phone lit up.

New message from SHANE.

CHAPTER 27

Shane: We met, didn't we? I thought it was a dream.

Me: It was real. We met at the park, and we touched.

Shane: I kissed you?

Me: We kissed. And then we drove around listening to music and we came across that street fair.

Shane: I'm sorry you had to learn about my deathly fear of carnival rides so early in our relationship.

Me: That was a little disappointing, I'll admit. But you made up for it, when you hijacked that paddle boat and took us out—

Shane: There was a lake?

Me: —on that magical lake that appeared out of nowhere.

Shane: What happened next?

Me: We paddled so far out we couldn't see a shore anymore. And it was just you and me, Jimmy Grace and Rosie Rose.

Shane: And afterward?

Me: I'm not sure.

Shane: Why did it have to end?

Me: Maybe it didn't.

Me: There's no shore, no desert, no Arizona. There's just James and Rosie, floating side by side in a daydream. And in a daydream they can do whatever they want.

Shane: I think they got married. Even though they both claimed they never wanted to.

Me: Okay. They got married, had kids, traveled the world, and wound up in a tree house on a cliff somewhere above the ocean, growing old together.

Shane: Someday their kid gets in trouble for making up stories and lying to people via the chip in her brain.

Me: Hahaha

Me: They can tell her that's how they met, the second time.

Me: When they first met, it was before they could even remember

Shane: And the second time, they were other people

Me: Good-bye, James and Rosie

Shane: Good-bye Rosie

James and Rosie receded from view, moving across the astral plane, leaving a shimmering path in their wake.

Shane: Ouch

Me: I'm sorry, Shane.

Shane: I'm sorry too.

Me: **Did you love me when we were twelve?**

Shane: **I don't know**

Me: **Did you love me when I bought you those cassette tapes?**

I could feel him working through it, trying to make sense of the ending we'd just written for our avatars.

Shane: **Yes**

Moving from darkness, to live in the light.

Me: **Can I come up?**

Shane moved, and the rivets on the pockets of his jeans scraped against the box above me. I tipped my head back and watched as his hand extended over the edge, outlined by a sky thick with stars.

A lizard scurried across the street and caught my eye. So much is hidden in the desert. Things happen inside plants, underground, in the shade beneath rocks. But the sun seeps into every crevice—it wants you to always look and see clearly.

I stood up, wiped the dirt off the back of my jeans, and reached for Shane's hand.

Rowan Maness lives in Los Angeles with her husband, who fell in love with a personality she created online. They have two daughters.